scent of butterflies

DORA LEVY MOSSANEN

sourcebooks landmark

Published by Sourcebooks Landmark, an imprint of Sourcebooks, Inc.
P.O. Box 4410, Naperville, Illinois 60567-4410
(630) 961-3900
Fax: (630) 961-2168
www.sourcebooks.com

Library of Congress Cataloging-in-Publication Data

Levy Mossanen, Dora
Scent of butterflies : a novel / Dora Levy Mossanen.
pages cm
(pbk. : alk. paper) 1. Adultery--Fiction. 2. Revenge--Fiction. 3. Iran--History--Fiction. I. Title.
PS3612.E94S34 2014
813'.6--dc23

2013031050

Printed and bound in the United States of America.
VP 10 9 8 7 6 5 4 3 2 1

This One is for

Paula, Maureen, Joan, Alexandra, and Leslie,

My
Cherished Friends and Colleagues

chapter 1

1999

I AM A RICH WOMAN from a backward country. A Jewish woman from Iran. I carry alien genes—green eyes, blond hair, fair skin, and a height of five feet, nine inches, which intimidates and offends Iranians. Such audacity, they murmur among themselves, to step beyond the permitted boundaries of our women. Boundaries drawn by men, I should add, whose masculinity depends on the diamond-studded leash they've wrapped twice around their women's ankles.

I am a photographer. A collector of exotic animals. A nurturer of rare plants.

Baba is convinced that the day I called myself an artist was the same day I lost touch with the reality of our culture. A sad, sad case of squandered femininity, he would say, his eyes twinkling like the Persian jester in one of our fourteenth-century miniature paintings. "What you need, my Nightingale, are sons to keep you busy and out of trouble."

I'm on Air France, destined for Los Angeles. Fleeing Aziz, my husband of twenty years, the man I married when I was fifteen. The only lover I've ever known. He believes that I will return to him. I will not. Why? Because I can't resist his drunken eyes, velvet words, and persuasive hands that know where to press softly and where to stroke hard, where to linger and where to slither away, where to cup and hold and warm.

And I won't return because I can't free myself from Parvaneh.

A turbaned *akhound mullah* shrouded in religious garb slips into the aisle seat next to me and, without as much as an acknowledging nod, removes the Koran tucked under his arm, touches the cover to his lips, and rests it gently on his lap.

I shift uneasily in my seat, farther away from him, a visceral reaction, I suppose, since I'm still properly sheathed by my stifling *roopoosh*, the dull brown, mandatory overcoat, not very different from the *aba* loose-sleeved garment he wears. I could have discarded the *roopoosh* in Paris, where I was no longer bound by the laws and regulations I left behind, and where I quickly trashed my thick, opaque stockings. I don't need to pretend any longer, to be who that society expects me to be. But a habit of twenty years can be as stubborn as a handful of bloodthirsty leeches.

The unfairness of it all, being forced to endure the company of a *mullah* for the next twelve hours, I silently complain. Then slowly, like a sneaky worm making its way into my head, the thought occurs to me that perhaps it's not that bad, after all. A *mullah* sitting next to me might yield endless opportunities.

He must be in his midfifties, the outline of his body muscular and solid under an ash-gray cloak, with Italian loafers polished to a high shine and a crisply folded black turban. Dark, well-clipped beard and mustache, arrogant nostrils and high forehead project a patrician air.

This same *mullah* was segregated from women on Iran Air on his way from Tehran to Paris, where we stopped to change planes. Now, he finds himself a desire's breath away from me. An exciting thought nudges my heart into life. How will he react if I slide up my sleeve and brush a bare wrist across his neck, on the lower-right corner where his turban has slipped up, or rest my head on his shoulder and pretend to wake up with a start? *Oops! Pardon me, an unfortunate accident.* What if I remove the scarf from my hair, lift up the *roopoosh* that covers my legs, and reveal my bare ankles?

I slip my hand down the collar of my *roopoosh* and trace the sharp angles of the Star of David dangling from the necklace Mamabozorg gave me. Will the pendant offend the *mullah*? Will he quarrel with Allah for seating him next to a Jewish woman who has the audacity to ignore the Islamic rules of *hejab*, or will he welcome my boldness?

Aziz's love-words explode behind my temples.

—Muslim men dream of fucking Jewish women, *Jounam*—

I lean my head against the window and close my eyes, stroking the chain around my neck. My grandmother's memories are sheltered in the translucent kernel of every amber bead.

I should have discovered the affair earlier. Yes, I should have, even if they had been discreet, Parvaneh and Aziz. Small mistakes were committed. Parvaneh accepting a sip from Aziz's tea; he, placing the most tender piece of kebab on her plate. She, going dizzy-eyed over his jokes; he, offering her a drag from his cigarette, or stealing an extra minute to comb his hair just right when we were on our way to meet the two of them, Parvaneh and her husband.

No, these intimacies did not alert me. I did not want to know. It takes courage to peel off the winding sheets of denial, to observe with wide open eyes, endure the consequences, the pain. Aziz is my lover, my friend, the lens through which my world comes into sharp focus.

The essence of licorice and mint wafts from the *mullah*'s breath. The smell of home, of my country, and of the *mullahs*, now the privileged elite. They empty our pockets, loot the deposed Shah's palaces, export our antiques and heirlooms, and purchase first-class tickets to America to drown themselves in the same excesses they condemn back home. They have replaced the Pahlavi dynasty, which robbed the country, too, but with style and aplomb.

Twenty years ago, in 1979, at the outset of the revolution,

and for some years after that, we, the so-called "aristocracy," believed—and, more than anything, hoped—that the Islamic Republic of Iran was the temporary madness of religious fanatics who would not and could not last. Iranians, we rationalized, at least those of us who had the courage to discuss matters among ourselves, were too modern, too educated, too Westernized to bow down to fundamentalists.

We were wrong. Their twenty-year-old roots have burrowed deep. They're here to stay.

The *mullah*'s forearm brushes against mine as he turns a page. "*Bebakhshid, khahar*, forgive me, sister," he murmurs under his breath without raising his head from his book.

I shift closer to the window and look out. Clusters of smoky clouds congregate and enclose the plane. It does not feel like the advent of Noruz, New Year, and the spring solstice, an intoxicating season in Tehran, when cherry blossoms are in full bloom and their scent of ripe fruit and bitter almonds permeates the mountain air. Up here, the cabin smells of cheap wine and restless discontent.

Soon, far from Aziz, I'll settle in America, where men are not allowed four legal wives and as many temporary wives as they desire, and where women are not stoned for committing adultery. America holds memories of previous visits with Aziz: our honeymoon, when we bathed in Lake Tahoe while it shimmered like woven diamonds, bike-rode on my thirtieth birthday on the bone-warming shores of the Pacific, and welcomed Hawaiian sunsets as grand as our desire for each other.

And more than one trip to visit fertility specialists. One strange treatment after another was suggested—baking-soda douches to promote an alkaline environment, temperature reading to establish the exact hour of ovulation, leg-lifting and twisting into yogic knots after sex so not one precious sperm was left unaccounted for. The verdict of one especially ignorant doctor was that we should consider adoption, since nothing could be done. Nothing at all!

My white blood cells, he announced in a conspiratorial, I-know-it-all tone, produced antibodies, some type of aggressive protein that neutralized my husband's sperm.

Despite everything I went through and put Aziz through, despite all the invasive tests I endured, the truth is that I have been on the pill since our wedding night. From the moment Aziz proposed, I decided not to become pregnant. The thought of sharing him with anyone, even our child, is unbearable. The sight of him holding someone else against his chest, whispering endearments in another ear...the prospect of a rival is unacceptable. So I concealed the pills in a small paper pouch I stapled to the back of a painting of a jester in the Ghajar dynasty court. And made sure never to miss a dose. Not even once.

When I lied to Aziz, telling him that the magazine I freelance for is sending me to America on a photographic mission, he said:

—I hate to let you go, but you have my blessing if you promise to be a good girl, *Jounam*—

Jounam, his life. How dare he call me that, I wanted to cry out. How dare he expect me to be "good" when he has been so very bad? But I kept my mouth shut and forced a meek smile because I wanted him to sign the legal documents that would permit me, his wife, to leave my country.

Madar likes Aziz. His name rolls like sweet candy in her mouth when she tells me, as if I don't already know, that the literal meaning of his name is "beloved," and that everything he's done for me proves him worthy of that name. Blowing a strand of well-coiffed hair away from her melancholy eyes, she declared that few men would tolerate the freedom he allows me, let alone permit a wife to travel on her own to America, which as far as Madar is concerned is the end of the world.

Baba, too, finds Aziz remarkable, but for a different reason—for his seemingly monogamous nature and for his unequivocal loyalty to his wife.

"Either he's impotent," Baba chuckled, twisting the tips of his peppered mustache, "or like me, he knows how to *kamarband ra seft konad*."

Yes, Aziz did keep his pants tightly buckled, I suppose. Until Parvaneh.

Aziz believes I'm ignorant of his infidelity. I had been until thirteen days and five hours ago when suspicion turned to certainty, when the cozy walls of matrimony cracked open, and I was forced to acknowledge the stench of betrayal.

The first thing I did that late afternoon—No! The second, after I rushed like a possessed creature to my mother—was to pay a visit to Settareh Shenas, a celebrated Isfahani astrologer.

Sitting cross-legged on a carpet in his herb garden by the side of a small pool, he aimed his bovine stare at me, demanding the exact date and time of my birth. The callused thumb he pointed my way seemed to stamp me with his seal of disapproval.

"You were born in the Year of the Tiger! Under the stubborn sign of Taurus, a time when the stars were in conflict with the moon and the rings of Jupiter tightened their grip around the giant planet. Comply, *Khanom* madame, comply!" he finally pronounced, "If you had bowed to your man's needs in the first place, he would not have looked elsewhere for satisfaction. Control your dark side, *Khanom*! Give him what he wants or you will face the fires of *jahanam*."

I turned on my heel to leave, but not before I gave the astrologer a piece of my mind, told him it was useless to threaten me with the fires of hell, since I was already burning in them.

Even as awareness continues to slice through me, I know with painful certainty that divorce—a clean, final break—total freedom—is not an option. I cringe at the prospect of a group of narrow-minded *mullahs* congregating in a dreary room to decide that Aziz's infidelity is not a valid enough reason for me to "destroy" my marriage. But even if I file for divorce and my request is granted, I won't be able to tolerate the life in Iran imposed on a *zaneh talagh gerefteh* divorcée, who would be looked upon as a whore for the sin of living alone or appearing in public with a male companion.

And the last thing I need is to return to my parents' home and to Baba's overpowering affection. Even now, sitting in the plane next to the *mullah*, I clearly see my father, his steel-gray eyes piercing, his mustache quivering, his hands clasped behind his back as if to support the slim, tall body he carries with the arrogance of a king.

I can hear his low, persuasive growl that can lure a snake out of its hole: "Divorce! What exactly do you mean, Soraya? If you intend to disgrace us all, then by all means go ahead. Otherwise, listen to your father. Go home to your family, instead of hauling cameras around town and squatting down like a porter *hamal* to snap pictures of friend and foe. And never mention divorce again! Neither to me nor to your mother, whose poor heart won't withstand such shame."

In America, I'll claim my own life and come to terms with the enormity of love and guilt I feel toward my father. Learn to carry the burden of his words: "My Nightingale, crown of my head. Ah! The ingratitude of stiff-necked children."

I'll take time away from Madar, who continues to punish Baba by hiding her emotions under a carapace of lethal silence. One day I might discover why she rebelled with such violent finality and what compelled her to bury the vivacious woman she once was.

I sense the *mullah*'s breath on my neck—warm, fast, and deep—sense his evaluating stare. I feel a spark of excitement. In silence and without budging in my seat, I turn and aim my questioning gaze toward him. Our eyes meet for a heartbeat. A shadow of a fleeting smile parts his lips.

As if my image is projected on his book, he looks down and murmurs into its well-thumbed pages, "*Salam*, *khahar*. Hello, sister."

"Soraya," I correct him. "My name is Soraya."

I owe my name to Madar. Concealing her triumphant smile behind her palm, she would recount her fights with Baba, who vehemently opposed the name. No one in their right mind, he declared, would name their daughter after a cluster of stars. "Name her Sarah, Rebecca, or Rachel, after our matriarchs!"

Madar, calm and unwavering, rested her condescending, pampered fingers on Baba's and instructed him in a gentle voice to stop bristling like a frightened porcupine or his simmering blood would damage his heart.

"Soraya," she had assured him, symbolized mystery and being out-of-reach, which would serve his daughter well in the future. And to add to the name's allure, the Shah's beautiful second wife was named Soraya, so that was that.

The *mullah* shifts in his seat, raising the smell of spices, the familiar, comforting scents of baked sweets and closeness I associate with saffron, warm butter, and browned flour, the ingredients my grandmother, Mamabozorg Emerald, stirred into her golden halvah. And, like a veil, another scent swirls around him. Expensive cologne, Paco Rabanne, imported from the West, from "the Great Satan," "the Great Arrogance," the same country he feels obligated to curse for the benefit of his colleagues.

An urge to jolt the *mullah* out of his religious stupor overcomes me. I stroke my camera, encased in ostrich leather and cradled in my lap. Snap the case open, tempted to turn my camera on and agitate his calm façade with the click, click of my shutter control. Perhaps I should ask the flight attendant to take a photograph of us, a record of him sitting next to a female stranger, even worse, next to a *taghouti*, a royalist and an aristocrat. Such devastating evidence, proof of his disregard for the commands of his supreme Ayatollah.

I survived the Islamic Revolution by developing ingenious ways of sidestepping its horrors—the splash of acid if found wearing lipstick or mascara on the streets, the pull and snap of scissors and razors if hair is visible from under the *chador*, interrogation and imprisonment if the Morality Police found me with a male stranger.

In Tehran, in place of the *chador*, I wore the dark, opaque stockings and *roopoosh* over dresses of the latest fashion purchased on trips to Europe. A scarf would cover my hair, and my face would have no makeup. But as soon as the chauffeur dropped me off at a friend or relative's house for our evening get-together, I'd remove my *roopoosh* and head cover and join other women in the makeup vestibule.

Secure in the knowledge that, in case of a raid, the host's private safe held millions of *toumans* in cash to bribe the Morality Police—the Committee for the Promotion of Virtue and Prevention of Vice—I'd apply makeup, a ritual each woman conducted in her own way, while the latest gossip swirled about. I accentuated the green of my eyes with lavender pencil and lengthened my lashes with soft black mascara, aware of sideways glances in the mirrors as other women attempted to duplicate my look on their own often darker complexions.

Once the swift transformation from Islamic to European—from one culture to another, one religion to another, even one century to another—had taken place, men and women would mingle freely. Banned alcoholic drinks swayed in Baccarat goblets, embraced by teasing hands. Guests swayed, danced, and flirted to forbidden *taghouti* Western music.

Here, high in the air, too close to a *mullah*, who reminds me of what I left behind, I peruse the menu, check the wine list, then signal the stewardess and ask her if she has anything better back there.

"All we have," she replies, before retreating down the aisle, her perfume as annihilating as Parvaneh's. Why do coy women insist on leaving the screeching echo of their scent behind? I spray a mist of Metal from my purse, a lingering whisper to chase the offensive odor away. I hear the subtle intake of the *mullah*'s breath and imagine his flaring nostrils drinking in the nuanced scents of my perfume.

The stewardess arrives with a bottle and displays the label. "1995 was a good year," she says.

Last night in our bedroom, Aziz uncorked a bottle of 1945

Chateau d'Yquem. He swirled the glittering liquid in a Saint-Louis glass, then warmed the wine in his mouth. My lips embraced his, yielding awareness to the scorch of alcohol as he folded me in his arms and murmured in my ear.

—I want your child, Soree—

The *mullah* flinches at the offensive pop of the cork, the releasing of the obscene smell of the forbidden. He shuts his Koran, shifts in his seat, and aims a reprimanding glance at me.

"*Sharab meil darid?*" I raise my glass and ask if he would like some wine. He is wearing expensive American cologne and Italian loafers, after all; why not have French wine?

His arm springs up as if to ward off the evil eye. "*Astagfirullah, Gonaheh!* God forbid, it's sinful!" He scratches the top of his turban as if his scalp has erupted into hives under it. The audacity of a woman not only ordering alcohol, but tempting him as well, must have sent his sensibilities reeling.

I drink half the glass in three swallows. The alcohol does not assuage the urge to spill out the chaos in my head. Even a *mullah*, to whom a man's infidelity is not an issue, would acknowledge the strangeness of their affair. The coupling of my lion with Parvaneh. A butterfly! All these years of friendship, since we were innocent children in kindergarten, and this is the first time I meditate on the meaning of my friend's name: Parvaneh. Butterfly. My husband, a sensible man anchored in the here and now, snared by a shameless sorceress called Butterfly.

There's a reason why her parents chose to name her Butterfly. She was born breech, doubled over and unable to breathe until the midwife slapped her on the buttocks and blew life into her. Butterflies are fragile. Their life is short. Very short. And when their wings become wet, they can't fly, but fall to the ground and flutter helplessly until they die.

How could this have happened to me, Soraya, an only child, the darling of my Baba, favorite of my Mamabozorg, and loved by a husband who had no qualms about falling on his knees in adoration at a formal gala? Aroused by wine, dazzling in a tuxedo, he knelt in front of five hundred guests, removed my pumps, plucked a hole in my nylons with his teeth, and pressed his lips to my toes, our public foreplay stoking our passion.

—Let them gossip, *Jounam*, I don't care—

The next glass tastes warmer, tangier, intensifies the rush in my veins, stirring possibilities. For a fleeting breath, my stare lingers on the *mullah*'s as I wipe my wine-wet mouth, push tendrils of blond hair back into my headscarf.

His lips part and his eyes light up as if noticing me for the first time.

Acidic words spill out of me like vomit. "You might not need alcohol, *agha*, sir, but I need it badly. I've escaped from my husband!"

The unburdening does not prove cathartic. The urge to take action is blinding. I cross my legs. Pale, defiant ankles flash through the slit of my *roopoosh*. I raise my wineglass and wish the *mullah salamati* good health, toss my head back, and empty the glass. "My husband is having an affair with my best friend!"

In a calm, soothing voice, he murmurs, "It happens more often than you think, *khahar*."

"*Nakheir*! No! Not to me, *agha*!"

"Even to you, sister," he replies, turning to gaze at me with such unexpected boldness that I feel the need to tuck my hair back into the safety of my headscarf but, hand in midair, decide against it.

"Let me explain, *khahar*. There are three types of women. Those who do not wear the *hejab* and do not cover themselves properly resemble public buses that everyone can freely ride. Those women, on the other hand, who opt to partially cover themselves are like taxis that only a few are allowed to ride. The third type who, like my modest wife, cover themselves properly, are like faithful donkeys. Only one man is permitted to ever ride them. Your friend, no doubt, resembles a bus. So, understandably, your husband was tempted to ride her."

I am rendered speechless by the appalling comparison. My

thoughts churn like dough in a mixer until ready to be delivered in that calm and deliberate manner I've mastered to perfection. I turn to face him, a poisonous cobra, ready to strike.

He slips to the edge of his seat. Leans sideways and thrusts one hand into his cloak pocket.

What is he doing? What is he looking for? I shift away from him and instinctively clutch my camera.

His hand appears. A white handkerchief is crumpled in his fist.

My heart slaps against my rib cage. Is a razor concealed in the folds of his handkerchief? Not so long ago, in the streets of Tehran, a woman's mouth was cut with a razor because she had worn lipstick. A young girl's face was mangled by acid because she wore mascara. My mind races to calculate the fastest route of escape from my window seat. If I step over his legs, he will easily grab and stop me. The idea shoots through my mind to smash my camera against his head. I'm about to jump up, to sprint over his legs and call for help.

He raises his hand and reaches the handkerchief toward me.

I grab his wrist, my grip tightening, rigid as a vise.

A look of surprise appears on his face. Then, as quickly, his features contort in anger. He attempts to release himself. I hold tight.

He seems to change his mind and calmly, as if resigned to my hold, transfers the handkerchief to his other hand. With a single fast motion, he wipes off the red lipstick I've applied for protection against the dry cabin air. "Islam forbids women to adorn their lips."

I release him and drop back in my seat, pass my tongue over chapped lips. My mouth stinging, my voice mocking, I say, "What if I'm not Muslim, *agha*? Will this restriction still apply?"

"Of course, *khahar*. Chastity is required of women of all faiths."

"I've lost my faith, *agha*."

He slaps the back of his hand twice, as if to awaken himself from a blasphemous nightmare. "*Astakhfor'Allah*, God forbid!

You do not know what you are saying, sister. You lost your way; you are confused."

"That I am." Yes, I am certainly confused, since I don't understand what my husband could ever see in a butterfly to make him risk losing me, his breath and life.

The *mullah* strokes a page of his book between forefinger and thumb, as if checking a bolt of gabardine to be custom-made into an elegant cloak. "That's normal, *khahar*. Most women are confused. A pious man can be of great help."

An urgent need to further offend him overtakes me, and I pour another glass. Turn the dial on my watch forward to American neutral time. I am done with this *mullah* and the rest of them! Done making myself invisible at home, while religious fundamentalism raged outside. They can all go to *jahanam* and dictate their restrictions and beliefs to their own timid wives.

I stand up and stretch my body to its full impressive height, untie my scarf, and loosen my straight blond hair to tumble all the way down to my waist.

Aziz's smoke-shattered voice vibrates in my head.

—The shapeliest legs in the universe, *Jounam*, the silkiest of hair—

I trace the embroidered sleeves of my overcoat, linger on every mother-of-pearl button meant to breathe life into an otherwise dreary coat, glide out of it as if shedding unwanted skin.

His stare slides up my bare calves, velvet skirt, silk camisole, and lingers on Mamabozorg's gift, the amber necklace. And hanging on the chain, wedged between my breasts, is the ruby-encrusted Star of David pendant.

A hint of a blush appears above his peppered beard, rises to his cheeks and onto his forehead. He tilts his head back and takes another good look at the Star of David. He shuts the Koran and touches his lips to the cover, a farewell kiss, before tucking it in the pocket of the front seat. He has finally distanced himself from his religious constraints, shed the pretenses forced upon him.

The revealed man is sexual, vigorous, and involved. He glances around as if looking for the hostess or assessing his surroundings. A tilt, a slightly amused expression, appears at the corners of his mouth. He pats his attractive beard, adjusts his turban, and sets it slightly at an angle like a Persian gigolo, revealing clean, angular sideburns.

He pulls out his handkerchief and wipes sweat off his forehead. A smudge of my lipstick remains behind.

I shift slightly closer to him, to his scent of baked goods and American cologne. Reach out and stroke the remnant of my lipstick off his forehead.

He touches his forehead. His dark eyes flicker into life like a cat catching sight of a plump mouse. "*Kheili moteshakeram*, many thanks."

Rising above the plane's roar, the captain's voice spills through the loudspeaker: "On your right is Las Vegas, the world capital of gambling."

The *mullah* brushes his arm against my bare shoulder, a fleeting touch, then runs his thumb down the length of my wrist, a bold move, flirting in public with this special treat, a Jewish woman. "Some more wine?"

"Yes," I reply eagerly, curiosity taking over. "Yes, please." Will he order a bottle, share a glass with me, toss all religious restrictions to the wind?

He raises the half-full bottle of wine on my tray and pours me a glass. I think I hear him murmur *khoshkel* under his breath, beautiful or lovely or some such pronouncement, before letting out a long-drawn sigh. "*Zane jalebi hastid, kheili motefavet.*" His breath laced with lust, he murmurs that I am an interesting woman, quite different from any other.

I assess with wonder this man who is full of contradictions, who seems to vacillate between two cultures, one moment a religious fanatic, the next moderately tolerant, even likable.

And then, like an afterthought, he asks, "Do you care to become my *sigheh*?"

"What! What did you say?" I blurt out as if I did not understand what he wants. "I'm Jewish, you know."

"Yes, I know. It is the proper thing to do. For a night, two, or as many as you wish, of course. Not much to it, I assure you. I'll perform the religious ceremony myself in private. At the Beverly Wilshire Hotel, where I will be staying."

This process the *mullah* is suggesting, of my becoming his *sigheh*, his temporary wife, is an easy procedure. A short prayer will legally join us as man and wife, removing religious barriers. Free him for sex. Once done with me, he will repeat "divorce" three times and the union will be annulled as if it had not occurred in the first place. Nothing to it! A respected Ayatollah recently endorsed temporary marriages based on the assumption that men are in need of "physical comfort" and the strained, post-war economy made marriage expensive.

A series of expressions scurry across his face, all of them appealing, each a testament to his desire for me.

Imagine! Just imagine Aziz's Soraya agreeing to become the temporary wife of a *mullah* she happened to meet on a plane ride to America.

I observe him with critical eyes, his carefully trimmed hair exposed below his turban at the nape of the neck and his crisp, white shirt under his religious garb. The well-shaped beard is masculine and his voice melodious. I attempt to clear my lungs of the assault of smells—licorice and cologne mingled with longing and deprivation. I could pinch my nostrils shut and tolerate him in order to relish the sound of Aziz's tormented voice.

—How could you, *Jounam*! How in the world could you—

I reach out and squeeze the *mullah*'s hand, lay it flat and willing on my palm. I am mesmerized by the long fingers, the nail beds square, the back of the hand fleshy, the nervous yet decisive gestures, a reminder of Ayatollah Khomeini's condemnatory wave that dismissed the Shah, ushering in an era of chaos, not only in Iran but eventually in my private life. I raise the hand

and press it to my lips, feel its dry warmth, the pulse at the tip of each finger.

—How could you, *Jounam*! How in the world could you—

Of course I can. Why not? I can and I will offer myself to this *mullah*, a man who embodies everything Aziz despises.

The hostesses are chatting behind the curtain; most of the passengers are asleep. Someone behind us has been writing for hours, his pen scratching, scratching like nails on sandpaper. My palm rests on my camera, an expensive piece of equipment my husband gave me as a gift, perhaps to assuage his guilt, or to keep me busy as he frolicked about.

I snap the case open and lift the camera, explain to the *mullah* that I am a photographer and would be honored to add his photograph to my private archives. It does not take him long to nod his permission.

Click!

I who have never, ever photographed a man other than my husband in that tender light reserved for lovers will now train myself to apply that same approach to snapshots of other men. I will become a collector of memories. Create an album, a compilation of photographs of men who will fall prey to my camera. I do not know what the stars have in store for me. What I know is that revenge must be extracted with calculated patience and complete emotional detachment.

The *mullah* retrieves a leather-bound notebook from his pocket. With an enamel, gold-tipped fountain pen, in elaborate royal-blue calligraphy, he inscribes his name—Mirharouni—and the phone number of the Beverly Wilshire Hotel, tears the page off, and hands it to me.

I fold the paper into a neat square and tuck it in my purse.

chapter 2

Beyond the window of my penthouse suite at the Peninsula Hotel, past the palms and the high-rises, smog furls in the air and the sky is the color of grief. Crows screech in treetops. Church bells ring somewhere in the distance. Nature is agitated.

I have been in Los Angeles for two days, walking the streets, observing, studying this place that I must call home one day. I miss Tehran. The languid afternoons, the late-night revelries, but especially Mamabozorg's wise words dispensed with juicy pomegranate seeds, dried berries, and cardamom-scented tea bags she purchased for me in the bazaar, aware I can't tolerate dark tea.

If you are ever forced to leave your country, she advised me the day Ayatollah Khomeini set foot in Iran, go to a place where the sky is the same color as Tehran's. Young and naïve then, I had taken her words literally and had laughed out loud, reminding her that the skies are the same color everywhere. How wrong I was. This horizon is foreign and forbidding. It is not mine.

Americans, too, might not accept me. Despite the passage of two decades, how could they forget the hostage crisis, the burning of their flag, the shouts of "Death to the Great Satan" as their people were led, blindfolded, around the walled compound of the

American Embassy, their humiliating images projected on television screens around the world?

Not many people walk the streets of Beverly Hills, and the few who do seem to be in a hurry. Commuters eat, drink, apply makeup in their cars. Joggers, speed walkers, and exercise fanatics behind health-club windows flaunt abnormally toned muscles. What function do these well-fed, well-exercised bodies have if they do not slow down to enjoy themselves, allow themselves to be admired? The neutral, sexless smells of perfumes and deodorants prevail in streets, restaurants, elevators. I miss the scents of excitement, fear, and arousal that permeated my past life.

Men's sensuality seems dulled here, their listless gazes turned inward. Aziz kissed with open eyes.

—Feel me with your mouth and your eyes, *Jounam*—

Does Parvaneh, that insect of a butterfly, lick the tips of your lashes, too, Aziz? Does she dream of your sleepy eyes that mirror the full range of your emotions—sadness, joy, and, above all, desire. Eyes that don't shed tears. Not the day we were married. Not the night you heard the news that your mother—still young—had died when her car veered out of control and toppled off the winding Chaloos Road. Not even that day in the doctor's office when you were convinced you'd never become a father.

Is Aziz attracted to her yearning to become a mother, the erotic longing she carries in full view? He must have succumbed to the softness in her womb, taken in by her seeming vulnerability, her seductive innocence. Is she as timid in private as she pretends to be in public? No! The Parvaneh I've known as my best friend must be very different from the woman he holds in his arms.

When did he first make love to her?

Despite my efforts to avoid the most painful question of all, it lingers like stale sin. Does Aziz have sex with her or make love to her? How could he bring himself to kiss her on the mouth, taste her saliva, the humid warmth he had searched for under my tongue? Our kisses, Aziz and mine, were wildly intimate. No one else, I assumed, would ever come to decode the language of our kisses.

I fooled myself into believing that I would welcome honest answers to my endless questions. But the last couple of days, in transient periods of clarity, I've come to realize that even if I had brought myself to ask, he would have been wise to lie. The truth is devastating.

I adjust the camera strap against my shoulder and lock the door of the suite behind me, cross the hotel hallway—an expanse of varying shades of persimmon—and take the elevator down to the bar. I have some time before I meet a real estate agent the concierge recommended. I grapple with a sense of excitement and dread at having to build a new life in unfamiliar territory—purchasing a house in a foreign land—a conclusive act, so final. Mamabozorg Emerald believed that no well-respected family would think of leasing—pay in cash, receive the goods in return, yours to own, forever.

—Forever mine, *Jounam*, and don't you ever forget!—

The hotel bar is bathed in the smoke and odor of cigars, greed, and burning cedar in the fireplace. A man in yellow spandex pants, better worn on the beach, occupies a stool by the bar; another man, lost in some other world, sits back in a leather chair, concern or sadness lining his handsomely tanned face. A young man smiles at me from a corner, a finger drumming on his temple as if to restructure his thoughts. The sight of a couple, clicking highballs of a chocolate-colored drink, overwhelms me with renewed grief and regret.

—*Besalamati, Jounam*, to your health, my life—

I raise the viewfinder to my eyes and take in the exceptional quiet in a place that bustles in the evenings with all types of men—American, Middle Eastern, European, and Iranian. I photograph the Cimmerian beauty of the mahogany walls, the anemic charm of the sconces, and the muted steps of servers who have been trained to beam at customers for no particular reason.

I pan my camera on the two men and ask if they would mind me taking a couple of pictures. Their lips part in smiles of approval. One man leans sideways in a charming pose against the bar; the other straightens his silk tie, then runs long fingers through his full hair. "What's the photo for, beautiful?"

"To make my husband jealous." My laughter sounds false, loud, and unconvincing to me, but not to the men, who reward me with conspiratorial, flirtatious poses.

"Then go ahead, beautiful, take as many as you want. Nothing's sexier than a healthy dose of jealousy."

The expected, magical reaction is occurring—actors at the beck and call of their tall, blond director and her camera. I snap a wide-angle shot as an overture, and then zoom in on their hungry-eyed and lust-flushed faces.

With the *click, click* of my camera, a pleasant echo in my chest, the discord in my head begins to unwind as I take one picture after another. "Thank you, gentlemen," I purr. Their bodies relax and mold back into the supple luxury of leather chairs. "A few more and I'll be on my way."

Click!

The flash of a row of keen teeth, a palm smoothing hair shiny with brilliantine, the spark of a pair of hazel-green eyes.

Click!

I press the rewind button and leave the bar in time for my appointment.

A broad-chested, elegantly dressed man is waiting in the foyer next to the mahogany table, by the flower arrangement, a burst of vulgar colors. An urge to rearrange and simplify his backdrop takes hold of me, the ever-nagging desire to honor aesthetical decorum.

He walks toward me and extends his hand. "Soraya?"

"Mrs. Aziz," I correct as my fingers get lost in his strong grip.

"Mrs. Aziz. Steve Rivers, Bel Air Real Estate." His stare lingers on the diamond studs on my earlobes and the amber necklace, my lifeline to Mamabozorg.

I take in his peppermint breath, glance at his broad chest and fair complexion. Good genes these American men have. Iranian men are rarely so tall, so blue-eyed, so utterly gullible, I've been told, and now believe, as he releases my hand as if letting go of embers. An Iranian man would have squeezed and held my hand, sized, undressed, and licked me with a gaze that spoke of a million possibilities.

"I lined up three exceptional properties for you," Mr. Rivers says.

"Which one has the most land?"

"One is fifteen acres. It's one of the largest properties in Bel Air. It's been on the market for three days and comes furnished."

"I'll see this one first."

He points to my Nikon camera. "A photographer, Mrs. Aziz?"

I remove the camera from its case, my glance sliding over his face and down his body, the sharp crease of his pants, the high gloss of his Gucci shoes. "A photographer, yes," I reply, but only of men, I want to add, but decide against it.

—Leave the camera behind, *Jounam*—Aziz would suggest when we were on our way for a stroll up the Tajrish overpass around the Shemiran Mountains—I want your undivided attention—

He will never know now that he always had that. Will never know that the camera was his best ally, that if ever a minute particle of my attention wandered off course, the viewfinder would attract and bring it back into focus like a magnet.

"May I take your picture, Mr. Rivers?"

"Of course." A smile lights up his pale eyes. He straightens his back, relaxes his knees, leans on the table.

I check him through the viewfinder. The masculine outline of his body is beautiful. I zoom in on the angles of his features—the indentation below his cheekbones, his strong mouth, the curve of his chin—and frame him within the window of my awareness as the zoom lens draws him into intimate proximity. My brain shuts off the surrounding humdrum and my senses converge into the center of my retina. The possibilities are endless for me, a foreigner in a hotel at the edge of the world. I could invite him up to my suite, douse the flames, calm this unbearable turmoil, and no one would need to find out…except Aziz.

For my purpose, an Iranian man will serve better, of course. Aziz's Soree in the arms of a man who shares the same geography, culture, and language. That might prove difficult in America. But I am a patient and stubborn woman.

Steve Rivers holds open the front door of the passenger seat of his black Mercedes Benz, and to his visible surprise, I announce that I prefer to sit in the back.

As we drive along Wilshire Boulevard, the thought occurs to me that I have traded the familiar, lawless, traffic-choked streets of Tehran for the orderly lanes and stop signs of America. Look right, then left. The pedestrian has the right of way—always. A fresh set of aches settles in my bones. I was familiar with the system back home. Learned to bribe the authorities, found ways to sidestep the law, even create my own rules in the limited boundaries of the Jewish community I occupied. Who will I become here? Will this country force me into blind compliance?

The traffic light on the corner of Westwood turns red. I observe Iranians among the pedestrians. I know their looks, expressions, mannerisms, even the way they walk, in deep thought and with their hands clasped behind their backs. Some were prominent in Iran, forced to abandon the products of decades of hard work, hand their mansions and great fortunes over to the Islamic Republic, uproot themselves, and become paupers of Westwood. Others, who did not have a dime or a title to their names back home, have become moguls of Beverly Hills, stuffed their houses with gilded antiques and colorful carpets, and still, at every opportunity, lament an unfair revolution that dealt them a bad hand.

"You are exceptionally tall for an Arab woman," Mr. Rivers says, shattering the positive image I had drawn of him.

"Iranians are not Arab, Mr. Rivers!"

"Pardon me, Mrs. Aziz. Didn't mean to offend you. Imagine experiencing a revolution. That's something!"

Certain that if I raise my camera, I'll capture this man's stupidity, I don't bother telling him that it would behoove him to pray to whatever God he believes in to never experience a revolution.

Up Sunset Boulevard and through the Bel Air east gate, mansions are wrapped in drowsy silence and the air is melancholy with ocean scents. The lush seascape of Ramsar, north of Tehran, comes alive like the deep cherry and azure shades of an Isfahan carpet. The lazy warmth of the Caspian Sea, the steaming peaks of its mountains, the seductive humidity under the jungle canopies.

Idle summers with Aziz.

Family trips with my friend, Parvaneh.

chapter 3

My friend and I attended the same school. I was the tallest and blondest girl, she the most petite, her wild hair ink-black. She was fragile and vulnerable and navigated her world with cautious pessimism, as if her Aunt Tala might spring out from behind unknown corners, able and more than willing to inflict yet another undeserved injury upon her charge.

I, on the other hand, was stubborn and fearless and trusting of my world then, a world that comprised Baba, a loving disciplinarian; Mamabozorg Emerald, always lenient when it came to me; and Madar, who adored and idealized Baba and supported his every decision.

We were in second grade, Parvaneh and I, when she weaved her way to me in the classroom, holding her lunch box tight against her chest. It was afternoon recess time, the empty room dense with the smells of leftover food in brown bags and lunch boxes.

"Do something, Soraya, please. Do something bad to Ahmad." She eyed a bully who had made her life miserable, calling her names and tearing the frilly *joupons* petticoats she wore under her skirts to fluff them up around her skinny thighs. There was something about Parvaneh in those days, a certain timidity and reluctance to fight back, that encouraged some boys into harassing her and others to follow her with puppy eyes.

"I know you can do it," she pleaded, wiping her tears with the back of one hand.

"Do what?"

"I don't know. Just make him go away. I beg you, Soraya. Do it for me."

Was it her seeming neediness or her admiring, hero-seeking expression that goaded me on? Perhaps it was the sense of vulnerability she exuded like a tempting invitation. At any rate, the need to step in and protect my friend from Ahmad, from her life, from the wiles of the world, was stronger than reason. So, I held her by the hand and led her into the school yard.

I would never again study a shrub, a flower, a tree, or an herb without recalling that time as the time I first became interested in the study of plants, their hidden healing powers, as well as their ability to hurt. Oh! I was a novice then—no, not even that. I was a curious child, hunched over in a patch of wild plants during recess, my friend leaning over me and watching me with stunned admiration as I picked and rubbed, smelled and tasted unknown plants in the laboratory of my mouth.

She encouraged me with her ceaseless mantra: "You can do it. You can do it, Soraya." To this day, I don't know whether the concoction I invented from some prickly plants, DDT-tainted soil, and water from a mosquito-infected puddle was poisonous or not. What I know is that the endeavor was a success.

I broke a piece off a bar of chocolate I had brought to snack on, dropped it in the concoction to mask the taste, then poured the whole mess into a half-full bottle of Coca-Cola. Bottle in hand, with Butterfly in tow, I marched toward the end of the school yard, where boys played soccer during lunch hour. We sat on a ledge by a garden of geraniums and waited for the game to end, the hiss of Parvaneh's anxious fingernails against her flesh louder than the whirr of sprinklers behind.

It was one of those bright days when the air smelt of rotting fruit and sweating leaves. I remember that day well. How could

I not? It was Wednesday, October 13, 1971. The day before, we had watched on television the opening ceremony that inaugurated the four-day festivities in honor of the anniversary of the 2,500-year-old Persian Empire. Iran was decked, groomed, and adorned beyond recognition.

Preparations had begun ten years before. New roads were built. Infrastructures strengthened. Airports renovated. A tent city was erected on 160 acres of desert land in the city of Persepolis. The desert was cleared of snakes, scorpions, and other poisonous creatures. Parisian architects, chefs, seamstresses, and all manner of artisans were flown in, as well as mature trees and flowers to turn the arid land into a green oasis. Mohammad Reza, the Shah of Iran, was holding what Orson Welles would call "the celebration of twenty-five centuries." And what the Ayatollah Khomeini would label the "Devil's Festival."

Proudly erect and decked in formal regalia, the Shah faced the tomb of Cyrus the Great and, with a strong voice filled with conviction, proclaimed: "Cyrus, we gather today around the tomb in which you eternally rest to tell you: rest in peace, for we are well awake and we will always be alert in order to preserve your proud legacy."

In eight years, the Pahlavi dynasty would be no more.

That day, still innocent and unaware of the future, I sat next to Parvaneh in the school yard and waited for Ahmad's soccer game to end. Afterward, we followed him to the water fountain, where he washed his face and dried it with his sleeves. I held out the bottle of Coca-Cola. Full of himself, rooster chest puffed out, certain this was a peace offering and that he had managed to bring Parvaneh to her knees, he gulped down half the concoction. He doubled over spewing and retching from the foul taste, but more so from embarrassment.

Parvaneh, breathless and flushed, raised my hands and pressed her lips to the back of one, then the other, as if to crown me the empress of the Persian Empire. "You are amazing, Soraya! You're never scared."

My heart darted around like a rabbit in my chest. From fear? From the pleasure of triumph? The reward of admiration? I'm not quite certain.

What I know is that all through elementary school, the responsibility of confronting bullies who crossed her path fell upon me, even if that meant having to lie to Baba to explain why I sometimes tossed all feminine restraint down the Rostam Gorge and behaved like a fatherless *dehati* village boy, or acted like a beggar from the boondocks of Samereh. It just felt good. Me, the benevolent keeper of my friend.

When we were twelve, Parvaneh became more serious and responsible. A bit more defiant. When her spinster aunt—who had moved into her home after Parvaneh's mother died—was present, Parvaneh no longer cast her eyes down, but looked her aunt straight in the eye and wrapped her arms across her chest as if to protect herself from Tala's lashing tongue.

Aunt Tala carried the stale smell of Turkish coffee on her breath and the biting odor of discontent on her ash-gray skin. She resembled a clacking skeleton rather than a woman with flesh on her bones. Her smoke-colored, ankle-length dresses with their winglike sleeves added to her funereal appearance. Contrary to her name, which meant "gold," her heart was made of cold stone.

It was around then that Parvaneh began to ask a lot of questions. She wanted to know why a God, who was "Our Father in Heaven," had allowed her mother to be invaded with a cancer that killed her in less than thirty-two days. And why, soon after, He struck again, storming her father's brain with petrifying images that rendered him a helpless idiot who whistled sad, outdated tunes, wandering aimlessly in his own home.

Having no one else to trust with her questions, she brought them to my Baba, who replied that God had his own mysterious ways and that we were too limited in our intelligence to understand. In answer to her dramatic declaration that she would die from grief, he chuckled under his breath and assured her that she would keep breathing and her pulse would continue to beat for a long, long time because it was far more stubborn than she could ever imagine.

And Madar, always there, always worrying in the periphery of Baba's world, ready to step in and validate, if he needed validating, would serve Parvaneh a cup of mint tea with rock sugar, pat her on the back of the hand, and offer her one of her restrained smiles. "Listen to Baba, Parvaneh. He is a wise man."

Madar did not mention that Baba was also the generous benefactor who paid for Parvaneh's tuition, uniforms, books, and stationery. But Parvaneh must have guessed because soon she was drafting two different essays on the same subject, outlining the reading assignments, copying them, and taking notes in classes I missed. I had more pressing matters on my mind. I was thirteen; I had just met Aziz.

Parvaneh, too, celebrated her thirteenth birthday that year. It was around then that a strain of deception that must have lain dormant began to yawn and stretch and shake itself awake. She studied hard and excelled in her grades, so she could someday move out and free herself from that witch. Not only that, but she spread out her colorful wings and transformed herself into a caring butterfly, attending to loving, motherly details: spit-cleaned a stain on my father's shoe, scolded him for losing weight, remembered to buy my mother a birthday gift, and visited her at home when she was out of sorts to shampoo and blow dry her hair.

Having adopted my parents as her own, she played the role of the obedient daughter. I, on the other hand, possessed the required intelligence, courage, and temerity to keep alive our family name and multiply my inherited wealth. I admired our differences. We complemented each other.

As she became older, Butterfly's body refused to grow round and voluptuous. I pulled down her bathing suit once to see for myself what her breasts looked like—those tiny buttons with no sway to them. At that moment, as young as I was, I comprehended the lure of a pair of arrogant, well-rounded breasts like mine.

That year, her aunt went to the bazaar and bought an extra-large, white kerchief, marched straight to the synagogue of our chief rabbi, Eshagh the Henna Beard, and demanded that he sign all four corners of the cloth with a black marker, to make sure his signature would not wash off or the kerchief be replaced for another. That, to my great horror, was the nuptial cloth Butterfly was expected to use on her wedding night to display her blood to her in-laws as proof of her virginity.

I hurried home from school that day and snuggled in Madar's comforting scent of talcum and violets. My words tripped over each other in my haste to tell her what I heard from Parvaneh and ask whether it was true that brides had to show a bloody piece of cloth the morning after their wedding. That was before Madar's inexplicable tantrum and before she turned her back on Baba, leaving me confused and angry. But that day, her silvery pallor heightened in the pearly mist that crept in from the window, she touched my lips with one manicured finger. "Yes, it's true, Soraya. It's an appalling custom. But you don't have to do it if you don't want to. I'll never force you."

"What if my future mother-in-law demands it? This bloody thing? Will you shut her up?"

"That's up to your father." She moved closer to me and wrapped her silk shawl about our shoulders as if to buffer us from the shock of what was to come.

What came was Aunt Tala's increasingly abusive behavior.

She framed and hung the nuptial cloth from a hook on the wall that faced Parvaneh's bed. Her aunt not only forbade her to remove the frame until her wedding day, but also demanded that she stand in front of it every night and repeat aloud that her virginity was her honor and that she'd guard it with her very last breath.

The first night Parvaneh braved the framed nuptial cloth, her aunt stood guard, legs apart, arms resting against the doorjamb like a bat about to take flight.

Butterfly tried to repeat the words Aunt Tala ordered her to recite, but the rabbi's ominous, spidery signatures threatened from all four corners and, as if a bird was stuck in her throat, nothing but croaking sounds came out.

Butterfly sank into a well of grief. I should have left her alone there, allowed her to drown in her black moods. But I did not. I held her hand and tried to teach her what I knew well. How to ignore her aunt and find her own way of snuggling into her own skin. She misunderstood.

She grew her fingernails long and painted them deep violet, shaded her eyes with smoky kohl, tainting her lips cherry red and braiding her hair with turquoise beads as if she were queen of Sheba.

Her aunt warned her that if she didn't trim her nails, rinse off her Valentino eyes and vampire lips, no one would ask for her hand and she would shrivel into a spinster, become wrinkled and sour like pickled cucumbers, and end up in New City, a one-penny whore.

Her father, a few gray hairs spiking the top of his head, his once cleft chin puckered like a cock's wattle, pointed a thick, yellow fingernail at his daughter and smiled one last time before catapulting into eternal silence.

Once we turned fourteen, an age when defiance was no longer tolerated in our community, and Parvaneh still refused to mature and settle down, I decided she was incapable of rising above her teenage mutiny. Born in a sexually repressed world and brought up by an abusive aunt, she was doomed to forever flap her wings against her gated boundaries.

I took it upon myself to free her from her cocoon. Why? I should have abandoned her there in the shallow darkness of her shell. What arrogance could have made me believe that I possessed the power to overcome all hurdles and change her world? Now, looking back, I recognize that I was young and reckless and rode high and proud on the egoistic conceit of an only child, the favorite of a grandmother who was nearly impossible to please and an iron-willed father who had, more often than not, given in to my demands. Yes, that was part of it. But I also longed for the friend I'd lost. The friend who was there to listen, encourage, praise, defend, and lie for me when necessary.

So that day, fourteen and fearless, I promised Parvaneh that I would encourage Aziz to introduce her to his business partner, Hamid.

Her eyes sparkled against her skin and her dark pupils narrowed like a cat's. Her lashes, exaggerated with midnight-blue mascara, cast spiky shadows on her flushed cheeks. Her small teeth glistened against bloody lips. The scent of the Chanel No. 5 she had splashed on her armpits intensified.

"Will Aziz mind?" she whispered in cautious delight. "I'm sort of embarrassed."

I imitated an old woman's warnings. "Get over your embarrassment, my dear girl, and find yourself a husband before your maidenhead shrivels and disappears between your legs."

She laughed so hard that she almost fell off her chair. "You sound scarier than Aunt Tala. All right, Soraya, you win."

"Go easy on the makeup. Men don't like too much."

Two teardrops sprang to her eyes and slid down her lashes. "Not sure I'm ready for this. You're so brave, Soraya, getting married when you turn fifteen. But me, I don't know."

Never in my young life had I seen such a sweep of emotions, such a chameleon quality in a person. I admired Parvaneh for her spontaneity, for her vacillating moods, for blushing violently when she, at last, met Hamid, and for having clipped her fingernails short and having the sense not to wear makeup that day.

Yes! Butterfly *did* marry Hamid, Aziz's partner. Yes! I am to blame. I am the one who, with wide open arms, invited her into our life, mine and my husband's.

I tossed lovely Butterfly with her transparent, engulfing wings between Aziz's inviting thighs, left the two of them free to roam the high mountains of my homeland, hike the lush trails by the Darakeh River, drink in the crisp air from the snow-capped peaks of the Alborz, lie under weeping willows, and revel in peach sunsets, while I exiled myself to a terrain as flat and foreign as a stranger's palm.

chapter 4

Steve Rivers steers the car through the gates of the Bel Air mansion and across a cobblestone driveway flanked by regal maple trees. The driveway leads onto a vast open space carpeted with saffron-colored gravel and bordered on both sides by a double-knot pattern of clipped boxwood.

My breath catches at the sight of the glorious French mansion of rosy brick and white stone beyond, a splendid two-story edifice with slanted slate roofs and numerous windows carved into the slopes of old-fashioned attics.

White bougainvillea cascades over balustrades of two staircases flanking the house. The staircases curve up toward the second level, extending into mock balconies that frame a marble placard onto which the name of the house is carved:

Chateau Laurier-Rose Blanc.

An odd name. Must have been left forgotten from earlier times when the grounds were planted with white oleander. Why would anyone name their home after the ugly, poisonous flower? The petals fall limply around the corolla, and the oblong leaves have a way of turning away from the flower as if appalled by its smell.

I turn around to survey the land through the back window of the car, the expansive driveway behind me, the geometrically accurate bordering. I am pleased. The purity of white and green is a respite from my personal chaos. "Show me the inside, Mr. Rivers."

Filtered sunlight pours through massive French windows, glazing the interior with copper hues. No! Not this excess. The ornate décor exacerbates the great clutter in my head. I want quiet. I want simplicity. In the dining room the crown moldings, the Louis XVI gilded chairs, gold-threaded upholstery, and engravings on the antique dining-room table are far too elaborate. I want a garden. A piece of land to care for. Enough space to create my own haven, a place to shelter my fragments, to plant, nurture, and hone my resentment.

The French windows in the drawing room open to a spacious veranda I walk out onto. Below, acres of rolling land stretch out to the horizon. On my right, a gazebo is hardly visible under a mass of climbing jasmine. The last half of the grounds, as far as the eye can see, is allotted to acres of land with all types of fruit trees. A bridge crosses a brook that snakes somewhere out of sight. Although the landscape that leads to the front of the house is meticulously cared for, these gardens in back are neglected. The weeds need uprooting, the dripping wisteria training, the climbing jasmine taming, and the iceberg roses spraying.

How could the owner have cared for his carpets and art, clipped the hedges in front with such diligence, yet abandoned an expanse of such valuable land? The nagging question lingering, I cross the veranda and take the steps down. I stroll among the vegetation and stroke the rough bark, the grainy leaves that creep up the gazebo, and the few petals that cling to parched stems. I kneel down and rub a fistful of dark, rich earth between my palms, smell its properties. Moist and full of minerals and humus, this soil is far superior to that in my Tehran garden. The possibilities are endless for such fertile earth. A wealth of plants can be cultivated, grafted, and left dormant in this friendly climate—as they certainly once were.

Baba would appreciate this piece of land, too.

One early morning, when I had come to tend to the plants in the greenhouse Aziz had built in our Tehran estate, I heard a cautious tap on the glass panel. This was my cloistered haven, a place where I loved my plants and nurtured my soul. My friends and family had learned to respect my time there, so I was surprised to find my father at the door.

I waved, encouraging him to enter, this lonely man who had sought me for comfort as the gulf between him and my mother widened and, in the process, had learned to share my interest in plants—so much so that he often brought me all types of exotic seeds from around the world. I welcomed the chance to show him that the emotional geography of plants was not that different from our own.

"They are magic! They will keep you busy and content without becoming cold and distant." I didn't add that they are more loyal and certainly more appreciative than Madar, whose silent withdrawal felt like betrayal.

Baba moved a pot of Pelargonium cordifolium aside and settled next to it on the wooden bench, then absentmindedly stroked the leaves of the plant on his other side.

"Don't touch that one. It's hemlock. It can poison you."

He locked his fingers in his lap. "You have a tender way with plants, Soraya. Didn't mean to disturb you, but it's hot. I couldn't sleep. So I walked here. Feels like *zelzeleh* weather."

"Relax, Baba, heat has nothing to do with earthquakes," I said as I pruned the Mexican Cestrum with the red leaves and inflated, purple tube flowers that resemble immodest creatures. He observed me as I tamed the Geranium harveyi, spraying each delicate, smoky leaf to a glossy shine and misting its flowers. Every embryonic tentacle, every baby leaf, every freshly produced bloom, I told him, was a show of gratitude and a testament to the competence of their creator.

He ambled among the plants, passing his palm over their leaves, their blossoms and stems, his usually erect body stooped.

It pained me to see him in such a state of resignation. I asked if he missed Madar.

"A wife shouldn't abandon her nuptial bed no matter what. Enough is enough. *Bebakhshim va faramoush konim.* Let us forgive and forget."

I shot him a questioning look. Struggled to keep my surprise out of my face. It was not in Baba's character to share such intimate matters. He must be in real pain.

Unaware of the source of Madar's anger, but wanting to patch things between my parents, I had once attempted to pry the truth from my mother. "You love your father far too much to be objective," she had sighed. "You won't understand. To him, I'm like a cockroach he might squash underfoot. Who am I, after all? A worthless wife who carried his child for nine months and raised her to become a capable and independent woman."

She had once again attempted to add a layer of guilt to a pile she imagined I had accumulated throughout the years. She, my own mother, did not realize that I was different from her, that I was not prone to carrying other people's guilt.

At the time, I didn't know that the role of martyrdom Madar chose granted her some kind of power. That's why she preferred to stay put in the sad upstairs bedroom she had moved into.

Baba stopped in front of a pot of Silver Beads, a rare plant with miniature, triangular, silver leaves, the juxtaposition of black and silver striking. I had brought the seeds from New Zealand and planted them in a pot Aziz and I purchased in the Marché aux Puces in Paris, a dragon-draped container etched with Japanese bamboo.

This one held a special place in my heart. The plant evolved from sapling to maturity, its wiry, coal-black stems coiling and looping until they came to resemble our chief rabbi's signature—the same one he had stamped on four corners of that cursed nuptial piece of cloth. Daddy Long Legs, Aziz had christened the Silver Bead in an intimate moment in my greenhouse.

Baba shut his eyes and inhaled the vapors that spiraled from the pot. The glass panels broke into sweat. I kissed Baba on the forehead. He had, like me, learned to identify the character of plants from the nuances of their scents.

He straightened his back, and the impish sparkle lighting his eyes made him look younger. "Will you humor your old Baba and spare this? It's for a dear friend."

A strained moment of silence passed between us. The sun made its way through the glass panels, painting everything sepia. I handed the plant to him, this treasure that continued to be the source of many private jokes between Aziz and me. "Of course, Baba, it's all yours. Who for?"

He tapped playfully on my nose with his finger. "Now, now, my Nightingale, you're not to put your Baba on the witness stand."

I would have done anything to hold on to that moment, to the rekindled mischief in his eyes, the lighthearted humor, the Baba who had suddenly shed his sadness like snakeskin.

Will I end up lonely like my father? Bitter like my mother?

I walk deeper into the Bel Air gardens, surprised anew at the extent of neglect. The thicket of weeds becomes denser as I move farther away from the house and into a vast grove of dried oranges clinging to branches, peaches half-eaten by squirrels, rotten apples underfoot. The layered silence is broken by the dry crack of dead branches and leaves crushing under our footsteps, mine and Mr. Rivers.

And then, just beyond a puddle of stale water, I notice a slab of pink marble. A stain of bloody liver among the leaves. I cautiously approach, brush away a blanket of dead leaves with my shoe, and bend closer. A muffled silence shrouds the place as if all bird life suddenly ceased. The marble feels cold. A shudder runs across my bones as I attempt to register the meaning of the engraved gold letters on the stone at my feet. *Beloved Friend and Husband, Your Memory Forever Lives*

I step back with a start. "What in the world is this, Mr. Rivers?"

He clears his throat and coughs into his palm. "Mrs. Aziz, I meant to tell you about this, um, grave." His mouth frames large, capped teeth that seem to speak honestly. "The husband passed away last year and the wife buried his ashes here. At that time she wanted him close by, I was told. Wouldn't allow the gardeners anywhere near the grave. But something must have happened lately and she…well…she decided to sell the house."

Some people can't bear their memories, and some of us can't let go of them.

I follow Mr. Rivers back inside the house and enter a vestibule that connects a set of suites. "These are the children's rooms."

"Don't bother. I don't have any children, Mr. Rivers. Show me the rest of the house."

Baba appeared unannounced on my doorstep one day fifteen years back. He did not bother to greet me with the usual kisses on both cheeks. I took the coat thrown over his shoulder and led him into the family room.

"No, thank you," he said curtly, insisting he would be more comfortable in the formal salon. Not a good sign. He refused the herbal drink of *gole-gav-zaban*, passion flower, and demanded dark tea. He sat erect in a high-backed armchair, the cup of tea steaming in his nicotine-stained grip.

"You have been married five years, Soraya. You are twenty, not growing any younger, and neither is Aziz. Time you had a son. A son would be the cane to support you in old age." Having delivered his verdict, he stood up, squeezed my face between his hands, and stared into my eyes as if my bleak future was reflected there. He kissed me on the forehead, tossed his coat across his shoulders, and disappeared in the heavy smog.

That night, I considered my choices. I could stop taking the pill. I could conceive. But the truth was that with the passing years, my need for Aziz's undivided attention had intensified. Other women could open their legs for their men to ejaculate tiny creatures in them. Other women could fuss about becoming pregnant, giving birth, and spending rewarding years raising kids. I had Aziz. Our life was in perfect harmony. I did not intend to shatter the exclusive wholeness of our love.

As if I had just revealed that I was terminally ill, Mr. Rivers quickly guides me away from the children's quarters and into the master suites.

I take in the Baccarat chandelier, the Savonnerie carpet, the drapery sheers, silk fauteuils, and damask wall covering. A door at the other end of the bedroom catches my eye. I step into a walk-in closet. There is electricity, possibility for plumbing, and ample space for a sink and counter. Narrow enough for everything to be easily reached. The space can be converted into a darkroom.

I like to work late into the night, escape to the darkroom for hours to watch images drift up and take shape from their white sheets. Here, I can develop the rolls of film from Iran—a history of the intimate years with my husband, a record of the rise and ebb of his moods and the slightest details of his physical changes: each additional gray hair, each wrinkle that complemented his elegant features, each degree of the deepening of his tan and the toning of yet another already fit muscle. The slight, imperceptible stages of transformation would shed light on what might have incited him to turn into the man he has become.

I follow Mr. Rivers into a circular, mahogany-paneled library. Onyx fireplaces, gilded sconces, demilune tables, chenille sofas, and ottomans crowd the area. Odors of leather, fabric, and wood compete for attention. The high ceilings allow ample circulation, more oxygen for my lungs. In a corner, a cherry-wood grandfather clock with bronze numbers ticks with metallic finality.

On all three walls, lacquered shelves display leather-bound encyclopedias, their spines embossed with gold, black, or silver letters, warm and supple to my touch. *The Encyclopedia of Magical Herbs*; *The Illustrated Encyclopedia of Butterflies*; *Complete Guide to Plants and Flowers of the Orient*; *Illustrated Encyclopedia of Butterflies and Moths*; *Orchids, Desert Cacti, Rare Flowers of the*

Tropics. I slide the last book out, leaving a dark void behind. The pages are earmarked. Delicate annotations in green ink crowd the margins:

Required temperatures of 90 and humidity of 80%. Aphrodisiac. Rarely blooms. Some species edible, others poisonous.

I return the encyclopedia to the shelf and select *Nymphalidae: A Dictionary of Zoology*, fascinated by the range of butterflies—admirals, brush-footed butterflies, map butterflies, Rajah Brooke and Saturn butterflies—a major order of insects characterized by wings with overlapping scales. Adults have a sucking proboscis. In rare cases they possess chewing mouth-parts. The larvae are plant feeders, have chewing parts, and are quite destructive. Butterflies land on the reproductive organs of flowers, where sticky nectar is stored, after which the insects transfer the pollen back and forth from the female to the male. Butterflies reach their peak of activity at noon.

Chimes of the grandfather clock come to life, and I stroke the cherry-wood frame. I like its musky scent, its bold, unassuming grandeur that dominates the library. Like the tune it bursts into on the hour. "The Blue Danube." First dance on my wedding night.

Diamond filaments gird my hair, his tousled over his forehead, we sail on the ruby-veined marble floor of the Darband Hotel high up among grand mountains and meandering streams, his legs tempting between mine, amid layers of white shantung, gauze, and satin crimping higher up my thighs, his eyes warming coals of laughter, goading, demanding, anticipating.

—Come, *Jounam*, come—

Mr. Rivers coughs, startling me back to the reality of now, and I slide the encyclopedia back in its proper place. My cheeks feel warm. Sweat trickles down my armpits. Twisting my hair into a knot, I secure it on top of my head with a pen I find in my purse.

We continue to walk through a series of corridors and antechambers. The surrounding light changes from soft copper to warm melon hues and then to a dreamy sepia as we enter a magnificent open-air courtyard in the center of the house. I grab hold of the wrought-iron railing that separates the house from the courtyard below.

An open-air, sunken courtyard—succulent, moody, and reminiscent of a fourteenth-century French chateau—is set right in the heart of the mansion. And in the center of the courtyard stands an atrium. An amber jewel that reflects the surrounding landscape on its glass panels.

Giant-sized terra-cotta pots with Italian cypress adorn the perimeters of the courtyard. Smaller planters brim with snapdragon, baby's breath, and bleeding heart—colorful but not overpowering, sensual but not vulgar. Marble daises display Greek goddesses who have lost one limb or another to the betrayals of time. Grecian columns engraved with mythological, stone-eyed beasts support a pair of granite benches.

An immense monkey tree, conical and majestic, rises tall above the courtyard, branches adorned with sharp-tipped leaves extending out like so many dismissive arms.

I descend the staircase that leads to the sunken courtyard and approach the glass-domed, high-ceilinged atrium in the center. Flies and insects are scattered at the foot of the atrium. I direct a questioning look at Mr. Rivers.

"Dead moths and butterflies," he says. "The owner is an amateur lepidopterist."

"Look! Butterflies with transparent wings." Hardly detectable, I think, like my friend, Parvaneh, who camouflaged herself to wiggle her way into my life and deceive me in more ways than one.

How in the world could I have been so blind? I should have known she would want Aziz. She always wanted what I have.

I press my face to one of the sweating glass panels of the atrium. Bubbles of steam adhere to the glass, making it difficult to see the interior.

Mr. Rivers positions himself in front of the atrium's door. A sweeping gesture of his arm encompasses the entire glass dome. "It's easy to dismantle and haul everything away. A couple of hours work and you won't even know it was here."

"Never!" I reprimand Mr. Rivers, "Never, ever destroy a greenhouse."

I wave him aside and step in.

My heart flips with surprise and pleasure at the magnificence I face.

I lean on Mr. Rivers' arm, just for a second, to steady and reorient myself because I've been yanked away from the courtyard of a mansion up here in the Bel Air hills and am transplanted to a humid, equatorial rain forest, face to face with a jewel I've admired for a long time.

Amorphophallus titanum.

Corpse Flower.

The most splendid plant in the world.

More than three meters tall, the plant burrows its roots in a heat-sensitive container. Out of an oversized, grasping leaf of mesmerizing shades of lettuce and pistachio green, the stem rises like an enormous erection, as if to pierce the high-ceilinged glass dome.

Amorphophallus titanum: giant, shapeless phallus.

Found only in the deep, equatorial rain forests of Sumatra, the giant, shapeless phallus dislikes the process of procreation. Even in the wild it blooms less than three times in fifteen years. The week before the flower comes into bloom, the stem will grow more than fifteen centimeters a day. Once in bloom, as if disgusted by its own senseless exhibitionism, the bud starts to emit pulsating puffs of rancid odor that can be detected from far away.

Years ago, I considered adding the plant to my own collection. After extensive research, numerous experts warned me that the Corpse Plant rarely grows in captivity and is better left in the wild, where under the fecund atmosphere of the forest canopy, its stench attracts pollinators—carrion beetles and sweat bees—morbid insects that feast on its flesh and speed the senseless process of procreation.

Here, in the atrium, with pipes spraying mist and gadgets to adjust the humidity and temperature, the plant is flourishing.

I gently curl my palm around the voluptuous, maroon stem and rise on my toes to smell it. The first whiff is sticky and sweet like molasses, then lemony like concentrate of orange sherbet. At the base of my nose, as the scent travels down my throat, it turns slightly pungent like sumac and…a slap of bitter almonds. Cyanide, perhaps. I wonder if the stench is associated with the onset of blooming.

Dusk is falling. The setting sun is reflected on the atrium's glass panels. It is growing chilly. I hug myself and step out to check the color of the sky.

If the Amorphophallus, uprooted from deep in the Sumatra forests, managed to adapt so well here, maybe I too might have a chance.

chapter 5

FOR ONE WEEK NOW, I have been working from dawn to dusk in the gardens with a crew of landscapers and a famous Persian landscape architect, a flamboyant, pompous, red-haired man with a penchant for pink cravats and two-toned gangster shoes. I was obliged to have a serious talk with him. Inform him that although I admire his brilliant job of redesigning the Garden of the Heart's Delight in Shiraz, a garden known for having attracted hordes of colorful butterflies, my garden is mine and the last word will be mine as well.

I want a eucalyptus grove.

Construction cranes are in the process of hoisting mature eucalyptus trees over the wall to replace the half-dead fruit trees.

I will create a friendly environment for gold-and-black Monarchs to winter in menthol-steeped leaves.

But the courtyard with its atrium must remain as is. It would be cruel to disturb the exquisite Amorphophallus, full of black magic and mystery.

The climbing jasmine that chokes the gazebo is being trimmed, and the inside cleaned and readied for outdoor furniture. A round, turquoise-tiled fountain with floating nightshades and discreet lighting comes to life at night with colorful jets of water to attract Glasswing butterflies. Not one is in sight yet.

But I am a patient woman. Glasswings will come. According to the encyclopedias in the library, these butterflies lay eggs on the nightshade, after which caterpillars feed on the plant and store the poisonous alkaloids in their tissues. The poisons are converted to pheromones in males, engulfing each insect in a fragrant net into which the female butterfly gladly and willingly tumbles.

I've left orders not to disturb the grave at the end of the grounds for now. To respect the previous owner's wishes, perhaps. It is not every day, after all, that a wife decides to bury her husband right in her garden. Still, in the short time I've lived here, I've come to believe that this house—with its pink marble grave at the end of the grove, its growing population of butterflies, and its magnificent Corpse Plant in the atrium—is worth far more than the sum of its bricks and mortar. For all I know, immersing myself in the scent of jasmine and pine and amnesia in this garden might one day prove cathartic, providing some respite from longings that cling to me like larvae to leaves.

One day, I might even consider this place home. This place, where the three full-time gardeners know to leave me in peace, where no *pasdar* policeman will sprint over walls to violate my privacy, and where I am free to wear shorts and a tank top, unleash my hair, and breathe heavily after strenuous gardening, without fear that the rise and fall of my breasts will provoke the foul-minded, eavesdropping Morality Police.

Mamabozorg despised the Morality Police, who prowled about town, forcing everyone to adhere to the Islamic code. Fearless and certain she had nothing to lose and that the Morality Police would not dare lock an old woman in prison, she had glared at a Morality Police once and, as she liked to say, sent the horned ignoramus yelping away with his useless tail between his legs. The young man had ordered her to wipe off the nail polish applied to her fingernails. In reply, she had poked a forefinger at his chest and had asked him whether he knew who he was ordering around.

Taken aback by her unexpected audacity, the man had replied that he neither knew, nor cared.

My grandmother had pointed her manicured finger at his left eye as if she would gouge it out if he uttered another word. Holding him captive with her incriminating stare, she announced that even if such an order would have come from high above, she would never, ever consider walking around with neglected hands, because hers were the hands that had set diamonds in the crown that graced the worthy heads of their Imperial Highnesses, Reza Shah Pahlavi and his son, Mohammad Reza.

Mamabozorg was only sixteen years old in 1926, the year of Reza Shah's coronation, yet she had already apprenticed for eleven months under the tutelage of Haj Serajeddin, the celebrated jeweler entrusted with the coveted task of creating the royal crown. Imperial orders went out to open the doors to the Iranian Treasury, allowing Haj Serajeddin to select some of the most magnificent precious stones in the world.

Her forefinger remained aimed at the Morality Police who, fascinated by her story and impressed by her sharp memory, remained rooted in place as Mamabozorg went about announcing the exact carat weight of the precious stones set in the crown—five emeralds weighing 199 carats, 368 rare matching pearls, two dazzling sapphires weighing nineteen carats. And then, with a flourish of her other hand, she announced that the four sunbursts on the four sides of the crown were set with 3,380 of the purest of diamonds, weighing 1,144 carats.

"And this hand," she declared to the Morality Police, "the one pointing at your foolish eyes, is the same hand that set twelve of these diamonds in His Majesty's crown. So don't tell me how to treat my hands," she had announced, sending the stunned man on his way.

I check my own hands. How long has it been since my last manicure? I run a thumb over my wedding band. The rarest of diamonds twinkle in symphony. But no one is here to crown. No one here to lace and ornament and tease and paint for. I have been spending every sleepless dawn pruning, raking, and shearing the blue spruce and rose bushes, the bordering sun-drenched hydrangeas and creeping jasmine; digging, feeding, watering, and feeling the earth with bare hands to manipulate, flirt with, and seduce until the land yields to me.

What only a week before was an expanse of unkempt land has been planted with a host of carefully selected shrubs to feed caterpillars, plus nectar flowers and milkweed leaves to attract adult butterflies. The white heliotrope and perennials such as lilac, blueberry, and pussy willow are already tempting droves of tiny, orange butterflies. These creatures, although smaller than a thumb, are as irritating as a fly stuck in the ear and are starting to wreak havoc upon their habitat. They suck flowers dry of nectar, then embark on a frenzy of mating as if to make up for their fleeting life of three days. They exhibit a wicked attraction to the passion vine, to its vulgar scent, its sticky nectar, and particularly to its grasping branches.

I ordered a delivery of hundreds of thousands of eggs to breed Monarch butterflies. I study their life cycles as they transform into caterpillars and then to chrysalides. Caterpillars are destructive, greedy nuisances. They make a hearty meal of the remains of the case of their eggs, after which they store enough food to carry themselves through their pupa stage. They chew holes into the surrounding plants and destroy every leaf in their path. Then they swell, some to ten thousand times their weight, before shedding their skin. And voila! A strangely resilient butterfly emerges.

Humans get buried under earthquake rubble, break their bones in tornadoes, drown in stormy seas. Butterflies, despite their fragility, are hardly affected by most of these natural disasters. Not only that, they are capable of migrating unimaginable distances. They simply float with the wind, staying on track with uncanny tenacity until they arrive at their intended destination, just as my friend did.

The noon sun is hot, and the gardeners are on their lunch break.

It is that time of the day when the gardens are at their full glory, and the contented birds snooze under the shade of furled leaves. The turquoise fountain reflects the drowsy pattern of the sky. I wash my hands, scrub mud from under clipped fingernails.

I pick up my camera and enter the house, where the interior designer, Olivier Du Boise, is busy with his entourage. He is a quiet man, balding despite his youth. His stout upper body seeming to run ahead of his short legs and arms as if his torso is in a race with his lower half.

According to my orders, he has replaced the previous chenille sofas and suede ottomans with minimalist furniture, the gilded sconces with modern floor lamps, and painted the mahogany panels with an eggshell color.

"Simplify, Mr. Du Boise. Simplify! Don't touch the books in the library. Those are for my research. Leave the grandfather clock alone."

I stand back and assess the décor that is in the last stages of completion. The onyx fireplaces on both sides of the room resemble two ancient tombs. "More control, Mr. Du Boise. No crown moldings. No elaborate carvings. Simplify!"

He blows air through puckered lips. "Not possible, madame! Important to follow the architectural esthetics of a house. This is not a contemporary chalet…"

"This is what I want, Mr. Du Boise. Understood?"

The only embellishments my house needs are the pair of collector's cabinets padded and lined with black satin. They flank a mirror in my drawing room that reflects the garden, where butterflies are drunk on nectar and the riot of colors hurts my eyes.

On the hardwood table, which I prefer without a tablecloth, is my butterfly-collecting paraphernalia.

Also on the table is a red, mohair-covered album.

The album, with its growing collection of photographs, is testament to how I will trap men like moths in my net, suffocate them in jars, pin them in cigar boxes.

chapter 6

I BUZZ THE GUESTHOUSE INTERCOM to call Mansour, the Iranian chauffeur I hired. He has no relatives in California and is to be at my beck and call at all hours.

Mansour arrives, wearing his brown uniform and holding his cap deferentially, pleased that I've decided to leave the house at last. His combed-back hair is wet, but as it dries, the curls spring back into the tight coils he can't tame with strong-smelling pomades. A badly healed scar runs down the length of his left cheek, digging into his upper lip and giving his weather-beaten face the lopsided look of a felon who flaunts his injury with pride.

The scar is the result of a knife brawl, I am certain, to protect his *namous*, his honor, his woman. Knife fights are part of daily life in the streets of Tehran. An innocent look at Mansour's wife, sister, or mother could have provoked him to go for the jugular.

"Where to, *Khanom*?" he asks, tucking his hat under his arm.

"Take me to a secluded place nearby."

I do not tell Mansour that I am going hunting. Hunting for men I will trap in the lens of my camera. Collect their photographs. Do with them what I want.

"Franklin Canyon is nearby, *Khanom*, a fifteen-minute drive."

We ride to the Santa Monica Mountains and Franklin Canyon, up North Beverly Drive, and higher still around the winding road that leads to the canyon. From afar, the panorama seems lush and content, but as we get closer, trees and bushes turn the shade of mud. Los Angeles is thirsty.

Mamabozorg was right. The trilling of birds sounds better from afar.

Mansour parks the car on Lake Drive and opens the door for me.

"Pick me up in an hour, Mansour."

"I beg you, *Khanom*, don't go up there alone. It's dangerous. A woman was murdered here."

"Go run your errands, Mansour. I know how to take care of myself."

"*Bebakhshid* pardon me, I am the dust beneath your feet. All types of criminals prowl these hills."

I shoulder my camera and tripod. Turn my back to Mansour to conceal my smile. He has no inkling that I am the one who is on the prowl.

I leave Lake Drive behind and walk around the pond and up the canyon, my ears tuned to the sound of footsteps.

Ducks sail on the pond. Bullfrogs honk like war trumpeters. I am saddened by the sight of two herons that huddle on a moss-covered plank, content in their togetherness. Long-lashed deer eyes flicker among bushes, the slight tremble of a blue jay's wings among thirst-mottled leaves. The *tap, tap* of a walking stick echoes in the surrounding hills. A man? I isolate details of nature through the viewfinder, observe the world with sharpened eyes—flight of a crow, scampering of a pair of squirrels, rattling of snakes.

A couple strolls toward me. They hold hands. The woman's pale eyes and arched eyebrows glitter in the sunlight. She raises the man's hand to her red mouth and holds it there, white marks visible on the back of her hand where he must have squeezed too hard. The language of his hand is repulsive to me, this soliciting attention, only to reject. Yet her eyes continue to lick him with adoring glances.

Butterfly, too, must have melted like sticky syrup all over my husband.

The woman guides the man's hand toward her belly. She is pregnant. Their shared smiles send my stomach heaving, and for an instant, I envision myself carrying Aziz's child. I quickly turn away.

Swiveling my camera around the hills, I search for my prey.

None to be found.

I point my camera toward the far bank of the pond, toward a narrow bend, zoom in on strong, masculine legs. A man is jogging around the pond. A pulse jumps in my neck. I tighten my grip around the camera.

A quick calculation of the width of the pond, the distance that separates us, and I conclude that if he maintains his pace, while I slightly add to mine without raising his suspicion, we will come face to face in less than five minutes.

I hold him in my gaze, slink forward, soft-footed and determined, the scent of fresh possibilities propelling me forward.

He suddenly stops, bends to pull up one sock, and then resumes his trot toward a bench ahead. He stretches one leg, then another on the bench, his T-shirt rippling against his muscled back.

I circle the pond and move closer, closer to this man, my prey, frame his profile within the world of my camera. Bring his features into focus: sharp cheekbones, strong chin, tamed-back hair. The similarity of his mouth to my husband's is startling, the plump outline and defiant lower lip.

Aziz is an excellent photographic subject. At different times and places, I would fall in love again and again with the Aziz framed in my viewfinder. Take pleasure in focusing on the fine pores across his warm skin, the masculine shadow of his well-shaven beard, the strong folds of his mouth, the beads of perspiration on the bridge of his nose.

I position the tripod next to me and squat into picture-taking position. A bee buzzes across my ear. I slap it off and inadvertently push on the shutter release.

Click!

He turns around. The corners of his eyes crinkle like caterpillar antennas. His drooping eyelids intensify the shock of his stare, which is as direct and bold as the four-eyed Peacock butterfly.

The man in my viewfinder narrows his eyes into slits. He takes one threatening step toward me. Another ten steps and he will easily circle his hands around my neck and squeeze.

Still, I remain where I am, too close to this stranger, to his privileged aloneness. I like this, like it very much, this capturing of his bold image in my zoom lens. And I am not about to shy away. Not now that he alone exists in the freeze-frame of the moment.

I manipulate the shutter into frenzy, shoot off frame after frame—tapered fingers, arrogant cheeks, determined mouth.

Click!

He pounces ahead with five long strides. His bared teeth flash in the sunlight. With an angry shove, he pushes my camera away. "How about I pose for you," he says, sarcasm dripping from his voice.

"Oh! No!" I croon, every muscle on the alert. "Don't change a thing. You are perfection."

The voice is a valuable weapon, Mamabozorg taught me. Use the pitch, tenor, mood, and tone to disarm, befriend, humble, or to simply assert yourself. How right she was. And never forget, Soraya, Mamabozorg reminds, at times, silence, dark and deep and mysterious, can be far more effective than words.

The silent eye of my camera is focused between his thighs, this man who will forever live in my collection, allowing him ample time to savor my attention before the lens zeros back in on his face. I feel seen, even recognized, as if Aziz's gaze is bent on excavating my every last secret. I become deaf to all surrounding noises and scents but to the thumping in the man's chest, the insistent beat of the artery at the crook of his neck, because Aziz, loud and demanding, occupies my mind and body as my viewfinder continues to tease and kiss and caress this stranger.

I lower my camera at last, press four fingers to my lips, and send him an aerial kiss. "Thank you, my David! My Adam! You are an artist's dream."

His head slightly tilted, he assesses me with a measure of arrogance and curiosity.

"Sorry I interrupted your workout," I murmur shyly. "I couldn't resist."

His features open up and soften into an imperceptible smile. He is ripe to tumble like a fish into my net, yes he certainly is. And I am hungry to have my share before tossing him back into the deep.

Mounting my camera on the tripod, I switch on the self-timer and go to stand next to him. I throw my arm around his neck. Rest my head on his shoulder as if we are longtime lovers.

His arm tightens around my waist, squeezing too hard. My eyes half-closed, my smile flirtatious, I spread my net wider.

Click!

I touch my forefinger on my mouth, then press it to his. "What an amazing model!"

He introduces himself, holding my hand in his. "I live close by. Free?"

Just like that! Free? As if mine is a world of choices, as if I am free to decide how to pass this night and the others and yet others that will inevitably follow.

"Depends," I reply.

"On what?" he asks.

"On you," I say, folding the tripod and placing my camera in its case.

I cock my head and hold him in my gaze as he struts his muscles as if he is a slave being displayed for sale in a public *souk* market, and I am the buyer.

My gaze travels the length of his body, assessing, with seemingly detached interest, the merchandise presented to me. I like what I see; I certainly do. Can't imagine a more appetizing morsel.

I throw my shoulders up and turn my back to him.

The sweet taste of triumph in my mouth, I circle the pond, past the ducks and the love-struck herons, climb up the wooden steps, take the dirt road to the car, and order Mansour to drive back home.

chapter 7

I PULL UP A CHAIR and sit at the table in my drawing room, gather my butterfly net in the center, lean back, and observe an Emerald Swallowtail that accidentally fluttered into my net and, in so doing, robbed me of the pleasure of the hunt. The terrified butterfly trembles and quivers and flaps, unrolling its coil into a tube as if searching to suck upon any available drop of fluid in my net.

I breed these butterflies in the humid warmth of the atrium. Collect eggs in small containers, check them every morning for hatched caterpillars, and then transfer them to lidded jars to keep them from wandering about and devouring the Amorphophallus. If allowed, the mean creatures will embark on cannibalism, the larger ones feasting on the smaller caterpillars.

The fleeting life cycles, habits, and preferences of butterflies as they metamorphose from egg to caterpillar to chrysalis to winged adult fascinate me. The larva matures, attaches like *sirishom* glue to the firm support of a leaf or stem before changing to naked pupa or chrysalis. This is all a butterfly's life amounts to. Evolving from egg to worm to adult, with nothing better to do than obsess over a quick sip of nectar so as to get on with the senseless frenzy of mating.

Not much different from the friend I once knew who became a

rebellious teenager, as if it was a prerequisite to casting off her skin, a necessary stage before she metamorphosed into the seducer she became, banishing me to a foreign continent.

"Those foreigners!" Mamabozorg had spat out one day. "Here they go again. Meddling in our affairs."

Mamabozorg's declaration had embedded itself in my two-year-old brain, continuing to change form over the next thirty-three years, igniting a spark of suspicion now and then—sometimes justified, often not—making me wonder, even today, whether "those foreign elements" *did* meddle too much in our internal politics. Years later, older and able to better understand how her past bled into her present, I asked Mamabozorg what had upset her that day in 1966.

"Soraya, I still cannot get over the insult. My ears still turn red with shame when I remember that our own Queen Farah commissioned Van Cleef & Arpels to make her coronation crown. Not only that, but Reza Shah's sisters and daughters had the audacity to follow suit. Such insult! An upward spit that landed on our own faces. The Imperial family ignored our own wonderful jewelers and handed the honor to foreigners. Traitors! Reza Shah's bones must have rattled in his grave. Yes, his own flesh and blood acted like traitors! As if a plague had wiped out all of our own jewelers, Reza Shah's son opened the doors to our National Treasury to a French *maison*."

Pierre Arpels spent days in the basement of the Central Bank of Iran, where the national jewels were housed during Mohammad Reza Shah's reign. Since the precious jewels were not allowed to leave Iran, a workshop was set up for the jeweler, his designer, and foreman in the National Treasury room, where they worked under heavy security for six months. The result was a crown of unprecedented beauty that boasted a stunning emerald weighing 4.3 pounds.

I check the Emerald Swallowtail in my net. She must be female. Her abdomen is visibly larger than any male's, in order to store the great amount of fluids she suckles during her lifetime. And down under, shadowed by the gray-bordered, emerald velvet of her wings, her sex protrudes from the end of her abdomen like a clasp. To better imprison the male in her grip. The males of the species have their own wiles, too. A certain type collects nectar with which it blends a perfume it hides in the pockets of its legs to attract females. Another type, a breed of male Clearwings, passes bitter alkaloids to females during mating to render the female repugnant to other males.

Aziz carries his smell of sandalwood, smoke, and power in full view and with no apologies. I fell in love with his base notes first, the initial scents that tickled my nose and warmed my lungs. Later, I got drunk on his top notes of passion, sweat, and sperm.

—*Jounam*, you are better at detecting smells than any reputable "nose"—

That I certainly am. Unlike experts, I don't have to go through a series of complicated rituals to detect the characteristics of a scent, the base notes and top notes, lock myself in dark rooms, or blow my nose clean, pinch my nostrils, sprinkle a handkerchief with perfume, and wave it in the air to bring out its gaseous state. No! I don't need any of these rituals to detect that live butterflies smell different from dead ones. Still alive and active, like the one trembling in my net, they give off the odor of predators, acidic and pungent, similar to the stench of Butterfly's Chanel No. 5.

Reaching into the net, I tenderly rub the butterfly's fuzzy warmth, caress the throbbing underbelly, stroke the quivering antennae. My forefinger crawls up to tease the erogenous spot on top of her head, the spot the aroused male fondles with his antennae.

And then gently. With the slightest of pressure. I squeeze the thorax.

Scarcely dead and still supple to my touch, she begins to give off the smell of public baths, humid and cloying and a bit dirty. And now, just this instant, limp and rendered harmless, she emits the bland odor of stale flowers.

I move quickly to prepare a relaxing jar of high humidity, place a wet sponge at the bottom of a plastic container the size of a shoe box, a wire mesh over the sponge, and then spread a paper towel on top. If the Emerald Swallowtail becomes wet, she will discolor and lose her beauty. I drop mothballs in the four corners of the box. One is more than enough to keep fungi and mold away; still, no harm done by taking extra precautions.

Careful not to cause any injuries, I lay the butterfly in the box, stick a wet paper towel under the lid, and snap the box shut. In a day or two, the butterfly will become pliable and ready to be pinned in position on a spreading board.

At that time, properly labeled for display, she will forever carry the odor of burnt wood, bitter, dry, and disintegrating.

Oni shuffles in, her razor-sharp, blue-black hair shining under the overhead light, her tight-lidded eyes seeking me as she holds out a tray with a bowl of cottage cheese and sliced apples.

"Lunch already?"

In this world, far from my family and friends and with my guts in knots, my stomach refuses to digest any elaborate food. I've been living on cereal and milk, cottage cheese and fruit. Simple and uncomplicated.

I see Baba yanking on his handlebar mustache, slapping his gloves against his thigh, and reaffirming his fear that his daughter, his *tajeh saram*, his precious crown, will end up a starving artist. I feel Mamabozorg's hand on my shoulder, hear her whispering in my ear: Don't disappoint me, Soraya. No man is worth starving yourself for.

Oni places the tray on the table. She is silent. A childhood trauma forever tied up her tongue into *gereh, gereh* knots. I understand trauma. Her written notes suit me quite well, as does her habit of melting away and disappearing as if her mere existence is an unfortunate accident.

When I moved into the house, I called a domestic agency. A horsey-voiced woman with a dry cough suggested Oni, an experienced housekeeper. Her sole shortcoming, I was informed in a conspiratorial whisper, is her inability to communicate because she is mute.

I hired her on the spot.

I feel enormous compassion and respect for this unassuming, quiet woman, who must be bristling with the weight of her past. She, unlike Butterfly, had the conviction to stop talking so as to sever her ties with the world.

Early mornings, I hear her leave the attic and come down the stairs, hear her wander around the house like a hard-working ghost in ballet slippers who evaporates like a wisp of leftover smoke whenever I appear.

"Thank you, Oni. I don't need food."

What I need is air, a place to wash my memories and hang them up to dry.

She glances at the relaxing box and then at me, totters on her toes, uncertain whether to stay or escape into the safety of her retreat.

I smile to put her at ease, to assure her that she need not fear anything down here and that it is important to leave the horrors of her past behind in the attic where they belong. "Come, Oni, see what I've got here," I encourage, opening the relaxing box. "Come look inside. It's beautiful, isn't it? Emerald Swallowtail! Smells bad, doesn't it? I wouldn't get this close."

Oni makes fists. The revival of a memory is drawing her to the butterfly. She bends to take a better look. I shield the butterfly with one hand and gesture to Oni to step back. I don't want her tears to wet the butterfly.

"Don't be sad, Oni. The victim always ends up triumphant."

chapter 8

I PULL THE BRIM OF my hat lower to shade my eyes against the sun and enter the glass-paneled atrium. Humidifiers and heating lamps adjust the temperature here. Not too dry, nor too hot or too cold; otherwise, the Corpse Plant will wither and die. I study the sweating stalk, the intense groping of the cabbage-like leaf, and the thermometer at the base of the root. Study the variation in the freshly unfurling leaf, no part exactly alike in color, texture, or feel.

The ravages of time and insects are beginning to show even on such a young leaf, discoloration at the tip, a slight drooping at the edges, holes created by the larvae of ghost moths that, if left alone, will munch and chew and grind until the leaf is rendered as fragile as a stretch of antique lace. Nature is restless, in a hurry to diminish and blemish, to assert her footprints.

I am startled by the screams of a bird. A certain familiar barking. I glance beyond the glass dome, searching for the source. A series of sad hoots follows, as if a group of women are crying out in terror. My heart flips with joy. I know this bird sound. I know it well.

I am back in Iran on a warm evening at the beginning of summer; the golden disk of a full moon is sailing above the plane trees. The air is fragrant with the scent of rose and jasmine. Water trickles in a brook nearby, and Mamabozorg is pouring tea from a samovar. Another bird cry! The dream is shattered.

I tiptoe across the atrium so as not to frighten the bird.

Locking the atrium door behind me, I step out into the courtyard in search of the bird. Despite the Santa Anas, it's easier to breathe here. I shade my eyes and gaze around. Don't even blink in fear of scaring the bird away. There's a slight rustle among the branches of the monkey tree, and before I have a chance to take a good look, the bird flies out and wheels out of sight. I stand there, disappointed, sending out a silent invitation for the bird to return and settle here because I recognize these mournful hoots that were my grandmother's companions for many years.

Close by, a turnip moth shudders. I send it off with an irritated flick. Butterfly is all around me, in the eucalyptus grove, on the lavender petals of nightshade in the fountain, and among the yellow lantana, violet aster, and lion's tail that provide nectar and larva food to these insects. A grasshopper leaps up and lands on my shoulder. Such an ugly creature.

From the midst of the nectar plants—purple coneflower, coreopsis, and black-eyed Susan—a brilliant, phosphorescent cloud explodes and separates into frenzied wings that take flight and scatter around the courtyard. The annoying nuisances lack a sense of time.

I turn my attention to a butterfly perched on a banana leaf, hopeful that a Glasswing has finally found its way here. No! Not a Glasswing. It is a large Peacock butterfly. What horror!

With the four circular designs on her wings, the Peacock is the most ghastly of all butterflies. Four eyes to hold evil. Four eyes to annihilate with.

"Believe in the Evil Eye," Mamabozorg advised. "Every time you encounter someone with protruding eyes and a stare that makes you cringe and crawl into yourself, spit to your right and left, toss a fistful of salt in water, and burn *espand* seeds of rue. Then, and only then, murmur, '*Cheshmeh bad dour* may the Evil Eye keep its distance.'"

The Evil Eye has assaulted my courtyard.

A leaf blower comes to life somewhere behind me. The noise does not scare the Peacock butterfly away. Are butterflies deaf? I bend closer, hopeful it is not dead because I do not want to be robbed of the adventure of the hunt. I pluck the butterfly off the banana leaf, detect a slight pulsing of the wings. Carrying the butterfly, I turn around and walk back into the house and straight into the kitchen.

Eight days ago, the real-estate agent had passed a loving hand over the stove here and had said that food for hundreds could be prepared on this. Yes. My chef in Iran did prepare food for hundreds. I enjoyed the task of decorating the desserts with edible flowers—day lilies, calendula, pansies, and chive blossoms. But entertaining here any time soon is not an option. I can hardly bear the presence of Oni and Mansour, who know to vanish when I'm around, let alone invite guests.

I turn the knob on the gas range. Blue flames burst into life and cast convoluted shadows on the metal backsplash. I find a set of barbecue tongs in one of the cupboards and secure the butterfly with them. The wiry legs wiggle, the worm-body twitches, the antennas shiver. I blow on the erogenous zone on top of her head. She is alive, all right.

How long after death do butterflies maintain their luster, these blunders of nature that, once past the larva stage, flutter away and disappear, these helpless creatures that lose the protective dustlike scales on their wings when handled intimately?

Oni shuffles into the kitchen, the soles of her slippers sweeping the marble floors. Her eyes narrow into shocked slits. She hesitates at the threshold, balancing herself hesitantly on the tips of her slippers. She crumples a note in her fist. Her gaze travels to the ceiling, past the circle of light from the oven, and returns to land on the tongs in my hand. Her mouth opens and it seems that the slightest encouragement will help her talk.

"Yes, Oni, tell me."

Her lips struggle to form words she is incapable or unwilling to voice. And then, she gestures toward the butterfly and mouths the word "help."

I wonder who she thinks needs help here, Oni herself or the Peacock butterfly. Perhaps she is one of those activists who have nothing better to do than save creatures that are on the brink of extinction. I wave the tongs in front of her eyes. "See this butterfly? It's evil! And it doesn't need your help."

Oni's hand flies to her mouth as if she didn't expect such a reply. She takes a few steps away, turns around, and hurries toward the door.

"Come back, Oni! Give me the note. What did you want?"

She takes cautious steps and puts the note on the counter. I read her note and am surprised by her willingness to risk her job by maintaining that she and Mansour have taken the liberty of stocking the pantry with food because I need help.

"Help! What makes you think I need help?"

She fumbles in her pocket for her pen and scribbles two words on the back of the note: "help cooking."

"Thank you, Oni. This one I'll cook myself." I want to comfort her, even hug her, assure her that I don't intend her any harm. No, not at all. On the contrary, I respect her stubborn willpower and the way she continues to uphold her principles, but by the time I form a reassuring smile she is fleeing the kitchen.

I hold the butterfly over the flame.

Peacock kebab.

Why is it that we humans, who have an appetite for every moving creature on earth—dogs, frogs, snakes, octopus, even monkey brain—do not consider butterflies delicious? We could steep their carcasses in boiling water and brew butterfly tea of a myriad of scents and flavors. Create colorful vests, soft slippers, and delicate ornaments from their rainbow fluff. Diminish their population, endanger the species.

I snatch my hand away from the flame. Not yet and not so fast.

I have all the time in the world in this paradise of butterflies. Swift actions result in regret and discontent. Scores must be settled gradually and patiently. To savor the sweet nuances of dessert, we must allow it to slowly melt on the tip of the tongue.

I cross my bedroom suite and enter my darkroom, still holding the butterfly in the tongs. Here, flanked by shelves of film and two counters with my photography paraphernalia, I am struck by renewed sorrow. Surrounding me are remnants of my other life, fragments of my shattered dreams. I hold the butterfly's wings between my teeth to free my hands, taking care not to suffocate the creature. Her antennas wiggle against my upper lip. I stifle a sneeze.

I gently remove her from between my teeth. Squeeze the thorax between thumb and forefinger. A flutter. A sigh. And the insect goes limp. I lay her on a translucent plexiglass sheet, curved at a ninety-degree angle, and carefully spread the wings and legs wide open. Place her inside a tent of white fabric to light her up and create a seamless white background.

I know exactly how the image of this Peacock butterfly, with four depraved eyes, will abide in my archive.

Click!

I load the roll of film into the developing reel, place it in the developing tank, and shake, twist, and twirl my wrist in a graceful dance to evenly coat the film in chemicals, so as not to cause air bubbles. I don't want to lose my precious images. Next, I pull out the reel, unroll the film, and wash it in water to rinse off the chemicals. After cutting the film into strips, I slip them in the negative carrier and the enlarger, exposing the paper.

My heart flutters around my chest, impatient to witness the birth of each contour and curve, each black wing, the grayish shades of fluff around the edges. It will not take long. The paper is immersed in developing chemicals. The image is shaping, rising from the foul-smelling chemicals like an embryonic ghost. Under a layer of stop bath the color of bile, one evil eye emerges on the wing, now three others darker than sin, then the two antennas and helpless legs surface as if floating in midair in the eerie red light of the darkroom.

The fully formed butterfly stares up at me with four greedy eyes that harbor lofty ambitions.

I immerse the paper in developing chemicals. Just before the image is fixed, I turn the light switch on and off for a deeper, grayish effect. Only a second or two. Enough for the image to slightly burn at the edges. Solarized!

The Peacock butterfly, wings wide open, stiff legs splayed in a stance of permanent solicitation, is immortalized.

I return to the drawing room, where I keep my collecting paraphernalia. A clear plastic box with my killing jars. At the bottom of each jar, a folded piece of paper towel saturated in ethyl acetate to relax the butterfly into a more pliable state and prepare it for mounting.

I secure the Peacock butterfly in the center channel of a spreading board, then step back and examine her with added curiosity, the beady eyes in the small head, the evil eyes on the wings, the wiry legs. And the brilliant colors of her fluff. I've read somewhere that it is possible to discover the sex of butterflies by examining their genitalia. What strange creatures, these insects are! Needling their vagina yields their secrets. I insert an insect pin through her heart. Then gently raise the wings with forceps, join the edges, and attach the wings with a drop of glue. In a few days, once she is dry, she will be ready for labeling.

chapter 9

I AM IN MY DARKROOM, alone but no longer lonely. Aziz is here. In the neat stack of film rolls lined up on the uppermost shelf, my memories are sealed in every black plastic cylinder, images I honed and heightened with white backgrounds, lamps, and filters to create the most dramatic effect.

I weigh one canister on my palm. Leave it alone, Soraya. Do not uncap the canister. Don't open it. Don't unwind the past and peel off the yet unformed scabs. There's only so much you can tolerate. One roll at a time. This I might tolerate.

The surrounding darkness is all consuming. The negatives are drowning in chemicals. My olfactory buds rebel against the stench of acid and deception. The thought occurs to me that the foul-smelling processing solutions might succeed where my camera failed. Erase all traces of humanity from the last picture I took of my husband's lovely face.

I hang the negatives to dry, cut them into strips, and place them in the negative carrier inside the enlarger. Then I switch on the light bulb for a few seconds, expose the photographic paper to light, and transfer the image. Now, the process of submerging the papers in developing chemicals. Ah! The pleasure of watching his image float in a bath of chemicals, the shade of blood in the eerie safelight, watch his image take shape and assert itself, then cease to develop once immersed in stop-bath, and finally establish itself permanently in chemical fixer. In the future, nothing—not even the harshest light of day—will succeed in altering the memory of this moment. Unless I decide to do so.

I abandon the embryonic night of my darkroom and walk across the hall to my studio. The cruel light hurts my eyeballs. I squeegee the wet prints and lay them on the drying rack, then pass the magnifying glass over each photo.

A kaleidoscope of lies parades in front of my eyes.

Photographs taken on my last trip to Mehrabad Airport. Aziz at the wheel while I once again marveled at how Iran had changed since the 1979 Islamic Revolution. A hamburger stand called McAli stood at the corner of our street. Stores were allowed to carry cosmetics, Walt Disney videos, and sad, Middle Eastern music tapes that had passed the government's moral tests. Outdated American magazines were back, although alcohol ads and "inappropriate" photos of models in revealing Western clothes were cut out or censored by heavy-handed ink strokes.

While the majority of anti-American slogans were gone, one remained plastered on the side of an eight-story building. Skulls replaced the stars of the American flag, the stripes missiles aimed at Iran. "Down with the USA," it announced. Now, a generation after the American hostage crisis, American tourists stood at the foot of the building and stared up in wonder and perhaps disgust. Some women wore hats instead of the head covers, and long pants and shirts rather than the *manteau.*

"What happened to the dangers of Westoxication?" I asked Aziz the day he drove me to the airport.

"I don't give a *goozeh khar* donkey's fart about Iran," he murmured. "What I'm worried about is that you'll become Westoxified in America."

I almost believed him that day, believed he might miss me, believed he felt protective of me, believed he regretted signing my exit papers. But no! The instant I stepped out of my home, Butterfly must have stepped in.

The magnifying glass exaggerates a photograph of her. The deceiving smile, the noxious pose that appears as virginal as the woman in Reza Abasi's portrait, *Youthful Lovers*. Did Aziz take this picture? I inspect the background. My blurry image peers from behind Butterfly's right shoulder. Even then, I was nothing but a faceless obstacle in the tapestry of their love.

I deface her features with a red marker. Toss the photograph aside. Check another under the light. Aziz and me in bathing suits. On a summer vacation in Ramsar, in northern Iran. The two of us are spewing seawater out of our mouths.

Dusk is the most beautiful hour in Ramsar. Shadows lap against shore, moonlight splashes the sea amber, and stars punctuate a melancholy sky. A beam of moonlight slices through the sea where Aziz swims, his thighs brushing against mine as he thrusts his head under, rises to the surface, and holds me in his arms, pressing his mouth to mine.

—Share the sea with me, *Jounam*—

I taste salt, sweet coral, and lush vegetation. I taste Aziz. I will always crave his taste. This is my punishment. For what? For loving him more than anyone has a right to love, perhaps. Or trusting more than sanity dictates. Or for a sin that will be revealed one day.

I enlarge the photograph. Cut myself out. Selecting the most delicate cat-hair brush from among brushes and acrylic paint of all colors lined in a row on the counter, I exaggerate the grain, deepen the shadows, thicken the eyebrows, paint the eyes acidic green, the complexion jaundiced yellow, and the mouth dripping blood. Scrape off a part of his luscious lips with the stub of a larger brush; distort his dreamy eyes, the drooping eyelids. Perfect! Taut facial muscles, acrimonious eyes, dark and cavernous nostrils, mean, spiky hair, and murderous teeth. Gothic mug shots. Gone and dead are the days when photography was a healing process.

Gone are the days when I prided myself on manipulating the camera, cajoling the lens, and battling with it to produce my own sensual style—the exquisite evanescence of a shy glance, the youthful recollection of a flirtatious hand, the sexual yearning of a tight-lipped cleavage, the sensual tang of a bloody strawberry, or the visual eroticism of a saliva-dipped banana. This is different. It is ferocious fare. But art, nonetheless.

I hang the photograph on the line and with felt-tipped pen scribble on the left top corner:

Wanted alive and competent to stand trial.

chapter 10

THE MOURNFUL BARKS OF the bird make their way from the courtyard and echo all night in my bedroom. I listen intently, wondering whether my guess is correct and what I hear are the cries of an owl. Mamabozorg believed that owls are a lucky omen for Jews. According to her, they heralded our freedom from Egypt. Trumpeted the completion of the Second Temple. And signaled the tumbling of the Walls of Jericho. She named her first owl, *Morgheh Hagh*, her Bird of Reason, and insisted that right after it moved into her garden in 1930, her luck took a turn for the better.

She was young and full of hope and energy then, when she began to frequent the bazaar in the south of Tehran to accumulate antique jewelry, rare pieces she had a special eye for. Jewelers, back-alley peddlers, black-market thieves, middlemen, and even housewives who were in dire need of cash for some secret endeavor discovered that dealing with Mamabozorg was a rewarding experience.

After thoroughly examining and appraising a special piece, she'd drop it in her hammered silver box lined and faced with royal blue velvet. It took her all of five minutes to calculate, on her small abacus, the fair market value of a diamond ring, gold bracelet, pearl earrings, or an emerald brooch. She found the common practice of bargaining to be barbaric and unbecoming of the Persian culture, especially at a time of change when Reza Shah was modernizing the country. Sellers had the right of refusal, of course, but few chose to. No one in all of Tehran could outbid Mamabozorg.

On a winter afternoon in 1936, when plane trees were snow-heavy and nightingales huddled on branches to seek warmth, a merchant, a supplier of spices to the royal kitchens, sought Mamabozorg and handed her a gold-embossed invitation. Her name had made its way into the royal court, and Reza Shah's wife was summoning her to the palace. Mamabozorg stroked the amber beads of her necklace when she told me about the ample bosoms the Almighty had sent her way to adorn with rare Caspian pearls, deep Burma rubies, and Indian cut emeralds. It was a sight to behold, she mused, her eyes dreamy with past memories of the royal quarters abuzz with women shorn of their *chadors*.

Reza Shah had issued one of his most controversial decrees, ordering women to appear in public without their traditional *chadors*. *Mullahs* raised their voices in objection. Pious women fought back by refusing to leave their homes. Modern women rejoiced, emerging in public with all types of fashionable hats set at coquettish angles.

The day Mamabozorg visited the palace, the king's women—flush with their newfound freedom of expression, coiffed and painted and primped—had strutted in their colorful hats like a party of peacocks. Mamabozorg was intrigued by Reza Shah's estranged wife, Taj-ol-Moluk, the crown prince's mother. It was rumored that she possessed the power to terrorize Reza Shah, a man whose piercing stare sent ministers and military men quaking in their boots.

"You should have seen these women, Soraya, the way they attacked my jewelry box. It was a miracle one of the trinkets didn't end up drowned in a cleavage. My favorite was one of the ministers' wives. Bless her soul, her generosity was second only to her wide hips. Two chairs were nailed together to fit her." Mamabozorg delighted in recounting the speed with which her fame had spread around town like juicy gossip and how she became *zabanzad* famous and rose to the enviable rank of favorite jeweler of the royal court.

A year or so went by. One day, Mamabozorg was summoned by Reza Shah himself. Why was she sent for? Sweat trickled down her back as she wondered whether she might have offended the queen, or even worse, Taj-ol-Moluk, the Shah's estranged wife. Was a blemish discovered in one of the diamonds, a crack in an emerald? Had a pearl lost its luster when coming in contact with perfumes or some unguent? These misfortunes were an expected part of her trade; yet no matter the cause, the jeweler was apt to be blamed.

She was led to the Sahebgaranieh Palace and straight into the formal Crystal Salon, her startled image staring back at her from shimmering cut glass that covered the surrounding walls.

The king was decked in full regalia and covered with medals, cape tossed over one shoulder as if expecting a visit from a notable dignitary. His photographs in the papers and in governmental offices depicted a much younger man, and she was taken aback at his graying handlebar mustache and thick, graying eyebrows, a shocking contrast to his black eyes. Despite having heard much about the lethal power of his glare, she was unprepared for the dark wells directed at her.

His stare swept the length of her body to rest on her green eyes. He gestured for her to approach. "You are Jewish!" The statement was pronounced in a controlled, low voice that sent a shiver up her spine.

"Yes, King of Kings," Mamabozorg replied, certain her good fortune had run its course, and she would be marched right out of the hall and tossed into a dank, rat-infested dungeon, forever forgotten.

"Jews, I understand, know when to keep their mouths shut and when to speak. Is this true, Emerald?"

At a loss as to how to respond, she cast her eyes down, finding it prudent to remain silent.

"Speak! Any unusual activity in the bazaar?"

Mamabozorg shifted from one foot to another, convinced she'd melt under the Shah's frown.

"We are waiting," he boomed. "Answer!"

"I am a simple jeweler, Your Majesty. I deal with precious stones and metals. I do not socialize with merchants of the bazaar."

"How are you paid?"

"Always in cash, Your Majesty, always. Well, until last week. Yes, two separate orders were placed with me last week. One for a turquoise bracelet and another for a mine-cut diamond medallion. On both occasions, I was compensated for the goods with foreign gold coins."

The Shah took a forward step. His stare burrowed through my grandmother, demanding the truth. "Emerald! Who gave you the coins?"

"They did not introduce themselves, Your Majesty. They were ayatollahs."

"*Akhound mullahs*!" The Shah spat the title as if to rid himself of a vile insect. This information confirmed his suspicion that "a bunch of blue-eyed scoundrels" were shipping boxfuls of British King George sovereigns to bazaars in Mashhad to bribe the clergy into an uprising to topple the Pahlavi dynasty.

The Shah was in conflict with the clergy. Two years back, he had violated the sanctity of the Shrine of Fatimah in Qom by ordering the beating of a *mullah* who had admonished the king's wife for entering a mosque while wearing a hat in place of a *chador*. Devout Muslims were furious at new laws requiring everyone to wear Western clothes, hats with a brim that prevented men from touching their foreheads to the ground during prayer, and especially by the policy allowing women to mix with men, study in colleges, freely attend cinemas, and patronize restaurants and hotels.

Mamabozorg kissed the hand the Shah had extended to her, thanking him profusely for supporting women. Encouraged by his seeming willingness to hear her out, she added that the Jewish community was especially grateful to him for ensuring their safety by instituting laws that separated politics from religion, a feat no other Shah had managed to achieve. "*Shahanshaha*, our King of Kings, bears mighty roots deep under and around our ancient Persian foundation. No blue-eyed scoundrel or dark-bearded clergy will ever topple the Pahlavi dynasty."

The pleased Reza Shah gifted Mamabozorg with sixteen sets of large gold coins, engraved with the likeness of himself and the royal prince. When, in 1941, the English exiled Reza Shah from Iran to Johannesburg and his son, Mohammed Reza Pahlavi, ascended the throne, the coins became collector's items. Mamabozorg promptly exchanged them for hectares of inexpensive land in the outskirts of Tehran. The capital expanded with such speed that in a few years her property was considered prime, valuable land in the heart of the city.

"Nothing is left of the splendor of the Pahlavi dynasty, not even the memory of their good deeds," she complained to Baba, after the Islamic Revolution. "We are at the mercy of a bunch of *dozd* crooked fundamentalists."

"How old is your Bird of Reason?" I asked her.

"Older than Reza Shah if he were alive," she replied. "Curse the thieves for ending him before his time. He had a strong disposition, you know. He would have lived for a hundred and twenty years, as long as *Hazrateh* Mousa lived, may his name be forever blessed."

"Do owls live long?" I had asked.

"Mine do. Because they are blessed with two hearts, one for love, the other for devotion."

Both of which I am in need of now, I muse, wondering whether the invisible bird is playing with my head. Its high-pitched barking makes its way from the courtyard, a constant echo in the house. Oni walks around with her hands pressed to her ears as if the sound hurts her. Mansour suggests erecting some type of partition around the courtyard to protect the house from the evil spirits.

"Who in their right minds," I heard him complain to Oni, "would build an open courtyard smack in the middle of a house?"

I ordered him to stay away from the monkey tree, around which I'd noticed him loiter one early morning, a long stick in hand.

Mamabozorg believed her owls communicated with her through feathers, antennas that link us to the supernatural. She, too, was fascinated by extraordinary phenomena and would inundate me with questions—Why do female cats scream during copulation? Wolves howl at the moon? Snakes have forked penises? The more tidal shrimp that flamingos consume, the pinker they become? How is it that the aurora borealis sounds like an orchestra of angels, and a mongoose can actually kill the deadly, fast-as-lightning cobra? "*Begoo*, tell me, Soraya, do animals sense our feelings and emotions?"

By the time I had an answer to her last question, Mamabozorg had become a recluse, and as much as I longed to, I had no way of telling her that animals are far more perceptive than humans. I had no way of telling her what had occurred on my last birthday in Iran.

Aziz had come home with a small box wrapped in black paper with imprints of ladybugs. Even then, he was attracted to insects, their spidery legs and useless bodies that carry nothing but the plague. I lifted the top of the box and peered in. A rainbow-colored creature raised its spiky neck, anxious green eyes and thin tongue darting about.

"A rhinoceros iguana of Haiti, *Jounam*. They exchange kisses like us and refuse to fuck unless in love."

Right then and there, on the Esfahan carpet with a border of royal blue scrolls and deep red arabesques, we made love with an urgency that left us soaking. We didn't bother with sending the carpet to be properly washed in a running stream. We liked the carpet better with traces of our passion.

Later that evening, we went to check on the iguana.

The animal was dead.

"It couldn't adapt to the new environment," Aziz announced.

"It's a bad omen!" I sobbed. "It died on my birthday."

I realize now that the insufferable air of duplicity in our house had suffocated the poor creature's love heart.

Aziz paid an expert embalmer to preserve the dead iguana. Its embalmed body, storing memories I could not abandon, has traveled from Iran to Los Angeles and now stands on the dressing table opposite my bed, stiff legs firmly planted in a bar of gold-flecked onyx, arms raised in eternal prayer. The vibrant colors of the animal's skin remain intact. The colors of our Persian carpet. The colors of butterflies. Purple and blue and blood-red. They hurt my eyes in the morning when I wake up and at night before I fall asleep.

I grab the embalmed iguana and hurl it across the bedroom. It crashes against the mirror, then falls with a muffled thump back on the dressing table. The cracked reflection of my face in the broken mirror is pale and haggard, green eyes lifeless, the pupils dilated, full lips twisted. A fragmented collage.

chapter 11

Tens of thousands of petrified Monarchs crunch under my shoes as I trudge deeper into the eucalyptus grove. The air is laced with the saccharine smell of rotting pumpkins. I can hardly breathe. What could have wreaked such havoc on my Monarchs? What disaster could have struck my eucalyptus grove last night in the dark to eliminate such a large population of Monarchs in the span of a few short hours?

Two days ago at half past three in the afternoon, hardly a day after the landscapers completed work on the eucalyptus grove, an orange cloud had darkened the skies overhead. Gardening shears in hand, I watched droves of purposeful Monarchs sail in my direction and make their way straight ahead to settle among the eucalyptus. In no time, the grove was transformed into a flurry of activity with tiny orange flames weighing the younger branches and sending leaves aflutter, thousands of fanning wings raising the scent of camphor.

What caused these Monarchs to lose their sense of direction and deviate from their normal course? What magical secret could have jumbled their inner compasses, steering them off course toward Bel Air, a place Monarchs do not normally migrate to? At that moment, strolling among them while they set up home, occupying every leaf, branch, and shallow nook carved into tree trunks, I turned my gaze upward and thanked Mamabozorg. Thanked her profusely for the blessing of her gift. Hordes of Monarchs to catch and dissect and experiment on, to study one after the other to discover what makes this breed so fertile, so flirtatious, so poisonous.

Now, surrounded by dead butterflies in my grove, I realize that they're not such a resilient species after all. For example, although known for their long migrations—southward in August and northward in spring—the life span of butterflies born in early summer is less than two months, and none live long enough to survive the entire round trip. Still, during these migrations, females drop millions of eggs, ensuring the birth of the next generation. I am not surprised that barren females born in late summer live longer than the fertile ones, three or four times as long. It makes sense that females who don't experience the rigors of producing eggs would live longer than those that do. Do women who take the pill extend their lives, too?

Mansour catches up with me in the eucalyptus grove. He warns me of hidden dangers. He prays under his breath, murmurs that he's never seen anything as macabre.

He is right. The grove is a mass graveyard. A lethal plague has infected every Monarch. They are everywhere! Dead at their roosts in the trees, carpeting leaves and branches underfoot, spread around roots and stuck to tree trunks, hanging on flaking bark. A few Monarchs that managed to survive huddle motionless, seeking warmth, or else dangle in clusters from branches.

Mansour slaps himself as dead butterflies rain down on us from roosts where they festooned tall trees. He throws his arms up in exasperation and stops, shuffling from foot to foot, before gathering the courage to face me.

"*Khanom*, it's not wise to go there." He gestures toward the end of the grove where the grave is. "Please look around at the death everywhere. Pay attention to all the corpses and sickness raining on us. A bad curse struck this place. It's the grave. Let's get rid of it. Burn everything down and plant other trees."

"Stop this superstition, Mansour. They're just dead butterflies! And if they're cursed, they deserve it. Come along, it's hard enough to breathe in this air without you grumbling in my ear."

"But forgive me, *Khanom*, it's a contagious plague. I am obligated to protect you from this…"

"I know what I am doing," I say, silencing him with an impatient wave of one hand as I continue to walk ahead, shoes sinking into the wet carpet of discolored butterflies stretching underfoot like pale, veined leaves.

I had read that as many as 250 million Monarchs were killed in a storm in the central mountains of Mexico, yet the loss of life, even at that extraordinary rate, did not render them extinct. How long will it take for the Monarch population to rebound this time?

An imperceptible movement, something struggling to be freed underneath the leaves, catches my attention. I kneel to examine the leaves underfoot, cautiously sweeping back an upper layer of death.

Mansour sprints toward me, horror further distorting his scarred face. "No! *Khanom*, I beg of you, please don't! It's very dangerous. Who knows what's buried here."

I'm taken aback by the enormity of his fear, but more so by his insolent grip on my arm, which he quickly releases when he realizes what he is doing. "Stand back, Mansour. I need to do this."

I plunge my hand deep, past corpses and leaves into the thick underlayer of twigs and branches to discover a bunch of limp butterflies underneath. I retrieve one and examine it on my palm. Its wiry legs twitch weakly; the wings tremble. Why did this one survive? I settle down cross-legged on the ground.

"*Khanom*, I beg of you. Be careful of snakes down there. They don't like to be disturbed. They hold grudges…They'll follow you until the end of time…" He slaps his forehead. "I don't know, *Khanom*. I don't like these butterflies. They came here dragging misery behind."

That they certainly did, I think, as Mansour crouches down next to me, sour-faced and stubborn, wincing when I stick my hands under layers of dead butterflies to free the few that cheated death.

"It's not proper for you to do this alone, *Khanom.*" He makes a face as if tasting something bitter, further contorting the scar across his mouth, and pressing his eyes shut before sinking one hand in to test the surroundings. He pulls out his hands and demonstrates his empty, mud-streaked palm. "See, *Khanom*, nothing. No sign of life."

I burrow around, then fish out another limp Monarch. Hardly alive, but breathing nonetheless. I drop it in one hand for inspection. It is larger than those that perished. Yes, its size must have worked to its advantage. An image flashes across the screen of my mind. Soraya, tall and confident; Butterfly, petite and timid. Who will survive?

Mansour mumbles under his breath, "Please pardon me, *Khanom*, but I don't understand why you care about these bad-luck creatures."

The truth is that I do not care much about the Monarchs. What I want is to find out what killed them, what differentiates the surviving ones from those that did not, learn their secret strengths and weaknesses. I am simply heeding Baba's advice that it is prudent to know my enemy as well as I know the palm of my hand.

Not daring to face me, yet feeling obligated to keep me company and lend a hand, Mansour drops another Monarch in my cupped hands.

I check it closely, flip it around, and feel its frail legs, limp antennas, the wings surprisingly warm to the touch. It must be the dry warmth underneath the leaves that saved the larger, sturdier ones. Perhaps the others perished because the temperature suddenly dropped last night. But it is spring in California. How cold could it become?

I continue to riffle deep among petrified corpses. A slow-spreading dull pain radiates from the center of my palm toward my fingers. I jerk my hand out and spring up to my feet. A sharp pain shoots from my hand toward my wrist and elbow. I take a close look at my hand and notice a small cut I'd incurred when gardening. My palm is turning a dark plum color. It is swelling, swelling fast.

Pale-faced and bewildered, Mansour shouts, "*Mar*! Snake! Help! Oni, quick. Here!"

Doubled over with pain, I am unable to speak. My fingertips are becoming numb. I check my fingernails and notice a slight bluish hue at the base.

Mansour makes way for Oni, who runs toward us with a first aid kit. She kneels and inspects my palm. She quickly snaps open the box and in silence begins to apply alcohol, ointments, and bandages.

I am relieved by her efficiency. She is taking all the right steps. Also assured by her calm demeanor, Mansour stops cursing and grumbling and begins to send *salavat* prayers to his Allah.

Having cleaned and applied antiseptics, Oni collects her supplies and bows to me a few times.

I massage my hand. Give myself a moment to catch my breath, time for the pain to take its course.

There's an unexpected chill in the weather. Nature herself is troubled. The hiss of agitated ghosts can be heard in the stale air.

"You are very good, Oni. Where did you learn to do this?"

She shrugs, endearing in her attempt at dismissing any compliment as undeserved. Assessing my situation and concluding, perhaps, that I am out of danger, she turns on her heels and disappears as silently and purposefully as she had appeared.

Mansour lets out a low growl: "I am getting the car, *Khanom*, taking you to a doctor! *Zahreh mar* snake venom can stop your heart faster than a sharp knife."

"Come back, Mansour! It's not a snake. Monarch caterpillars are filled with the toxin of milkweed leaves that's poisonous to humans if consumed. But here, with thousands around and such a concentrated amount of toxins, the smallest of nicks on the skin allows the toxin into the bloodstream, causing severe reaction."

My throbbing hand pressed against me, I continue to walk deeper into the grove and toward the direction of the grave.

Mansour begins to mumble and curse anew, voicing all types of incantations to ward off evil djinns and spirits.

The grave is covered by a velvety quilt in different shades of orange, embroidered with black veins and strewn with pearls. A blanket of Monarchs with wings spread out to heaven as if praying for salvation. Their flamboyant wings are lovelier than the most ornate Japanese fans. Dead, they are so beautiful. So harmless.

I like this specific posture. Like the idea of trapping and displaying praying Monarchs on glass shelves in my cabinets. An homage to my best friend, who once raised her hands in prayer to a framed nuptial kerchief.

Had she, even then, prayed for what was mine?

chapter 12

MANSOUR GLANCES AT THE rearview mirror as he maneuvers the car down the silent streets of Bel Air toward Sunset. He must be wondering why I would wake him at midnight and ask him to drive me to the Beverly Wilshire Hotel. Why I am not asleep after a hard day in the eucalyptus grove, overseeing a group of lepidopterists who took hours to study thousands of dead Monarchs, poking and prodding the earth and trees with scientific instruments.

A parade of thought, regarding the lepidopterists' final conclusion, churned in my head all night to the stubborn calls from the courtyard of the yet unseen bird. After the painstaking process of gathering scientific evidence, the lepidopterists had developed a perfunctory theory that supposedly added up to some meteorological equations about what happened to the Monarch population—changes in temperature, air pressure, moisture, and wind direction in the troposphere.

I am not convinced.

The truth is that the reality of life does not add up so neatly. As far as I am concerned, the outbreak is nature's way of rubbing the mortality of this sinful species in its own arrogant face.

At that thought, I was propelled out of bed by an uncontrollable urge to hurt Aziz, to yank him out of his sheltered cocoon of trust, naked and unsuspecting, into the painful uncertainty of suspicion.

I unzip the side pocket of my purse and fish out the folded note *Mullah* Mirharouni gave me ten days ago on the airplane on my way to America. His elegantly looped script brings his image back to life, the patrician forehead, the tidy hairline winking below his turban, his masculine voice when he offered to make me his temporary wife.

I enter the quiet lobby of the Beverly Wilshire Hotel, nearly run to the house telephone and, my words tripping over each other, ask the operator to connect me to *Mullah* Mirharouni's room. I suffer the pulse of each ring against my eardrum, damning rings that sound louder and louder. Yet. I don't drop the phone on the cradle and flee as I should, until the operator informs me that Mr. Mirharouni is not in his room and that I may leave a message if I wish. I drop the phone on its cradle and steal away as if it might come back to life and wrap its cord around my neck.

I decide to go to the bar because I can't bear the thought of returning to my cold bed. And there he is, crossing the lobby with resolute steps, head down and in deep thought. And before I have a chance to collect myself, *Mullah* Mirharouni raises his head and looks me straight in the eye. I have an inexplicable urge to fasten the top two buttons of my blouse.

He lifts an eyebrow. "You didn't call me."

"No," I reply with a shy smile.

"I'm waiting," he says, touching a finger to my wrist before turning on his heels and marching out.

I observe his retreating back as he steps out the door and disappears from my sight. The thought occurs to me that we are not that different, this *mullah* and I, both of us up and about this late of a time, restless and searching and unable to sleep.

In the dim bar of the hotel, shadows loiter amid opulent wood paneling and tangerine lights from gilded sconces that frame belly-dancing candle flames. There's an air of apathy as if nothing is left undone past midnight, nothing left unsaid. Two men are in deep conversation, one stirring his highball with a speared olive. These potent mixtures should be forbidden. They rush the brain, destroying inhibitions and all sense of grace and decorum. Iranian men stay away from complicated drinks. They prefer them simple like their women. Scotch and soda on ice. Vodka, straight up. A snifter of cognac just neat.

I check the men for signs that they might be Iranian. No, their complexions are either darker or lighter. The jewelry of one is too flashy and his suit, despite being elegant, not of the latest fashion. I glance at a red-haired man. Scottish? Norwegian? Israeli?

A woman in her midforties perches on a bar stool. Her round eyes are emphasized by blue pencil, her yellow braided hair rolled on top of her head like an inverted cone. Fishnet stockings strangle her short legs. A prostitute, I am certain. Not so long ago, I would rather have choked on *zahreh mar* than to step alone into a bar with such types. Yet here I am, at a most indecent hour, wearing a tight skirt and clingy blouse that would be more appropriate for a *jendeh* whore.

A middle-aged man seated by the fireplace tugs at his crisp, white cuffs and jerks his neck to the left, the right. His stare pounces on me, then slithers toward the vacant chair next to him and, with the accompaniment of a slight gesture of his pinkie, invites me over. I know that arrogant, self-serving look well. The two of us, Aziz and I, had no patience for this breed of men, who flaunt their wealth by wearing gaudy turquoise rings on their short, chubby fingers.

I want to turn around and flee, run away from this man and this bar, but more so from myself, from the woman I have become and no longer recognize, but I remain fixed in place, waiting for him to make his next move.

His joints protest as he stands and smooths his hair back with both palms. He walks straight to me and, without a second of hesitation, bows elegantly and plants a kiss on the back of my right hand. Ah! I would have expected nothing less than impeccable manners from an Iranian on the prowl. He squeezes my hand in his, and I do not pull back but step closer, towering over him. I ask him to buy me a drink as if my life depends on this one gallant act of his. He leaves the imprint of another kiss on my palm, then pulls a chair over for me.

I pass my right hand under my nose to smell the residual odor of his handshake. My heart misses a beat at the unfamiliar odors of pepper, Hennessy, and curry.

"What would you like to drink?" he asks, vowels tumbling heavily in his throat.

My stomach rumbles with disappointment at his guttural foreign accent, which I don't recognize. I don't want to waste tonight on a non-Iranian. Yet, I hear myself tell this man that I would love a glass of red wine. I say this because my thoughts are muddled with Aziz and how to hurt him, muddled with the power he continues to exert upon me, the pain he continues to inflict on me.

A waitress with capped teeth and flowing pants sets a glass of wine in front of me. The strong smell sends my empty stomach reeling.

"Are you married?" I blurt out to the man.

He removes a cigar from a gold case and, with a silver pin, punches a hole in its head. "Does it matter?"

I point to my heart. "Yes. Here."

He squirms in his seat, the corner of his left eye twitches, and I know that I have my answer, know that the time has come for me to stand up and leave.

I set the glass of wine on the table, snap open the case of my camera, and cross the short space that separates us. I sit on his armchair and wrap my arm around his neck. I tell him that I find him quite handsome, that I was attracted to him the moment I entered the bar, that the color of his eyes remind me of the mountains around my homeland. I spew these lies because I want him relaxed, smiling, and aroused. Aziz is a perceptive man.

I signal to the waitress and ask her to step farther away so that the bottles of alcohol on the counter can be visible in the photograph, hand her the camera, and demonstrate how to take a picture.

The man's hand firmly around my waist, I put my head on his shoulder and half-close my eyes.

Click!

There will be other men. Better men. Iranian men.

chapter 13

I PAMPER THE AMORPHOPHALLUS, CHECK on the temperature and humidity in the atrium, feed the plant, oil its stem, and murmur encouraging endearments. And my plant rewards me by swiveling to face me like a lover. Music and caressing have been proven to hasten the growth of plants. My conversations entice this one. I rise on my toes and stroke its stem. "I am a lonely woman in this strange land. And I'm sad. But I like you. I'll visit you every day and take care of you, if you promise to bloom for me. Will you? Are you happy here? Is the humidity right? What about the light?"

I tell the Amorphophallus that now that I've been here for eleven days, I wonder if it would have been better to remain back home, tint my hair the color of the sun, wear my most seductive *petit robe,* my highest high heels, and dig them into Butterfly until I drew blood.

Despite our daily tête-à-tête, true to its nature, the Amorphophallus refuses to bloom. Contradictory feelings—impatient curiosity to meet the flower and lingering worry about what it might produce—churn my blood. I've been warned about the stench and am prepared for it. But why this sense of premonition, a nagging whisper that once it blooms the bud might yield some inexplicable horror to haunt me? Like rotten food that's sure to birth maggots that appear out of nowhere and refuse to die even with the strongest repellents, multiplying like the revolutionary guards who overnight invaded the streets and narrow alleys of Tehran.

They harassed us for no reason other than that they could and because they suddenly found themselves in a position of power, owing to a revolution gone wrong. They assaulted women, snipped off hair visible from edges of veils, wreaked havoc on faces with a bit of makeup, or stoned women who were accused of committing adultery.

It was 1985, fourteen years ago. The new regime surprised us by surviving for six years. If we drove a decent car, wore respectable clothing, and bore ourselves with the slightest display of feminine dignity, we became targets and vulnerable to assaults from religious zealots and their followers.

One Friday afternoon, Aziz and I were returning from a lunch of *chelo kebab* at the hotel that had been the Hilton before the revolution and was now renamed *Esteqlal* or "Independence." Aziz negotiated the car around the impossibly loud, chaotic traffic. A store, once named Kentucky Fried Chicken, was "Our Fried Chicken" now, the colonel metamorphosed into a turban-sporting *mullah*.

Kiosks at the edge of streets that once carried *Newsweek*, *Time*, *Cosmopolitan*, and *The Wall Street Journal* now displayed magazines that instructed the populace on how to cleanse their backsides in the bathroom without defiling the right hand, which must be used only for pure activities such as eating. We reached the intersection of what had been Pahlavi Avenue, now named *Vali-ye-Asr* or "the Expected One." Smoke, gasoline fumes, and the shimmering, dry sun made it difficult to breathe.

Aziz stepped on the brakes to allow a group of *pasdaran* revolutionary guards in dull, green uniforms to cross the street.

I pushed my hair further back under my scarf and lowered it over my brows, buttoned my *roopoosh* up to my chin, and hid my shaking hands under my thighs. A chill forced its way into the car and into my bones.

"I'm here, *Jounam*," Aziz whispered, comforting me with the metallic click of his wedding band against mine.

A *pasdar* signaled us to stop. Took his sweet time to approach our car. He tapped the barrel of his Uzi on my window. Aziz unlocked his door to step out, but the *pasdar* ordered him to remain in the car. I took a deep breath, shifted closer to Aziz, and rolled the window down.

"Who is this?" the guard barked, his breath reeking of fried onion and annoyance.

"My husband," I replied, aware that punishment for being found with a male stranger could be anything from harassing or flogging to being forgotten in the dreaded Evin Prison.

"Your papers," he barked across to Aziz.

Aziz fumbled in his coat pocket.

The guard raised his Uzi, extended it into the car past my chest, and pointed the barrel at Aziz's temple.

Aziz's hand froze in his pocket. "*Ejazeh bedid* if you permit, I'm about to produce our marriage license."

"Son of a dog! Hurry up!" the guard, all claws and teeth, barked while avoiding eye contact with me, as a good Muslim must when facing a woman other than his wife and sister.

But I could not avert my eyes from the gun pressed to Aziz's temple. My heart flipped in my chest. Did I remember to remove the document from his suit before it was sent to the cleaners?

He held out a neatly folded yellowing paper. Concealed in the document, recorded in the elegant Farsi language, in Arabic alphabet, was our date of marriage: December 21, the winter solstice.

The guard balanced the original document on the barrel of his Uzi, then slid the cold metal against my breasts and out of the window. He flipped the document onto the palm of his other hand and unfolded it harshly, tearing it in half.

He held the two torn pieces together, took a cursory look, then screeched in a fetid, pubescent voice, the sparse hair on his chin trembling. "*Bifayedeh!* Worthless! Can't tell if the names are yours."

With his acrid breath too close to mine, the *pasdar* took his time examining and comparing our names to the one on the driver's license Aziz presented. The man pointed at me with a long-nailed index finger, no doubt uncut to dig leftovers from between his molars. "*Your* driver's license!"

Aziz's face turned the color of fear. His smoke-filled lungs rasped. I wanted to slap the *pasdar*'s oily snout. There was no driver's license to present. "I don't drive, *agha*."

"This will not do! Not at all. *Khanom* must present some type of identification!" the guard growled, ordering me to step out of the car. Directing his Uzi toward my breasts, his gaze never meeting mine, he pressed on one breast, then the other, the icy impudence of the Uzi eye burning imprints on my nipples.

Aziz flung the car door open and sprang out. Before I had time to utter a word, he was at my side and glaring at the Uzi with a murderous gaze. A stray dog emerged unexpectedly and snarled with bared teeth at the *pasdar*, who kicked the dog, sending it yelping away. Aziz pushed the Uzi away from me and held on to the gun's barrel as if that might stop a bullet. A scream echoed behind my eardrums.

I hurriedly snapped my purse open and, fumbling inside with trembling fingers, took out a matchbox and held it out to the guard.

On our wedding night, in front of every place setting sat three party favors. A filigreed silver box containing sugared almonds. A miniature version of our wedding invitation, mounted in an enamel frame. And a matchbox with the photograph of the bride and groom on one side, and on the other in calligraphy: Aziz and Soraya's wedding, December 21, 1977.

The guard yanked the Uzi away from Aziz, then snatched the matchbox and held it at a distance. He passed his hand over the photo, leaving lewd fingerprints on the image of my face. He tossed the matchbox underfoot and crushed it with mud-caked boots. Bow-tied groom and lace-clad bride, innocently radiant and idealistically smiling, melted into the tar-warm asphalt.

I freed myself from Aziz's grip and took a step toward the *pasdar*, my shadow preceding me like a warning. "If you are man enough, *agha*, raise your head and look into my eyes! Or leave before I report you to the authorities."

The *pasdar* doubled over with laughter, straightened up, tilted his gun on the pavement, and leaned on it, addressing his boots, "Report *me*! Who are *you* to report *me*?"

"Sister to His Honor Judge Sharifi and cousin to Chief Rostami. Does that suffice, or shall I go on?"

"Go!" he yelled into my ear. "Get out of my sight! Before I smash your arrogant little nose."

Aziz held the door as I climbed into the car. I longed to bang the door shut, but didn't think it would be prudent to do so. The car lurched into the dusty city of Tehran, with its amalgam of high-rises and one-story buildings, modern and dilapidated, new and old, thrust next to each other, forced to tolerate each other.

"That's my Soree," Aziz said. "But never, ever do that again. You could have gotten yourself killed. Luckily, this one must have had a dubious file he didn't want revisited."

I wiped my forehead of fear and grabbed Aziz's hand, twirling his wedding band.

He removed and slipped it onto my thumb. "Here, *Jounam*, a piece of my heart forever yours."

chapter 14

I STILL WEAR AZIZ'S PLAIN gold wedding band. A piece of his heart forever mine. Never removed his wedding band, not even on the day my suspicion turned to certainty and time extended into years, even decades, before scorching itself in my memory. In minutes, perhaps seconds, one by one, the protective fortresses of denial split open to the tune of "The Blue Danube," and I was forced to acknowledge the stench of betrayal.

I didn't have a camera. I didn't need one. I've replayed these moments over and over again, drawn with meticulous care the geography of their affair, its every devious outline and silhouette, until the blueprint is embedded in every layer of my consciousness.

Candlelight. Music. "The Blue Danube." Sighs. Twisting flesh and frenzied legs. Damp heat and fogged mirrors. Glasses of wine. One empty. The other, half full, lipstick stained. Witnesses on the surrounding walls: my photographs gazing down at them. Freeze frame.

Click!

Our bed in Iran faces west toward Jerusalem, a religious custom Baba insisted we honor. Unaware that I did not intend to become pregnant, my father was adamant we follow a tradition that would guarantee us a firstborn son. As far as I was concerned, as long as we loved each other on that bed, it did not matter if our bed faced Sodom and Gomorrah.

That afternoon, twenty-four days and four hours ago, the bed's placement made it impossible for them to see me standing at the door. But even if that was not the case, I doubt they would have noticed anything or anyone but themselves, being entangled in and consumed by each other as they were. Butterfly's long hair imprisoned Aziz like a morbid net. His thighs held her in their grip. Sweat glistened on her skin as she clawed at the hair on my husband's chest.

The web of her curls parted. Their profiles came into view and I saw what I should not have seen.

I turned on my heel and fled. Ran out of my own home, shoe soles scuffing the carpet, breath tangled in my throat.

I sat erect in the backseat of the car as the chauffeur drove around Vanak Circle and up Jordan Avenue, renamed Africa Avenue after the revolution. I was dry-eyed, indifferent to the cherry blossoms, velvet sky, spring sun. Like the protective fences of denial I had once erected around myself, a thick layer of paint on walls around the city now concealed anti-American slogans and a series of tragic images that, nonetheless, endured underneath. Posters and murals of mothers crying bloody tears for their martyred sons; men crumpled lifeless against walls, shot in the head, broken-necked and hanging from makeshift gallows. Hoveyda, prime minister during Mohammad Reza Shah's reign, shot at close range, dark welts disfiguring his face, bottomless sockets for eyes.

Perhaps posters were removed and murals painted over in hope that we would forget the horrible atrocities of the revolution and the tragic consequences of the Iran-Iraq war. Forget the senseless death of our youth. Forget the tortured bodies that dangled from cranes in streets. Forget how we struggled with the aftereffects of poison gas, how our widowed women and mothers were forced into prostitution. Forget the acrid stench of spilt blood and gunpowder that continued to lace our lives. Perhaps the authorities assumed that having witnessed endless horrors for so long, we had become desensitized, so the images were painted over to give us temporary respite before even more offensive ones emerged to haunt us anew.

The watchman flung open the wrought-iron gates of the mansion my father had built before the revolution, the beloved home he refused to abandon, lest the authorities confiscate everything, partition the rooms into cubicles, and move "needy, impoverished" families in.

I ran into our high-ceilinged hall, the Esfahan carpets muffling the anger of my tinder-smelling heels, but not the chaos in my head. I did not care that I had only tossed a coat over my shoulders without taking time to wear stockings, nor that I cut my arm against the gilded console as I ran across my parents' hallway. I wiped my bloody arm and licked my fingers, thinking of the Fountain of Martyrs that gushes red-colored water in the center of the Heaven of Zahra Cemetery. There was a time when the staining of water to resemble blood seemed a senseless act of a desperate people. But that day, I was bleeding from every pore, so why shouldn't a fountain?

Madar held me as I cried out Aziz's name. He was with a woman. In my bedroom. I pressed my palms against my ears to stop "The Blue Danube" playing in my head, the notes that evoked our shared secrets, smells, and memories. He fucked her in our house, on our bed. Such recklessness! How could he toss all precaution to hell? The answer was obvious. He was in love.

"Cry," Madar advised, with a wary little gesture of rubbing her eyelids. She forced half a bottle of Passiflorine, a calming tonic of French passion flowers, down my throat. "I know how hard it is."

"No! You don't!" Baba would never fuck my mother's best friend. Never! And on their bed, no less, and to a tune the two of them had danced to on their wedding night.

Now, the notes reverberate in my head, hurting my eardrums with a different breed of secrets. The truth is that neither the music and the wine, nor the candles and the indignity of my photographs looking down on them, had the power to destroy me. What devastated me beyond repair was what I saw when her hair parted, revealing their profiles.

Their lips were glued in a kiss. My husband's tongue was buried in Butterfly's mouth. The horror of their melded bodies paled at the sight of that gesture of deep intimacy.

"They were naked," I whispered to Madar that day.

"Who is she?" Madar asked.

I turned to her with all the force of my pain and told her it didn't matter who she was. The kernel of a resolution was beginning to harden even then. It was important to pull myself together, to take care of this betrayal in my own time and in my own way.

Madar's tears left dark stains on her silk blouse. "Whoever she is, she's a passing whim, I'm certain. These types don't last. Anyway, Soraya, nothing you can do."

"Don't say that, Madar. Please don't!"

"I am being realistic, Soraya. Remember when I left? Remember what happened?"

Of course I did. Five years had gone by, yet that incident remained seared into my consciousness.

Madar and Baba fought furiously while I, who had come to spend the weekend with them because Aziz was away on business, sat in the next room, pretending to read and trying hard not to intrude. Baba insisted that no one but he had the right to decide how to dispose of his assets after his death. Madar snapped her fingers like castanets, reminding him that she had been his wife for more than thirty years and that he had no right to change his will without consulting her.

"I'm leaving more than enough for you and Soraya. It doesn't matter what I do with the rest."

"Oh! Yes! Yes! It matters. It certainly does." Like a chirping bird, Madar stressed every syllable as if to preface a profound statement. "You better change your will back or...I'll...yes, I assure you...I'll get a divorce."

"*Barayeh chi*?" Baba asked. "Why would you do that?"

"Because I can!"

"Of course," Baba replied calmly. "You can do anything you want."

I respected Baba for not losing his composure and for refusing to intimidate or be intimidated. Any other man would have mentioned the Jewish *ketubah*—an ancient religious agreement that entitles a divorcee to no more than her weight in gold.

"*Etemad behet nemikonam*," Madar declared, and the small hairs on my arms rebelled at that rare flash of anger, a glimpse of seldom revealed fang.

At his wife's proclamation that she did not trust him anymore, I heard Baba jump out of his chair, which crashed behind him with startling finality. "This is it, then! There's nothing left to say." Having delivered his verdict, Baba marched out of the house and slammed the door nearly off its hinges.

The swish of sprinklers came to life outside. The gardener whistled a melancholy tune. The snap of sheers grated on my nerves.

Madar shuffled into the living room, sat on the sofa, and patted a space next to her. She stared at the clasped hands she cradled in her lap, then unlocked her fingers and ran them through her carefully tinted hair that did not show a hint of gray at the roots. "Baba and I have had our differences, but not this serious."

I put aside my book and pressed my damp handkerchief against my eyes. "Why did Baba change his will?"

"It doesn't make a difference, Soraya. I want you to know that whatever happens, I love you very much."

I felt helpless and miserable as I observed Madar toss a few pieces of her silks, chiffons, and mink into a suitcase, letting loose the scent of her talc and violets. She removed her wedding band. Her bright eyes gazed at it as if the answer to her problems lay there. She pressed it to her lips before leaving it on the dressing table.

"Where are you going?" I asked.

"I'm not sure, Soraya."

"Come stay with us, then. Until you both calm down."

"No, Soraya, I won't calm down. And I'll never stay at my son-in-law's."

"But it's my home, too, Madar."

"Not really," she replied. "A home belongs to the man."

From the window of my parents' home, my devastated gaze trailed her as she passed our neighbor's house, a consulate that sported a flag from a faraway land, and then past a café with dark-tinted windows, past the green grocer who was in the process of haggling with a pregnant customer, before disappearing at the end of the avenue, leaving behind her scent of *Je Reviens*, her pearl earrings, her Peykan car parked at the door, and the high-heeled pumps she wore out of the house, and without having teased her hair into the curls that normally framed her translucent face.

My father, despite his total loss of self in her absence, despite the melancholy liquidity in his eyes, continued to slick back his hair with the pomade that smelled of leather, continued to wear his formal three-piece suits and colorful bow ties.

In less than two weeks, at the same open window from which my gaze had raked the street when I came to visit, I watched my mother unexpectedly reappear on foot around the bend. I was surprised and saddened by the change in her. In such a short time, she had hardened into middle age. She wore the same slippers she had left in, her hair tucked behind her ears, gray visible at the temples, frailer than I remembered her.

What later continued to devastate and humiliate her was that she had no choice but to return because our culture ostracized a divorced woman and would not allow her to continue to live the life she was accustomed to among her circle of friends. She had returned to the place she would from then on call "my husband's home," with the added awareness that my father had the legal right to draw his will as he pleased and that, in the end, there was nothing she could do.

In a short time, she turned old and bitter, with a rough edge to her fragility.

To punish Baba, Madar stitched together the remnants of her pride with the ancient thread of martyrdom. She transformed herself into a living saint. Her skirts became longer, her fingernails shorter, her lips paler, and the style of her hair matronly. She separated her bed from my father's and moved into a sparsely furnished room on the second floor. She padlocked all emotions in a chest as impenetrable as steel.

That day, five years later in my parents' home, my blood beginning to thicken with the recent discovery of my husband's betrayal, I did not understand Madar. I stood up, smoothed my dress, and asked her to keep my husband's betrayal to herself. If Baba ever found out, he would certainly punish Aziz. And that was my business. I did not intend to follow in Madar's footsteps. I did not intend to allow Aziz to transform me into a martyr.

I am from a different generation.

I will shape my own fate.

chapter 15

THE LAMENTING HOWLS OF the bird reverberate around the courtyard from somewhere up high among the darkest branches of the monkey tree, where its cries echo its lonely existence. I can't help but think of my grandmother's barking owl, can't help but believe that there must be a reason for this bird's appearance in my courtyard in another country at this time of my life. I whistle once, twice, and then murmur soothingly in hope of seducing the bird out into the open. Failing to do so, I summon Mansour to the courtyard and tell him that I need his help. I will tame the owl.

Mansour, his eyes rounded in shock, lowers his head and mumbles under his breath that I should keep my distance because owls are bad-luck creatures of the night. "Please, *Khanom*, they are messengers of the Devil! Evil spirits you shouldn't see in daylight! They are funereal birds!"

"Are you done, Mansour? Now go buy a kilo of raw meat, find some beetles if possible, maybe a dead rat or two, and come back."

He stuffs his hands in his pants pockets and huffs under his breath. "With your permission, *Khanom*, there's no need for rats. I keep a few kilos of meat in the refrigerator for Oni and myself. Maybe that will do."

"Flavor a piece with seasoning, some salt, and turmeric. They like that. And bring it to me with a tall ladder. I'll be waiting here. And bring a bowl. Do we have an extra-long hook and handle?"

"Yes, in the garage. For trimming treetops."

"Bring that, too."

I rest against the trunk of the monkey tree and glance up every now and then to check for the slightest movement among the still branches.

The air is sweet with the scent of lemons. Leaves are the pale green of spring. Our wedding anniversary is fast approaching. A ray of sun falls across the carpet of grass like a trail of splashed gold. Nature is in a festive mood, braided and rouged and powdered. What is there to delight in? A Red Admiral lands on the back of my hand. I blow off a powdery layer of its bright red shade and marvel at how fast its luster is lost. I trap it under my cupped hand and imprison it in darkness. Butterflies are cold-blooded. They need the sun to fly.

I remove my hand and off it flaps. Gone!

Mansour appears with a bowl of seasoned meat. With the help of the ladder and the hook and handle, he slides the bowl onto the top of the atrium skylight and quickly scrambles down.

"Leave the hook and handle here in case I need it."

The scar across his mouth is a tortured zipper. "With your permission, *Khanom*, I will stay with you. Owls are jealous creatures. They attack and blind women."

"No, this owl is a blessing. Thank you, Mansour. I want to be alone now."

He slaps his forehead in disapproval and, with a stiff nod and heavy steps, crosses the courtyard, climbs the stairs to the terrace, and disappears into the house.

I will stay out here as long as it takes, even sleep here if I need to, until I earn the bird's trust. I do so in silence, motionless as a corpse, transporting myself to my grandmother's garden in Iran, where with great patience and wisdom, she managed to tame an owl into a pet, feed it from her heavily gloved hand, and later tempt the bird out of hiding by simply dangling a dead rat, frogmouth, or opossum in front of its bespectacled face.

The owl made its home in a walnut tree next to her bedroom window, in a dilapidated nest abandoned by other large birds that had migrated long before to other places. During the first months, the owl raised a racket with its despondent barks as it strove to establish ownership of its territory and while hunting at dusk and dawn. In time, this strong and unfriendly bird would gently bite into its daily meal out of Mamabozorg's hand, careful not to hurt her.

With persistence and a healthy dose of compassion, you can domesticate anything or anyone, she would advise me.

But my patience is running low and the sun is beginning to wreak havoc on my face, yet my illusive bird is proving to be far more stubborn than my grandmother's owl. I throw my hands up.

In a neighbor's garden, musicians are tuning their instruments in preparation for a party. It is Sunday. A luncheon. Cars are arriving. The band begins to play "Bridge," an old song of the Iranian pop singer Googoosh: "Help me weave a bed of flowers for our innocent sleep of love…Help me weave a tent of songs to shadow us…I am not scared of night because you handed me the sun…" Tales of fragile loves and broken hearts, virgin brides and eager grooms, nuptial moons shimmering through diaphanous skies.

Struck by an overwhelming urge to cry, I fold down on the damp grass, lean against the tree bark, and swallow my nostalgia. We loved to dance to Googoosh's songs, Aziz and I, admired the way she managed to reinvent herself year after year. Now, like many of my expatriates, she must have fled Iran, where creating music is a crime worthy of flogging, imprisonment, or other punishments.

I gaze up at the tree above me and call with a pleading voice that is louder than I intended, "*Khaheshmikonam* please, Mamabozorg, I'm alone and lonely here and desperate for your guidance."

Mamabozorg's image flits behind my eyelids, veiled in her silks and scents of jasmine and powder. Her embroidered sleeves rest like fans on her ample breasts. She strokes the amber beads slung about her neck, raising their scent of possibilities. My eyes squeeze shut to keep her from fleeing.

Like an answer to my prayer, a flurry of movement occurs among the branches. I jump to my feet and step back to survey the tree from a distance. A shadow flutters about. The silence is broken by the creak of twigs and rustle of leaves. The bird quietly emerges to settle on one of the prickly branches. I freeze in place, afraid to breathe or even wink, lest I scare it away. And then, as if playing a game of teasing Soraya, it hops down to a lower branch, then another, and before I have time to take a good look, swoops to circle and spiral overhead once, twice. Then it lands on a branch almost level with my field of vision, spreads its mottled wings, and preens itself, showing off for me.

I try hard not to cry and laugh with joy and wonder, not to scare it away because it is a barking owl. Right here in my courtyard. The elusive "screaming woman." I am certain because its similarity to Mamabozorg's owl is unquestionable. The same mottled plumage in shades of brown, cream, and auburn, some the color of burnt chocolate. Its large head rests on a short neck. Framing its shining, yellow eyes is a circular pattern of white, as perfectly round and seamless as a platinum wedding band.

With a flurry of flirtatious hopping and flapping, the owl takes flight, wheels around the atrium, and with great purpose lands on the dome of the atrium, where the sun reflects on the glass panels like so many fireballs. The owl observes with interest the bowl with its offering. Please, I beg, my heart will break if you reject my meal.

An imperceptible growl emanates from its throat. The compact head rotates one complete circle, then turns back to the bowl. Head flailing, it tears with its beak and devours morsels of raw meat held between strong talons. Having finished its meal, it lets out low barks and pecks on one glass panel, then another, as if conducting a conversation with the Corpse Plant in the atrium below.

I take a deep breath, slowly approach the ladder, climb a few rungs, and await the bird's reaction. Encouraged, I climb higher for a closer look. I draw shallow breaths as its inquisitive eyes inspect me like double camera lenses. Then, as if in acknowledgment, it lets out a low, groaning hoot of a bark, sharp and short and far reaching.

The size of its stocky body and broad, white-dotted wings leave no doubt that the owl is female.

My grandmother is making her presence known to me.

chapter 16

WE HAVE GROWN TO trust each other, my owl and I. Her lingering gaze follows me from wherever she happens to be: perched on top of the atrium, on one of the granite benches in the sunken courtyard, on the lip of the reflecting pool, swooping down nearby while I tame a creeping jasmine around the gazebo, or recently barking behind as I enter the eucalyptus grove to check on the newly arriving Monarchs.

I stroke her plumes that in sunlight are the russet shades of autumn leaves, caress the silky parting in the middle of her breast and the slightly damp feathers of her warm belly. Snippets of my developing history take shape in the mirror of my owl's eyes, where my grandmother's image is reflected. I see her plant her footstool nearby. She is here to help me reconstruct memories, to locate the time and place Aziz and Butterfly's affair began.

Mamabozorg must have been aware of the betrayal the day she had summoned us to tea in her rose garden. She must have known that the plague of whores had struck her own beloved granddaughter.

That day, five years before, my father, Butterfly, and I sat on a wrought-iron bench opposite a table of Italian stone set with rice cookies and narrow-waisted teacups with filigreed holders. Baba wore a double-breasted, pin-striped three-piece suit and wide burgundy bow tie. With his slicked-back hair and clutching a pair of leather gloves, he resembled a displaced prince among Mamabozorg's roses and Persian jasmines, his backdrop a turquoise-tiled pool. I liked my grandmother's garden, enjoyed engaging in conversations amid the magnificent setting of rare hybrid roses flown in from Holland.

Butterfly sat erect at the edge of her seat, the scent of her perfume heightened by perspiration. She never felt at ease in my grandmother's company. I did not blame her.

Mamabozorg was a formidable presence. Although illiterate, she ruled her family with wisdom and a sharp tongue. She had opinions on every matter, and nothing could stop her from voicing them in an emphatic manner.

Her indispensable footstool tucked under her arm, she emerged under the marble arches of the veranda and stepped down the stairs, approaching through an arbor of jasmines. Her Owl of Reason sailed overhead, casting its shadow like a protective *chador*. Despite her short stature and her weight that made it difficult for her to walk, she dressed in the latest European fashions and the most expensive Parisian fabrics. No matter the color or style of her dresses and shawls, year after year, and for as long as I can remember, the same chain of amber beads lay coiled on her generous breasts, her blue-gray curls twisted into a tight bun at the nape of her neck, and her nails painted the shade of onion peel.

She set her footstool among the rose bushes, shifting it slightly farther back to better observe us all with a sweep of her sharp eyes. Translucent powder collected in her well-seamed face, proof of a life spent more in her garden than inside her mansion. She paused to catch her breath, then signaled for the servants to serve tea steeped with cardamom and sprigs of mint. The owl settled on her lap. Another pair of eyes to scrutinize us.

Mamabozorg clasped her hands around her bird and appraised Baba and me for what felt like an unbearably long time. She dismissed Butterfly as if she was not worthy of much consideration.

It was a brilliant autumn day, the previous day's rain marks still visible on surrounding bushes and trees. I wondered about the unexpected chill in the air. Why was there no sign of the nightingales? Even the normally inebriating scent of roses was muted.

Without bothering to welcome us in her usually warm manner, Mamabozorg abruptly addressed my father. "Son, the situation is dire. Tragic! We are losing our young and old to a plague of temptation. Look around you! Whores are thriving like water hyacinths in the polluted waters of our society. These women breed contagious diseases. Suffocate everything in their path. Green plague! That's what they are. Do something."

It was a well-known fact that after the Iran-Iraq war many women who had lost their husbands to war were forced into prostitution to support their families. Even today, in 1999, prostitution remains widespread, not only in the southern new city and the red light district, but also in affluent northern areas of the capital, where late in the evenings, *chador*-clad women by roadsides tempt with an expert opening and closing of the veil that reveals naked bodies. On that day in my grandmother's garden, six years had passed since the war ended, yet the government did not show any interest in improving the situation.

Baba slapped his gloves against his palm. The threatening thump of leather against skin. "What exactly do you expect me to do, Madar? It's hard enough to keep my own family in line, let alone change the world. Unless *you* have a brilliant solution."

"But *you* are the one with all the brilliant solutions, son."

"Please do not *taarof*, Madar," my father replied. "Anyway, what exactly is all this fuss about?"

True to her Persian heritage, Mamabozorg had begun with *taarof*, the ritual of sitting on ceremony, being polite and seemingly sincere, but concealing her true intentions. "Now that you ask, son, I'll tell you."

A passing plane overhead muffled all sound. We glanced up. Mamabozorg shuddered, pressing her eyes shut. She must have evoked the memory of Reza Shah and Iran during World War II. No matter how often the political situation of the time was explained, she never came to terms with the decision of the allies to drive her beloved king out of his homeland. She touched a finger to her lips as if to tame and soften the impact of her next words.

"Tell me, son. Tell me why you changed your will. It is very *mashkook* to me. Quite suspicious. Didn't you do more than enough for her?" An amethyst ring flashed on the forefinger Mamabozorg directed at Butterfly, who seemed to shrink in her skin.

I held back a gasp of surprise. A trickle of cold sweat carved a path down my spine. Here, at last, was the reason we were summoned, the reason my mother was not included in this meeting. Why would Baba change his will in Butterfly's favor? He was a kind man and certainly generous, that much I knew, but this was a remarkable act, especially in the face of Madar's disapproval.

My father sat there, seething, uneasy that Butterfly and I, thirty-two-year-old married women, were present while Mamabozorg scolded him as if he were a naughty teenager.

Butterfly did not move from the edge of her seat, her knuckles white as death from gripping the stone tabletop. She appeared small and frail, as if a slight breeze might snuff her out. I longed to console her. But Mamabozorg would allow nothing to temper the gravity of the moment.

Baba knotted his eyebrows and pressed his steel-gray eyes shut, as if to squeeze an offensive idea out of his brain. "I have my own reasons, Madar, among them my promise to Butterfly's dying mother. And if you have to know, I will *not* allow excessive wealth to warp my wife and daughter's moral compass, especially when I'm not around to rein them in."

"Nonsense!" Mamabozorg lashed out, startling the owl into a flutter on her lap. "Your wife and daughter are not horses to be reined in, and since when have you become such an extraordinary *asbsavar* horseman?"

Baba removed the cushion from under himself and tossed it aside on the bench. "Madar *jan*, my family is *my* responsibility, not yours."

Mamabozorg's voice turned soft. "Yes, my son, of course. In that case let me remind you that *cheraghi keh beh khaneh halal ast beh masjed haram ast*." She stroked her owl's underbelly as she reminded her son that he needed to take care of his own before showing charity to others.

Baba stood up, brushed imaginary dust from his trousers, and announced that Mamabozorg had the right to do whatever she chose with her own wealth, as he had the right to dispense with his own as he saw fit. If, in the process, he kept his promise to a dear friend, so be it. He planted a kiss on his mother's forehead and then motioned to Butterfly and me to take our leave with him.

I held on to the chair handles and attempted to pull myself up. But my legs had turned to sawdust and I couldn't move. How could Baba encourage my independence, yet attempt to control me by withholding his money?

"Sit down, Soraya," Mamabozorg ordered. "I'm not done with you."

My heart reacted, giving up a beat, slapping against my chest. What now? What had I done?

Sunlight filtered through Mamabozorg's hair, turning each to silver filament. She drew a great breath, and her eyes acquired that faraway look of being embroiled in her own thoughts.

My father turned his back to us and, with Butterfly in tow, marched under the arbor and climbed the steps onto the veranda. His stiff gait and retreating back conveyed the enormity of his anger. Butterfly glanced back at me with pleading eyes and then smoothed down her skirt with nervous urgency as the two of them disappeared into the house.

A breeze from the Alborz Mountains ruffled the gray curls at the nape of Mamabozorg's neck. A pulse beat at the corner of her mouth. Demanding complete silence, she clapped to startle away a group of chattering pigeons that had appeared to peck on leftover cookie crumbs. The owl flapped its wings against her belly. She nuzzled its feathers and it let out a low bark, puffed up, and settled back. She cupped the bird's head in her palm. Was she attempting to calm the bird or to communicate with it in the ancient language of silence?

"Listen to me, Soraya," she said at last. "I am leaving everything I have to you."

"Oh! No, Mamabozorg," I cried out in shock. "What's wrong? Are you sick?"

"Don't interrupt, Soraya! Have I taught you nothing? Patience! Bite your tongue for a second. I'll explain. You have always been like the daughter I wanted but never had. The independent woman I aspired to become but never entirely succeeded. Yes, I know. Becoming the Shah's jeweler was not a small feat, but my dream was to become a doctor. Not an ordinary medical doctor. I wanted to mend souls. They're called therapists these days.

"I wanted to help abused women who conceal their pain in their hearts and their bruises under *chadors*, especially women traumatized by the illegal abortions those cursed backwater charlatans perform every day." She tapped on her heart. "It still hurts here after all these years. I was only a child when I lost my mother to one of those botched abortions."

I pushed back my chair and stood, my shadow rising with me, moving ahead to embrace her. "I didn't know any of this."

"Sit, my dear. There's so much about me you don't know. Did you know how deeply I loved your grandfather? No. I never talk about that either. Nor do I like to talk about that black year of gloom after he died. I was young and hopeless and ready to end my own life. But the angel of death had more pressing matters to attend to. So, I picked myself up and dusted my grief off. I survived a lot of ups and downs. Yes, I did. And God blessed me with a good life. But I'm old and tired now and have one last wish,

Soraya. I want you to break this chain of oppression. I want you to fulfill the dream I wasn't allowed."

I slowly settle back in my seat. "Please, Mamabozorg, stop saying these things. You're scaring me. Are you sure you're well?"

"Yes, my child, I am well if one can call this well." She waved her arm up and down her short frame. "My body still acts like an eighteen-year-old, although I can't say the same for my spirit. Anyhow, I want you to open an account in *yengeh donya*, somewhere civilized and far from here, Soraya. I'll wire-transfer everything into your account. And, Soraya, not a word to your father or husband. Promise."

I was stunned not only at the enormity of her decision, which would make me an even wealthier woman, but also at the repercussions she would face when my father would inevitably discover that she had refused to leave her fortune to him, her only son. Although Baba had told Mamabozorg she had the right to dispense with her wealth as she saw fit, he surely did not expect *this*. "I don't need your money, Mamabozorg. And, anyway, you'll live many, many more years."

"Don't argue with me, Soraya. Do this for me."

"Mamabozorg," I whispered, afraid the servants might be eavesdropping. "Let me share this honor with Baba and Aziz."

"Don't let me down," she sighed. "*Eltemas mikonam*, I beg of you. No one must know, not even after I am dead and long gone. I want this account to be in your name alone. Be realistic, will you? No sentimental 'we' and 'us' and 'husband and wife must share everything.' Aziz and your father are good men. Yes, they are. They are also strong men, smart men. And like all such men, they are manipulative and controlling."

I tucked a strand of her thinning hair behind her ear and pressed my lips to her temple to inhale the lavender scent of her skin. "But they are family...It would be a betrayal."

"Grow up, Soraya!" Mamabozorg cried out, throwing her arms up and sending her owl into a flurry of protesting growls.

"Loyalty is not about blurting out everything that's on the tip of your tongue. Didn't you hear me? Don't give your man the *aslaheh* ammunition he will use against you."

"I love and respect you, Mamabozorg, but I can't accept your gift. I don't know how to keep secrets from Aziz, or even Baba..."

"Listen, you stubborn girl. Now that you force me, I'll tell you that I decided to do this recently after I had a nightmare. Didn't want you to worry, nor tell your father, who doesn't believe in dreams. I dreamt that my family was lost in a desert, surrounded by a network of endless, dark paths, the earth shaking violently under our feet and about to swallow us all up.

"Suddenly I saw a bright path, as if illuminated by hundreds of candles. But I was being sucked into a sand tunnel and couldn't move, so I gestured to your father and husband to lead you toward that illuminated path. But they gaped at me with glazed eyes and toothless mouths, never reacting, not even when the earth roared and yawned and swallowed every single one of you.

"Do you understand the significance of this dream? What it means is that I can't help you, and no one else will if you won't help yourself. Not a word! *Divar moush dareh moush ham goush dareh.*" She reminded me that walls have mice and mice have ears. "And, Soraya, one day you and Aziz will leave Iran. I am certain. I see it as clearly as my own tears. So swear on my life, Soraya, that when the time comes you'll go to a place where you'll learn to love the sky and the plants it feeds. Stay away from wet, cloudy climates. They have a way of getting under your skin and rotting you before your time."

Unwilling to argue further with my beloved mentor, the source of encouragement in my life, I promised Mamabozorg I would follow her advice and never set foot in Britain, the country she refused to forgive for having exiled her beloved Reza Shah.

"One more thing, my child, at your age, you must be done idolizing your father. Sever the umbilical cord." With an impatient wave of her hand, she stopped me from asking how it was possible to end a devotion that seemed older than myself, and why she called it idolization when my idol was my father, who deeply loved and cared for me.

She rubbed her amber beads between palms that had stroked resistant gems and velvet petals. Lifting the necklace over her head, she curled it once around her wrist and smelled the spicy scent of the beads that evoked her past. She ordered me to kneel in front of her and draped the necklace around my neck. "Reza Shah gave it to me. I want you to have it."

I hurriedly removed the necklace. Like giant drops of honey, the beads coiled in my palms. "I can't accept, Mamabozorg. It means too much to you." I could not endure the weight of her memories.

"Take it! I'm done with the past."

She held my face between her hands, her once brilliantly green eyes dulled, yet full of the pleasure of seeing me. "Listen to me, Soraya, listen well. You might not know that a tiny mosquito can kill an elephant, but it can. If a mosquito finds its way into an elephant's ear and starts buzzing, to get rid of it the elephant will hit its head so hard and so often against a stone that it will eventually smash its skull and die."

"Why are you telling me this, Mamabozorg *jan*?"

"Because I want you to be watchful of petty betrayals before they become insurmountable miseries."

"You've always been my cynic, Mamabozorg."

"No," she sighed, stroking the owl in her lap. "I'm your *Morgheh Hagh*, your Bird of Reason. Now go. I'm tired."

❧ ❧ ❧

On the day of her eightieth birthday, Mamabozorg Emerald, the matriarch and framework of my family, informed us that she had had enough of the petty familial revolutions in her own house and more than enough of the not-so-petty religio-political revolutions in the streets.

She summoned Mashti Gholdor, the famous blacksmith who catered to upscale mansions in Shemiran, north of Tehran.

Mashti the Bully entered the Alley of *Mullah* Sadra and marched toward Mamabozorg's mansion as if he were a one-man army coming to single-handedly fight off a squadron of enemies. The length of his bare arms and bulging biceps were tattooed with images from the great poet Ferdowsi's mythical *Epic of Kings*—Shah Kaiumars clad in tiger skins and seated on the Persian throne; the combat of Rostam and Sohrab that tragically ended in death because father and son were unaware of their familial ties; the seven knights of Turan wrestling with the valiant Rakush.

Mashti Gholdor came to a halt in front of Mamabozorg's gate, removed the decorative chains around his neck, and dropped them with a big clang at his feet. He turned to the neighborhood, cupped his mouth with his enormous hands, and bellowed, "Ohoy! Hear me, one and all! Ohoy! From now on, no one will step past this threshold without my permission. No one will disturb the respected *Khanom*!"

He worked day and night to raise a towering iron fence around the perimeter of my grandmother's mansion. On the seventh day, with much huffing and puffing and exaggerated petitioning of Allah and Akbar, he produced a massive, copper padlock to secure the gate. On a plaque that dangled with a chain from the padlock was engraved:

There is nothing more I wish to see.

Mamabozorg allowed no one in and out of the mansion except Asghar, the night watch, who was also her confidant and gardener, and Fatemeh, who had helped Mamabozorg raise her son.

She became a recluse in her own home.

Once Baba had silently mourned his loss and was ready to broach the subject, he said that he understood why his mother had exiled herself into the safe haven of her home. In her lifetime, she had experienced major political upheavals, wars, and revolutions: the 1941 invasion of Iran by Britain and the Soviets; the nationalist revolt of 1953; and the most enduring one, the Islamic Revolution of 1979. The last one, Baba was certain, had crumbled his mother's hopes and memories to such tiny slivers that she didn't even attempt to collect the shreds.

I, on the other hand, believed that a more profound incident must have caused Mamabozorg's abrupt retreat. I also knew that she would not easily divulge her secret to me or to anyone else. But I assumed that she would make an exception in my case and allow me to visit her. I was wrong. She refused my repeated pleas. Even when I sent word through her gardener that I was in a predicament and in dire need of guidance, she would not unlock her gates to me.

My world fell apart in her absence.

Mamabozorg withdrew and Butterfly emerged.

chapter 17

THE PLANT HAS CHANGED in the last day and a half. The lavender stem has turned a lewd purple, a shade darker than liver. The leaf that hugs the stem is now a glassy, almost transparent green. The stem is like fire, the engulfing veined leaf the hue of pistachio ice. And something else! Two centimeters below the tip, on the left, a fleshy knoblike growth that resembles a strange fruit. But in none of the books I've read, nor in my extensive research, is it mentioned that the Amorphophallus might bear fruit the color of clouds with a peculiar smell. Not quite unpleasant, nor inviting, but suggestive of concoctions Butterfly once steeped.

My dear friend, Butterfly, with lips like blood and vampire fingernails.

Not yet fifteen, she substituted her taffeta skirts for ankle-length dresses, toned down the kohl eyeliner, applied lip gloss in place of red lipstick, ironed her curls straight, and braided her hair into a thick plait tossed over one shoulder like a cobra.

Even now, miles from home, I recall with great clarity the afternoon she came to our house after school to complain to Baba about Aunt Tala. His face a mask of rage, he summoned our chauffeur and ordered him to drive through the hectic streets of Tehran and straight into the dirt road alley. The car came into a noisy halt in front of Butterfly's mustard-colored brick house, with its wide-open door and depressingly gray laundry limp on balcony railings.

The immigrant prostitute from a Communist country, who occupied the first floor, was leaning against the doorframe that day. She wore a camisole, green satin pants, and silver slippers. Two golden braids framed her chubby, yogurt-pale face. Numerous wrinkled shar-pei puppies yelped and skipped between her legs. She curled an inviting forefinger at Baba and, finding him unreceptive, shrugged her shoulders and winked at a man who happened to exit the Saraf Bakery next door.

More than once, fights had broken out between one man and another, each insisting that the lady's soliciting finger and flirtatious lashes were meant for him. More than once, sharp switchblades or broken bottles of *arragh* vodka were used as weapons aimed at an artery, and more than once the knives or bottles had been hurled at the bakery windows, scattering shreds of glass, cookies, blood, and guts onto the sidewalk.

Years later, during the first months of the revolution, Butterfly's neighbor was among the first of many prostitutes who faced the firing squad of Khalkhali, a *mullah* known for his sadistic delight in strangling cats.

That afternoon, Baba marched past the prostitute, straight up the stairs, and into Butterfly's home. He let loose his baritone into the small apartment, calling out, "Tala! Tala!" as if he was a general on his way to punish a petty officer.

Aunt Tala came running out of her bedroom, her black jersey dress and bat sleeves twisting like poisonous snakes around her skeletal frame.

Baba thrust his hands under her armpits and lifted her off the ground, dangling her in the air like an emaciated scarecrow hanging from the gallows. "As of this moment you'll have a pot of food simmering on the stove when Parvaneh comes home from school. Do you hear me! I will weigh her myself in two weeks, and if she doesn't gain three kilos, you'll be responsible for your own blood."

I felt a twitch of jealousy that day, and again sometime later, when Baba took time off from work to invite us to Saraf Bakery after school. Even now, in my house in America, I can taste the bleached cardamom cookies and golden *guitty* pastries laced with saffron and pistachio and the glistening, honey-soaked baklava perfumed with rosewater. I am still able to summon the smooth, voluptuous taste of *naneh khamei*, pastry shells pregnant with fresh cream from the milk of goats that fed on clover pastures.

Butterfly looked forward to the visits to the bakery. Baba enjoyed them, too. He felt useful and needed. And Butterfly, who seldom benefited from fatherly advice, was hungry to learn and please. Baba discussed the *vazifeh* duties of a wife, the importance of being independent, yet appearing vulnerable, so our future husbands would presume they wore the pants around the house, even if the reality was otherwise. "Voice your opinions, by all means. But present them in a diplomatic way so your husband ends up believing the idea is his."

The day after Butterfly received her high school diploma, she married Hamid, Aziz's good friend and partner in the import and distribution of pharmaceutical products.

Hamid was of medium height, but the resonant timbre of his voice and the way he carried himself made him seem taller than he was. Like me, he must have had foreign genes in his far past. He had light, chestnut-colored hair and mischievous hazel eyes. Unlike most Iranian men, Hamid found it unfair that women were not allowed to date like men.

He also did not believe in outdated customs that demanded girls to remain virgins until their wedding night, when men were not held to the same standards. He did end up marrying a virgin, however, because Butterfly did not have the backbone to defy her aunt and toss away that ridiculous nuptial piece of framed cloth signed by an ignorant rabbi.

On her wedding, Baba played the role of Butterfly's father, who by then was far gone, hopelessly lost in his own labyrinthine void and incapable of giving his daughter away. Aziz was the best man. He suggested that the wedding ceremony be held in his house, which, with my help, no longer resembled a bachelor's den.

My parents took care of Butterfly's dowry. Madar, who had volunteered to oversee the wedding party coordinators, went to work with a passion and interest in detail that she had not yet lost.

That night, creamy roses and snowy baby's breath spilled over Baccarat vases. Marble consoles were set with caramelized almonds and dates rolled in coconut; mounds of rock sugar and cones of sugar were displayed for good luck. I decorated a six-tiered Napoleon cake with edible chrysanthemums, daffodils, bachelor's buttons, and carnations.

More than two thousand identical, peach-colored rosebuds had been flown in from Holland and strewn on the table that displayed the bridal gifts. A set of antique candelabra with burnished cherubs held up marbleized candles. Ten obsidian marble slaves carried an antique clock. An ancient mirror that had lost its mercury to time was framed in bronze encrusted with agate, opal, and turquoise.

Two sets of enamel combs, brushes, hand mirrors, and other toiletries were on view in royal blue velvet boxes. A watch for the groom; emerald earrings, necklace, and bracelet for the bride. An antique trunk brimmed with evening gowns, satin slippers, and silk underwear. And, on a separate table, silver vases held sugared candies for each guest to take home as a memento. Madar had outdone herself.

Butterfly appeared in a swirl of white gauze and the rustle of shantung skirts, red lips and dark-lashed eyes gleaming behind layered veils. My father, in black tuxedo and wide satin cummerbund, ushered Butterfly in with pride, a pair of gloves in one of his hands and the other holding her elbow. Aunt Tala followed, hanging on to Butterfly's father and hardly able to keep him at bay. Having given up her funereal dresses for the occasion, she sported a multi-tiered, crushed velvet skirt and green taffeta blouse that gave her the air of a puffed-up parrot. She was visibly overjoyed that she would, at last, be left alone with her older brother, who could hardly differentiate between day and night, let alone meddle in her suspicious visits to the Synagogue of Rabbi Eshagh the Henna Beard, with whom she had forged a romantic liaison.

To the joyous tune of "Congratulations, My Beloved," the wedding guests rose as one. Applause echoed around the house. Women tossed sugared candies in the air and ululated in an ancient cry of joy.

Musicians tuned their instruments. Waiters ceased serving and, silver trays in hand, retreated to the perimeters. Ladies gathered their skirts and stepped closer to surround the bride. A faint scent of roast lamb and saffron rice wafted into the salon. The crash of plates could be heard from the kitchen.

Baba lifted Butterfly's veils and kissed her on both cheeks, smoothing her veils back over her tiara before stepping back to relinquish her to her future husband.

Hamid carried her in his arms to a sofa upholstered with a fabric woven with the design of tulips. At the time, we were still dazed from the unexpected fall of the Shah and the rise of Khomeini and his cronies, so the sight of the tulips that *mullahs* believed grew from the blood of martyrs brought the acrid smell of death into my throat.

Hamid came down on one knee in front of his radiant bride, who was holding court in a cloud of Chanel perfume and crowded by blood-of-martyr tulip prints. He snapped open a satin box. A ten-carat diamond solitaire reflected stars on her tiara, surely exceptional by anyone's standards, let alone Butterfly's.

Her eyes shifted, dismissing her wedding ring and her future husband at her feet, and wandered in pursuit of another.

Click!

What I captured in that frame should have warned me.

chapter 18

Noruz, the Iranian New Year, is a time of joy and celebration, a time when the advent of the spring equinox and extended daylight triumphs over darkness. Not so for me and my busy mind, which continues to birth endless memories that throb in my head like a persistent headache.

Still innocent then, I recall with a sweet aftertaste the last Noruz I spent with my parents. The ornate tables were laden with the customary seven foods symbolizing spring, rebirth, fertility, joy, and prosperity. Goldfish swam in crystal bowls set on the Limoges cabinet in the dining room. The aroma of freshly baked *sangak* flat bread and the perfume of rosewater pasties and hyacinth swirled around the house. Whitefish spiced with mint and coriander sizzled in ovens, and rice with aromatic herbs steamed in copper pots. Boiled lamb, stuffed with dried fruit and nuts, lay on polished silver trays ready for garnish.

Wearing a gray, pin-striped suit and a Sulka cravat, his hair slicked back with brilliantine, Baba looked younger than his fifty-seven years. He strolled around his domain with an absent look in his wise eyes, rearranging objects that did not need rearranging, a vase of roses a centimeter toward the center of the coffee table, a bowl of fruit slightly to the right, the glasses in neat rows on a silver tray. With the passing years and a certain mellowing of character, he demonstrated an added fondness for his home and the stability it represented.

We gathered in the salon after dinner to watch *Casablanca* on video acquired through the black market. Foreign films were forbidden due to unacceptable subject matter or because the actors were not dressed in proper Islamic attire. The drapes were drawn in fear of the Morality Police jumping over the gate to check through the windows in case anyone was watching satellite television or videos or drank alcohol. That Noruz, years after the revolution, the Islamic government had become more lenient, and Baba was prepared to offer any intruding police a cup of tea before handing him a thick wad of cash kept under lock for such purposes.

Half an hour past midnight, a frantic call from Hamid startled us. Butterfly had left the house in a state. Hamid had discovered an empty bottle of Valium at her bedside. He was driving around the city looking for her. Could we search a different part of town?

Aziz and I rushed out to drive around the streets of Tehran. Why, I asked myself, why would she do such a thing? My mind whirled as I summoned events of the past weeks and months in an effort to locate the catalyst. Suddenly there it was, clear as a raindrop.

The day before, after eighteen years of marriage, doctors had informed Butterfly that they had exhausted all possibilities and that although both she and Hamid were healthy, for some inexplicable reason Butterfly's egg rejected her husband's sperm.

We found her not far from her house, barefoot and in her nightgown, braid undone, disheveled hair tumbling to her waist. Aziz tossed his coat over her shoulders and carried her to the car, mumbling that he didn't want the Morality Police to find her in that condition. We called Hamid with the news before driving to the emergency department of Tehran Clinic on Avenue Mirza Shirazi, Avenue Shah Abbas before the revolution.

Hamid explained to a thick-lipped, ruddy-faced nurse that the bottle of Valium was nearly full in the morning when he left for work. "I remember well. There were at least thirty in there, if not more."

Silent and scared as a fenced colt, Butterfly did not resist the nurse as she wheeled her into the operating room to pump her stomach.

Invaded by a myriad of medicinal smells, I curled up on a dilapidated sofa in the waiting room. Aziz sat next to me, a cigarette idle between his lips. Hamid stood in a corner, his hands clasped behind his back, staring at his shoes as if the answer to his wife's strange behavior was reflected there. An ugly clock with noisy hands announced the lingering minutes.

I began an earnest negotiation with God, offered my solemn promise to become a better Jew if He saved Butterfly. Promised to stop pursuing astrology or any other divination forbidden in Judaism, pledged to ask our rabbi to sacrifice chickens and disperse them to the poor. I reprimanded myself for my lack of compassion. Butterfly was different from me, after all. She was desperate for a child. To relinquish hope of motherhood must have been devastating. I should have been more understanding and present.

The doctor entered the waiting room. Sweat glistened on his oily forehead. Behind his glasses, giant, incriminating eyes inspected each of us. "Husband?"

The offensive clank of the clock announced three in the morning.

He took time to glare at Hamid before barking: "Clear! Absolutely clean. Nothing in her stomach. Not a trace of Valium or any other drug. Take her home!"

"Are you certain?" Hamid asked. "I don't understand."

"I do!" The doctor's myopic eyes continued to dissect Hamid, the neon lights reflecting garishly in his thick lenses. "I see it all the time. Simple boredom, disease of the spoiled *taghouti* royalists! We're too busy with the sick and dying to tend to…" He made a sweeping motion with his thick-fingered hand as if to encompass the entire rotten world out there, then turned on his heel and marched out.

Aziz led Hamid out the door. "Shower her with love and

attention, my friend. Nothing that a nice gift and a bunch of roses won't fix."

We drove Butterfly home, washed her face, and gave her a sherbet of rosewater and diced apples. While Hamid tucked her in, I searched the medicine cabinet in their bathroom. I was amazed at the many different pills and syrups for insomnia and anxiety I emptied into the wastebasket.

"Why?" I asked the moment I was alone with her.

"Not now, Soraya. I can't talk now. I'll tell you everything tomorrow."

The next day, her house was steamy with the aroma of *gole-gav-zaban*, passion flower tea. She poured two cups of the dark, calming tea and offered me juicy balls of watermelon she dug out one by one from the bloody heart of the melon.

"Why, Parvaneh, why in God's name?"

She stirred sugar in my tea. Beads of perspiration glistened on her upper lip. Butterfly did not sweat easily. "I lost him, Soraya, lost him for good."

"Hamid?"

"No!"

I stared at her in disbelief, fighting to keep curiosity at bay, as well as an ominous feeling that I'd better run away from this place my friend was inviting me into, away from this other place of intimacy that would burden us for the rest of our lives.

She hugged me, her fingers leaving pockmarks on my flesh. "I am in love. Please, Soraya, don't scold. Try to understand. I need you. Can't do this alone."

I grappled to identify the moral boundaries between friends, tried to make sense of this woman, so different from the friend I believed I knew so well. "I thought you loved Hamid."

"I do. Very much."

"Then why? I don't understand."

"It's different…I don't know how to explain. Maybe I'm in love with two men. Or in love with how he makes me feel. I don't know. Am I crazy? Sometimes I think so. Maybe the nuptial kerchief and all that stuff with Aunt Tala made me crazy. But, you know what, Soraya? *He* doesn't think that. He thinks I'm very special."

"Who is he?"

She took a quick sip of scalding tea, wincing with the pain of her burned mouth. "I can't tell. Not even you."

"Don't be ridiculous! Why can't you? Is he handsome? Rich? How old is he?"

It was a sunny morning. The light filtering through the window turned her cheeks bright. "I didn't think to ask," she replied.

I fell silent to digest the emergence of this unexpected crack in our friendship as well as to grapple with a horde of clashing emotions: confusion, anger, compassion, the constant sense of responsibility I still carried. I did not want to frighten her away because this other Butterfly fascinated me, her obsession with this man, her courage or impudence that seemed to bubble out of nowhere like a just-awakened volcano.

Adultery for women could result in exile from family and society—or even from life by imprisonment, lashing, or stoning. At best, Hamid would surely divorce her if he found out. Then, she would have nowhere to turn but to the misery of her mad father and cruel aunt.

Despite the ordeal she had endured at the hospital the night before, Butterfly's eyes suddenly turned to shiny marbles. "Don't blame me, Soraya. I don't understand it myself, but everything is different with him. Even something as simple as going to the Grand Bazaar. Everything looked different, the path of hard-packed earth hardened by years of traffic, the octagonal hole in the vaulted ceiling, even the bolts of material, the spices, and the jewelry looked different.

"He is very wise, you know. He said that Iran is a heterogeneous country of numerous ethnic groups, religions, languages, and regions that are diverse and interesting like me. Isn't this a wonderful thing to say? He didn't even hold my hand. I asked if I'd done something wrong. He just glanced at his watch and said it was late, as if the devil was at his heels. I didn't hear from him again."

"You acted like a child. A full bottle of Valium could have killed you." And then, still ignorant of certain betrayals that can shatter your heart and leave nothing but ruin in their wake, I held her hand and told her that no one was worth dying for.

She pressed two fingers to her lips and glanced around, then sashayed toward the door on high-heeled sandals. She checked behind the door before locking it. She raised wide, pleading eyes that reminded me of the day she had begged me to help her poison a bully in school. "Swear! Right now, Soraya. Swear to never, ever repeat this. I lied. Flushed the pills down the toilet. I want him to think I'll kill myself if he leaves me."

"But how will he know?" I asked.

She cupped her small left breast in her palm, a nervous habit she had acquired in her adolescent years when her budding breasts concealed a much frailer heart. "Trust me. He will."

I, who consider myself an authority in recognizing the first whiffs of an ominous smell long before it blooms into a full-fledged stench, failed to detect the odor of deceit. I, who consider myself an expert in smelling the undercurrent of every emotion, had Butterfly's Chanel No. 5 top notes of orris and ylang-ylang so embedded in my nose that I did not recognize her base notes of cat piss and rotten eggs.

chapter 19

AN HOUR HAS ELAPSED, or maybe two, since I began sitting at my desk in the library, surrounded by framed butterflies and a variety of moths flaunting themselves in provocative poses—a Sphinx balanced on her wings with her underbelly exposed to temptation, the stiff legs of a Peacock suggestively splayed, and the wings of a Red Admiral stiff as double erections. The stale odor of olive soap and nicotine wafts from the lacquered box where the letters Aziz mailed to me at a rented post office box remain sealed and unread. I push the box away, select a sheet of paper, smooth it on the desk, and prepare to compose a string of lies:

Happy Noruz, my love, and happy anniversary. Sorry I missed your calls. I'm often out on shoots. Photographing Los Angeles is fascinating, and an altogether different style has emerged in my work. Can't wait to finish my assignment and return to you. The house I've rented is lovely, especially its garden, my only safe harbor away from you. I miss you terribly, my love. Every cell aches for you.

I select the deepest red lipstick I can find among my makeup and paint my mouth scarlet, then press my slightly parted lips to the paper.

I unlock the glass door of the cabinet that holds different types of butterflies—the Red Admiral, the orange tip, the Camberwell beauty, also known as the mourning cloak butterfly, and the strangest of them all: the Sphinx, or death's-head hawk moth. This one is a shameless thief that raids beehives for honey and gets away with it because it's able to mimic the smell of bees. It lets out an irritating squeak when bothered and its belly flashes red with rage.

I reach out for this one and then change my mind. Careful not to cause damage, I pinch the skewered Peacock butterfly off the center of the black satin wall. It is the very first butterfly I caught in my net. It has four incriminating eyes on its wings. Its similarity to Butterfly is unquestionable, the spine rigid with desire, eager legs splayed like a whore.

I lay the carcass inside the folded letter and slide it into the envelope. Then, I pick up my pen and write:

Wish Butterfly and Hamid a happy Noruz. Extend an invitation to Butterfly on my behalf to visit me here. I'll make sure to show her a good time. Give her this token of my love.

I lick the flap shut and wipe my tongue clean with the back of my hand.

The library clock strikes twelve midnight, reverberating throughout the house to announce that five hours, sixteen minutes, and twenty-nine seconds have elapsed since the arrival of Noruz, the Persian New Year.

Mamabozorg Emerald, too, must be alone tonight in these first hours of the New Year. I am certain now that there was more to my grandmother's self-exile than what Baba had conjectured. Her feisty spirit would not be snuffed out by revolutions, wars, or the loss of a dictatorial Shah. She must have known about Aziz and Butterfly. Her story of the elephant and the mosquito was meant to alert me to their betrayal.

Who is the mosquito? Aziz or Butterfly? Who is the elephant?

Mansour has set *haft-seen*, the seven S's on the table in the salon for the New Year ritual. *Samanu*, sweet wheat pudding for sweetness; *sonbol*, hyacinth for beauty; *seer*, garlic for health; *senjed*, dried fruit of the lotus tree for love; *serkeh*, vinegar for patience; *seebeh sorkh*, red apple for health.

Soft spears of *sabzeh*, sprouts for rebirth and fertility, bristle against my palm. My uterus closes into a protesting fist. I press a hand against my stomach until the contractions subside. I could have been back home now. We could have celebrated our twentieth wedding anniversary.

Sekeh, fake gold coins for wealth, are spread on the tablecloth; Lit candles, symbols of fire and happiness, illuminate the chickpea, almond, and rice cookies Mansour purchased from Persian markets in Westwood. I turn away from the image of my pale complexion, feverish eyes, and pinched lips, reflected in the mirror that presumably represents the sky and honesty.

My wedding bands have become loose. On my ring finger, twelve one-carat marquis *bleu-blanc* diamonds set in platinum; on my thumb, Aziz's simple gold band, testimony to a love gone sour. I am not ready to part with them yet. Neither will I wear them forever like a yoke.

My empty stomach heaves and revolts against the cloying sweetness of a sugar-coated almond I drop in my mouth. I bite on a chickpea cookie. My insides turn at the sticky paste that coats my tongue and the roof of my mouth. This is not what I crave tonight. I crave the fulfilling, smoky taste of Madar's lamb kebab skewered with onion, green peppers, and eggplant. I crave tender lamb shank in *ghormeh sabzi* herb stew and a fulfilling slice of roast to top it off.

—You crave me, *Jounam*, you're lonely—

How would you feel, Aziz, if I told you that it is possible for me to be alone without you but not lonely? Perhaps your arrogance would not permit such a possibility. Perhaps the fault is mine for pampering you rotten, for being a fool and subscribing to blind trust. In any case, the night is young and you will not like the way it will unfold.

I yank the embroidered tablecloth off the *haft-seen* table. Apples and garlic, vinegar and pudding, gold coins and pots of hyacinth tumble over each other and crash to the floor. That's more like it! All of these symbolize nothing but ruin. Candles slide to the edge of the table. An angry shove and they topple down, dragging their flames behind them like blazing tails. Hungry flames feed on woolen threads of the carpet, stroke, and lick the lacquered leg of the table. How quickly and purposefully they devour what does not belong to them. I lift my leg and grind the sole of my shoe into the greedy flames, grab the tablecloth, and whip the flames back into life.

Mansour appears at the door and rushes to snatch the pitcher of water from the table. Stone-faced and in silence, he pours the water over the flames until they die. How quickly rage can consume, leaving nothing in its wake but ash and wisps of pungent smoke. He falls to his knees and begins to clear the mess, shards of crystal and china, strewn flowerpots and potting soil, apples and cookies, and pieces of singed cloth curled into itself.

"Don't bother," I tell him. "Bring the car. We are going out."

He faces me with bewildered eyes and murmurs, "*Saleh no mobarak, Khanom.*"

"Happy New Year to you, too, Mansour. Any news from your family?"

"They called, *Khanom*. They wish you a year of health and prosperity, as well."

"*Insha'Allah*, God willing, next year is going to be different. Drive me to the Beverly Wilshire Hotel, please. Here! Drop this letter in a mailbox on the way."

I lean back against the headrest and close my eyes as we drive south through dark streets toward Wilshire Boulevard. I have become sensitive to all sounds, even Mansour's breathing, and I think he knows this because when he eases the car to the curb and stops to drop my letter with Butterfly's gift into a mailbox, he shuts the door behind him quietly and with great care.

The night is shrouded in vapors, the sky the color of tar. The constant hum of traffic can be heard from the freeway, and the wind transports the faint scent of possibilities.

Thoughts whirl in my head as I march past a red-cheeked doorman and straight into the lobby of the Beverly Wilshire Hotel. I should have been alerted to Butterfly's betrayal the Noruz she pretended to kill herself with sleeping pills. I should have known Aziz was her lover. Why else would she keep his name a secret from me, her close friend?

I nearly run to the hotel's house phone as if I am being driven by invisible forces. "Mr. Mirharouni's room," I tell the operator, expecting—and even hoping—not to find the *mullah* in his room tonight. Why would he want to be alone in a hotel room these first hours of Noruz?

"*Befarmaieed.*" His sleepy voice rattles me as if I am the one who has been awakened into the dark reality of night.

I take a second to compose myself, muster a steady tone. "This is Soraya. From the plane. I'm downstairs."

Without a moment's hesitation, not a second to summon forth past information, he says, "Don't go anywhere, sister. Give me ten minutes."

A man appears in the lobby and walks toward me with powerful strides, his Italian loafers making brisk, nimble slaps on marble. I lace my fingers behind and blink a few times. This cannot be the *mullah* I met in the plane. He is sporting a charcoal-gray suit, silk cravat, and gold cufflinks studded with diamonds. His every approaching step ushers in a sense of purpose, a virile intensity. Shorn of his religious garb and his turban, *Mullah* Mirharouni is very attractive. He exudes a sense of power and charm.

He faces me, a step away, so close his knees might touch mine. There's a naughty twinkle in his eyes as he cups my hand between his palms and raises it to his mouth. The light kiss planted on the back of my hand lingers like a sweet aftertaste. My cheeks are on fire, mottled with shame. His gaze slithers up my legs, scuffing my hips, ripping my white T-shirt open to lick one breast, then the other.

I yank myself back to my reality. "I'm hungry," I announce, sidestepping formality. "I want dinner first."

My attention-demanding high heels punctuating the marble underfoot, I enter the restaurant and seat myself unceremoniously at one of the many empty tables. I will my breathing to normalize, my flushed cheeks and cantering heart to settle.

He rests his powerful hands on the back of the chair on the opposite side of the table. A turquoise ring encircles his right pinkie. The thought occurs to me that Ayatollah Ruhollah Khomeini would have worn a ring, but not turquoise. His would be a large agate one, etched with Arabic letters. And he would have approved and even encouraged his followers to sport such a ring. The prophet Mohammad was known for being well-dressed and for his love of perfumes, which Islam endorses.

The lights from the chandelier fail to penetrate the plane of *Mullah* Mirharouni's eyes, which are smeared with a butter-like layer of lust. "You have been in my thoughts. Your mesmerizing corn-silk hair and graceful tallness."

I offer him a smile and gesture toward the chair.

He accepts with a low bow and a dramatic sweep of one hand.

I reach across the table and slap the back of his hand. "Bad boy, where's your Islamic cloak? If your brothers back home knew, they'd punish you."

"Don't you like me like this, *azizam* my dear?"

I lower my eyes and caress the embroidered emblem on my T-shirt, fondling my breast as Butterfly did when she flirted. As much as my show of coyness is revolting to me, it seems to please and excite the *mullah*. An unexpected surge of laughter begins to bubble in my chest. I fumble for my napkin and raise it to my mouth, mimicking one of those horrible, in-the-chest feminine sneezes that could blow one up if one were truly holding a sneeze back. I rest my elbows on the table and lean toward the *mullah* and whisper, "Suit, *gabaa*, pajamas, I don't care what you wear, *agha*, as long as you prove to be a man."

He plucks at one starched sleeve cuff, then the other. "It is settled then. Shall we order?"

"I'll have a rare filet mignon." Yes, I want a nice juicy piece of meat to dig my molars into.

I imagine Madar glancing down with disgust and sighing, "Look at you, Soraya, eating a piece of live cow! All because you are angry with your husband. Didn't I tell you this is life! Men betray women. There's nothing you can do."

No, Madar, you are wrong! There's a lot I can do. I am not powerless! You will see. And right now, with a wild, almost savage edge to my hunger, I crave rare, bloody meat and that's what I will have.

The *mullah*'s pupils widen like a leopard's. His breath rattles. Cigarette lungs. Smoke-ash breath. He gestures toward a waiter and tells him in a heavy guttural accent that: "Mademoiselle desires a very, very uncooked filet mignon."

The waiter apologizes, informing us that the kitchen is closed, but room service is available around the clock. The *mullah* settles that problem by pressing two hundred dollars into the waiter's hand.

The fibrous meat, when it arrives, is satisfying, the oily french fries hard on my system. How long since I've had real food, lost weight, starved myself inside a cocoon woven of bitter yarns? Would I, like a butterfly, emerge without difficulty out of my chrysalis? Or like a moth need to exert great effort to break through my cocoon? I bite into another piece of raw steak, chew on it, grind the fiber into pulp, hold the bloody juice in my mouth.

No! I am not a feeble moth.

I sigh contentedly and settle back in my seat. I glance at him and wink. "I'm happy now. Ready to share something rich and sweet."

He unbuttons his collar, loosens his tie, smiles at me, and says: "Yes, of course! We will share something rich and sweet upstairs. I can arrange for that." His hand moves toward me on the table and squeezes my hand. He gestures for the bill. Fumbles in his coat pocket for his wallet.

"No, not yet," I say, casting my eyes down flirtatiously. "What I mean is…well…what I want is dessert first."

"Yes, of course, very smart to think ahead. Sugar fuels the body, gives extra energy." He snaps his fingers and calls out to the waiter, "Mademoiselle desires something very, very sugary."

The waiter returns with a dessert tray for me to choose from. I burrow a forefinger into the tiramisu and lick a dollop of cream off my finger. "I want this." I swivel two fingers in the crème brulée. "This, too." I bend close to the pear tart and sniff the pulpy smell of over-ripe fruit, a relentless, tangy scent I don't like. "And two, no, three of these." I take my time to carefully arrange the plates on the table.

The *mullah* studies me with narrowed eyes, then draws a pear tart toward himself and digs his fork into the crust.

I lean forward and scuff the back of his hand with my fingernails, settle back with a sweet smile and enjoy his puzzled expression. I am disappointed at the speed with which he seems to shed his confidence and composure, shed the arrogance he carries with undeserved pride. I want him to attempt to stop this charade. I want him to be a worthy adversary, show more backbone, be more like his Imam and leader, Ayatollah Khomeini, who succeeded in exiling Mohammed Reza Shah, the king of kings, from the country he ruled for thirty-eight years.

In 1979, on a cold, dreary January day twenty years ago, I watched on the television screen the once omnipotent Shah, with a fur-clad Empress Farah, shiver on the tarmac as they bade a tearful good-bye to the once invincible Royal Guards. The Shah carried a small box filled with Persian soil in his pocket. But he took with him much more. He took our peace of mind.

A mere fifteen days after the Shah and his Empress left, Ayatollah Khomeini's plane landed at Tehran's Mehrabad Airport. Although I despised Khomeini for upturning our lives and destroying our country, I admired him for his dogged perseverance, for his meticulous planning and endless patience that had eventually culminated in his triumph. That day, back on Iranian soil to address a nation of worshippers, he had at last managed to bring revenge on the Shah, whose secret police had presumably murdered Khomeini's son, Mustapha, who was found dead in bed.

This *mullah* sitting opposite me, who left his religious garb upstairs in his posh suite at the Beverly Wilshire Hotel, is made of weaker cloth.

He squares his shoulders and attempts to compose himself after my inexplicable dessert orgy. "Let us go up before daybreak."

I want to dig my heel into his polished alligator loafer and scream that the day has already broken and that I am mortified at the prospect of spending the night with him, to tell him I've never been alone in a hotel room or any other room with a stranger and that my husband is the only man I've ever made love to, but that I will still join him in his hotel room because I am being guided by inexplicable forces that are beyond my control. He is only a conduit, I console myself, here to propel me closer to my goal. I am the one who solicited his company to hurt Aziz. That is what matters and nothing else.

Mullah Mirharouni glances at the check, slides his hand into his coat pocket and retrieves his wallet, pulls out a thick wad of cash and counts out hundred dollar bills.

I hold his hand back. I do not want to be indebted to him. Before he has a chance to make sense of the prospect of a woman not only paying for her meal, but his as well, I leave a couple of hundred-dollar bills on the table and rise.

The lady behind the registration desk glances at us from under lashless eyelids that she swiftly averts as we turn toward the elevator.

I refuse the arm he offers to lead me into his suite, all silk and damask and velvet and smelling of the demanding bodies that had previously occupied the king-size bed. I turn to him and stroke his sleeve with a soft touch. "Are you married?"

"Yes," he replies without hesitation. Lies are unnecessary, as is foreplay, for the unspoken deal the two of us have struck. Tonight he is here with me, and in a few weeks he will return to his home and his wife. And after a quick angry fuck of revenge, where will I find myself but back to my solitude? Back to my Amorphophallus titanum, my misshapen phallic plant, my Corpse Plant with its decomposing rat stink. Back to my bordello of colorful butterflies.

"Tell me, *Agha* Mirharouni, have you ever loved two women at one time?"

"Of course, *azizam*, of course I have." The answer comes too fast, too certain, too easily. Like an electrical switch. On! Off! Now this one, next another. "What about your wife?"

"This has nothing to do with her. Allah blessed men with sophisticated...how shall I say...complex neurological wiring. We can compartmentalize our emotions so they won't bleed into our private life."

To my horror, I watch my fist spring forward and crash against his chest.

His arm circles my waist. "You're nervous, *azizam*. It's normal. Come, I'll calm you down. Give me a moment."

He shuts his eyes, and without letting go of my hand, his lips begin to move. Distinguishing a few Arabic words, I cringe at the realization that he is in the process of reciting the prayer that would make me his *sigheh*, his concubine, his temporary wife, *halal*, permissible to him according to Islamic law.

He draws me close, his sonorous voice transporting me to that other place inside of me, into my head and heart, and soon enough Aziz is observing *Mullah* Mirharouni slide his hand down my vertebrae, crawl lower, brush against my buttocks, climb back up and slip my shirt off, his stare creeping around my shoulders and breasts to naked curves at the mercy of his licking eyes that linger between my thighs.

My husband's face flames and his lovely eyes rage as the *mullah* coaxes me toward the bed, unfolds the corner of the puffed-up goose quilt, pats the yielding mattress, and gives my back an encouraging tap.

—*Jounam*, you've the sexiest back in all of Tehran—

I slip under the sheets. Pull the covers up to my chin. The king-size bed is far too small to hold all three of us.

—*Jounam*, keep away from other men. They'll break your lovely heart—

The *mullah*'s fingers crawl on my stomach, slide up my waist, and squeeze my breast. His lips circle my nipple, kiss one, then the other, graze my earlobe, blow into my ear. His breath scorches my temple, my cheek, comes too close to my mouth. My muscles tense; my nipples stiffen in protest. My hands spring up to shield my mouth. Not my mouth. Not this. Anywhere but my mouth. Not a kiss.

Our kisses, Aziz and mine, are our cherished intimate language.

—*Jounam*, give me your tongue—

I pull the sheets high up over my breasts to cover my nakedness from the *mullah*'s vengeful eyes.

chapter 20

I FIRST SAW SIMILAR CAULDRONS of vengeance on the television screen when I was seventeen years old.

It was 1979.

A stiff, stern seventy-eight-year-old Ayatollah Ruhollah Khomeini descended the stairs of a chartered Air France plane, knelt down, and kissed Iranian soil. His vengeful stare pierced through the jubilant crowd gathered in the airport to welcome him. After fifteen years of exile, first in Iraq, then Neauple-le-Chateau in the suburbs of Paris, his eminence arrived to the overwhelming chant of: "*Agha amad!* Our Sir is Here!"

"*Vaveilla!*" Mamabozorg had cried, in the ancient wail of mourning women. "He is back to take revenge on us all. Revenge!"

"It's the end of us Jews!" Baba declared as he paced the room with cane and gloves in hand, as if ready to leave at the next sign of trouble. "We've lost the Shah, our only ally in the Muslim world."

Baba had tears in his eyes as he vowed not to abandon everything to our cook, driver, and guard, naming just a few, who were waiting for us to flee, as many of our friends had, in order to confiscate our house, furniture, carpets, antiques, and cars, and then inform the authorities, whoever they might be at the time, of our vast real estate holdings and demand, in exchange for their loyalty, a portion of that fortune, too. The prospect of living among Muslim fundamentalists without the backing and support of the Shah sent a collective shudder through our core.

That day, in my parents' home, crowded by antiques and art, the grounds adorned with ancient plane, mulberry, and walnut trees, Baba and Madar, Mamabozorg Emerald and Butterfly, who had joined us to find answers to her own future, pondered the possibility of the CIA arranging the royal couple's return. This had happened in 1953 when the Shah and his second wife, Soraya, had fled Iran after a coup Dr. Mossadegh, prime minister of the time, had initiated. It could happen again, *Insha'Allah*. The Pahlavi dynasty is not dead.

"Such an uprising was inevitable." Baba said, "First, the Shah turned into a cotton-brained megalomaniac, forgetting he was America's puppet, after all. Second, he ignored the importance of religion to his people and of oil to the world. Once he did that, his fate was sealed."

"Oil?" Butterfly asked in a reverential tone, as if afraid to agitate the sacred aura my father wore like a crown.

Baba brought fingers of both hands together like a prayer dome. "Black gold! A blessing and a curse." In 1971 the Shah had raised the price of oil, stoking the first embers of the revolution. By 1973 he had quadrupled the price. By 1977 Iran was acquiring weapons as if preparing for World War III. Baba slapped his thigh with his gloves.

"Someone should have told him: 'My man, America depends on oil. You depend on America. Don't forget that the CIA reinstated you, or you would have rotted somewhere in exile. So don't play political roulette with America. Don't yank at the lion's tail.' By the end, when the Shah was lonely and friendless, the lion turned around and chopped off his head."

I tried to imagine the Shah's royal skull being crushed between the jaws of a vicious lion with AMERICA tattooed on its forehead. It was difficult to envision America as my father's ferocious, Shah-eating lion, or as Khomeini's "Great Satan." I had attended the Community School, a private American school in Tehran. My American friends did not resemble ruthless lions. If anything, the Ayatollah Khomeini, on the television screen that day, was the one who resembled a furious lion being escorted across the tarmac.

What I did not know then was that before I'd have the chance to digest the whirlwind events of the next few months, the "disinherited"—one of the exaggerated titles granted the poor or the working classes—would turn against the *taghouti*, or supposed royalist elite, storm their vacant mansions, settle in, and distribute their wealth as they saw fit.

I did not know that before long we would watch in disbelief as strangers settled in the house of our neighbors, who had fled the country in fear of being imprisoned for the sin of having the deposed Shah's photographs in their family album.

And that we would end up being one of a handful of wealthy families, part of a small Jewish community, to remain behind after tens of thousands fled. We managed to go unnoticed only because we did not own large factories or have business or political involvements with Israel. Nor did we have any dealings with the royal family or the SAVAK, the Shah's dreaded secret police.

We made sure to donate part of our wealth to the recent Islamic regime. We banned alcoholic drinks from our home, burned photographs that were reminders of the Pahlavi era, and dressed first in the *chador* and later in kerchiefs, opaque stockings, and the *manteau*. Baba believed these were necessary adjustments, a temporary and passive fight against either subjugation or inevitable exile.

We would not abandon our country and home. We would remain and pretend that nothing much had changed so as to protect what belonged to us in the first place. The newly established authorities had confiscated our freedom; we would not allow them total victory by handing over our wealth, too.

I did not know then that Butterfly would succeed one day where a revolution and the cunning Ayatollah Seyyed Ruhollah Musavi Khomeini had failed. I did not know that she would thrust me from family and home into exile to a country that might not want me.

That day, we watched Khomeini on our television screen as he was being ushered up to a podium to deliver his speech.

"We became *gharbzadeh*!" Mamabozorg coughed up "Westernized" as if it were a chicken bone stuck in her throat. "We're neither here nor there. Westerners invade us as if we're Bedouins with a camel culture. And now this! Will this *mullah* drag us back to the Middle Ages? Will he bring back the barbaric ritual of whipping with chains and maiming themselves during religious mourning? God bless his soul, Reza Shah must be rolling over in his grave. If his son had his father's grit, he'd have stayed put and protected his country."

Baba curled his handlebar mustache, tossed one long leg over the other. "The Shah had to go. People didn't want him." He gestured toward me and Butterfly. "You're surprised, of course, having lived a sheltered life. The poor resent us. Call us the One Thousand Families. You haven't been exposed to the poverty and restlessness brewing just a few kilometers south of us. The *mullahs*..."

Mamabozorg cried out in disgust, "If Reza Shah was our ruler, he would have flushed each and every *mullah* down the toilet, where they belong."

"Reza Shah! He was a worse dictator than his son," Baba replied. "Do not forget, Madar, that he would have handed Iran to the Nazis if he remained in power. The Nazis were practically at our border. God only knows how many Germans were living in Tehran during World War II. The truth is, if you'd scratched Reza Shah's skin, you'd have found a Nazi underneath."

Mamabozorg lifted herself up from her stool, tossed her shawl on the carpet, and trampled it with her orthopedic boots. She could not bear the disillusionment of more than four decades of cherished memories. She had developed her own conclusions regarding the politics of Iran. Many were accurate, some tainted by her obsession with the late Reza Shah. And she never forgave the British who had, during World War II, forced him into exile in Johannesburg, where he died. Having achieved their objective, the allies facilitated the way for Reza Shah's inexperienced son, Mohammad Reza, to occupy the Pahlavi throne.

I lifted her shawl and coaxed her back to her stool. "You should have converted to Islam and married the Shah, Mamabozorg. He really liked you. Then I'd have been a princess."

She coiled a strand of my hair around her finger and gave it a hard tug. "It's the way of life, I suppose, for young fish to dare to peck at their elders." She rubbed the beads of her necklace, raising the scent of sun-drenched fruit, powdered cinnamon, and ancient longing. "Genuine amber, Soraya, his gift to me."

"*Agha amad! Agha amad!*" Khomeini's intense speech, the first of many to follow on Persian soil, whipped the crowd in Mehrabad Airport into a frenzy. "Our Sir is here! Our Sir is here!"

"What now?" Mamabozorg wailed. "Will this bearded Seyyed force us to hide ourselves behind *chadors*? Make temporary marriages legal again?"

I was still young and innocent at the time and wrongly believed that the source of Khomeini's rage was political. I had assumed that he would rest once he achieved his nationalistic and religious ideals. Although I was aware that the Shah had arrested Khomeini's son, and that Khomeini blamed the Shah for his son's mysterious death in Najaf, I didn't know how long pain could brew and simmer and survive in lethal and deceiving stages.

I had not yet been cheated of my lover and friend and had not yet experienced the madness that endures like smoldering embers until the source is, at the very least, humbled.

⁂

Mullah Mirharouni, with or without his religious attire, at home in Iran or in a hotel room in America, could never boast of Ayatollah Khomeini's attributes—endurance, cunning, and the never-dying ambition to retaliate.

His breath is hot and demanding on my breasts, this *mullah*, who must have deceived a harem of temporary wives, this *mullah* who helped give birth to a generation that knows nothing but repression.

I, too, am a product of this revolution and have been deeply affected by it in many ways. The fear-ridden atmosphere of the first years is fresh in my memory. We tucked our makeup bags, miniskirts, and fur coats in moth-filled closets and in their place donned the *chador*. The Shah's portraits came down and Khomeini's went up. The Shah's statues were toppled in squares, and in their place a heap of rubble remained, on which appeared cranes with dangling, lifeless bodies to sow fear in the heart of an already traumatized nation.

Arms from the Shah's arsenal passed into the hands of riff-raff militia, and we locked ourselves in our estates for fear of a stray bullet finding its way into our confused brains. I woke each morning to news of more senseless executions, more internal struggles for power among different religious factions.

And then, as if we Iranians had not caused enough damage and suffering to ourselves, we plunged into the horror of eight years of war with Iraq. We, who could not bear to be called Arabs because we considered ourselves cultured Aryans; we, who blamed the Arabs for conquering the high Persian culture and displacing the religion of Zoroaster, locked ourselves into war with Arabs. Thousands of our children marched defenselessly across minefields and into the heart of the enemy with the promise that the small plastic key around their neck would open the doors to heaven. The end of the war left us scarred. A nation of martyrs. And we have no one to blame but the likes of *Mullah* Mirharouni, who is sniffing his way between my legs.

My mouth puckers with disgust at the sight of the man who represents everything I despise. I grab him by the hair and push him away with one leg as if he were a wayward dog. Disentangling myself from the surrounding mess, I slip out of bed and step back into my clothing.

chapter 21

IT WAS HOT IN the smoke-filled restaurant on Vali Asre Street at the foot of the Alborz Mountains. Once extending onto the sidewalk and under the shade of ancient sycamores, the restaurant had retreated behind tinted glass doors after the Revolution. Now, years later, the *pasdaran* had become less strict and couples were allowed to share a table if they wore proper Islamic attire. Some women opted to discard the *chador* in favor of the *manteau,* opaque stockings, and kerchiefs. Still, we carried our marriage documents in case the *pasdaran* raided the restaurant. I wore mascara and a touch of blush, tossed a shawl about my shoulders, my defiance against senseless insults and demands to conform.

Copper trays were set on the table around which Aziz and I, Hamid and Butterfly, and Madar and Baba sat. Butterfly heaped our plates with saffron rice laced with slivers of almond and pistachio, eggplant stew, and crispy rice *tahdig*, selected for each, according to our tastes. Veal shank for Madar, *polo* rice with more nuts for Baba, an extra serving of roasted eggplant for me.

I was aware of Butterfly's every glance, every small move. Only a few days ago, she'd demonstrated exceptional courage, or stupidity, by pretending to commit suicide. I wanted to know for whom she was ready to die. Her gaze momentarily fell on a musician dressed in a colorful vest and billowing pants who sat cross-legged on a platform playing classical Persian music on his sitar. I dismissed that possibility. The musician was too young and dull for her taste.

I uncrossed my legs and held out my plate to facilitate Butterfly's reach as she offered me some crunchy rice. My high heel caught another high heel. I held my foot in midair. Butterfly's leg was not where it was supposed to be. Pretending to search for my purse, I raised the tablecloth and peered underneath. Her legs were primly crossed at the ankles. Hamid's patent leather shoes tapped a silent tune on the floor. Mother's legs were concealed under her *crepe de chine* skirt. Father's hands rested on his thighs. The sharp crease of Aziz's meticulously pressed gabardine pants grazed brown crocodile shoes. He placed his hand on my knee. It was cold.

I should have been alerted. But I was not. A seed of suspicion might have planted itself in my subconscious. Perhaps that was the reason I felt sudden anger at Butterfly for withholding the identity of her lover from me. I let out a cry of pain and pulled out a handkerchief from Aziz's coat pocket. I wiped imaginary perspiration off my forehead and then, as if at my wit's end, I jumped up, startling everyone to their feet. "Let's go! This headache is killing me."

"That was abrupt," Aziz said when we were in our car.

"I had a sudden urge to make love to you."

"My beautiful liar!" he replied, his fingers climbing my thigh, lowering the waistband of my stockings, and sliding under my lace panties to the spot he knew well.

❧ ❧ ❧

Aziz stood at the threshold of our house the next day, his face concealed behind six-dozen baccarat roses that gave off the rancid stench of suspicion.

"What are you hiding?" I asked.

"My passion," he replied, ambling to the bathroom.

I sat on the edge of the bathtub and watched him loosen his tie with a single flip of his hand, slide the loop over his head, and toss the tie in my lap. He unzipped his pants with one fluid movement, revealing the outline of his bulging penis. He squeezed me to his chest, bit my shoulder, sucked my lips.

I drank his scent of sex and afternoon sweat, and another lingering smell, not quite his.

I should have recognized Butterfly's perfume, the top notes of ylang-ylang and neroli of her Chanel No. 5, perhaps even the base notes of sandalwood and vetiver. I did not. The instant I was alone, I picked up the phone and called her. I, who had always mentored and protected Butterfly, sought her advice now.

The chauffeur drove through the traffic of Avenue Vali Asre that snaked north toward the chain of the Alborz Mountains. I cursed the slow minutes, the honking, the madness in the streets, but most of all my own impatience. The snow-capped summit of the mythic Damavand volcano scintillated under the sun. It is an active volcano, emitting sulfur and volcanic heat. Yet, history does not record any eruption. What did that mean to us, the inhabitants of Tehran, who lived at the foot of this awesome volcano? Constant vigilance, I mused, the importance of being on our guard. Always! The potential for an eruption is constant.

"I smell another woman on Aziz," I blurted out the instant I stepped into Butterfly's house.

She hooked her arm in mine. "Come, let's have some tea." She led me to the kitchen, poured herself a cup of steaming chamomile tea, and dropped a tea bag in my cup. Leaning her arm on the table, she rested her chin on her fist, directing questioning eyes at me. "Are you sure?"

"A woman knows."

"A wife is the last to know, they say."

"He smells of sex and fear."

A smile tugged at the corners of her mouth. "Come now, Soraya! How can you smell fear?"

"It's not funny, Parvaneh. I really do."

She released my hand. "You're probably imagining things. Anyway, he's too smart to come home smelling of a woman."

Butterfly was right. Aziz was a meticulous planner, never missed anything, never forgot anything. He would surely have asked his mistress not to wear perfume.

"Is it possible for a man to love two women and have great sex with both?"

She bit her lip. Rested her hand on mine. "I don't know about men, Soraya, but it can happen to a woman."

"Of course, you'd know!" I snapped at her. "And you won't even tell me his name."

I should have noticed the blooming blush on her cheeks, her slight shifting away to minimize her scent of perfume. I should have wondered why, soon after, she changed her perfume. But I did not.

The day I left for America, weighted by the awareness of his betrayal, I asked Aziz whether it was possible for a man to betray the woman he loves.

He clucked his tongue against the roof of his mouth. "Why ask?"

"Just curious."

"Well!" He chuckled. "*Mullahs* say men need more than one woman. That might be true for them. Me, I'm more than fine with my one lady!" Then, as if that was the eleventh commandment, he rubbed his palms, signaling the end of the discussion, lifted me off the ground, and sat me on his lap.

"Keep your eyes open, *Jounam*, and give me your tongue."

Even then, despite the bitter awareness poisoning my mind, my body softened in his embrace. I gave him my tongue, and he cradled it in his mouth one last time and sucked the tip like a relished delicacy.

chapter 22

STARTLED AWAKE, I SIT up in bed and rub my eyes. Why this sense of premonition? Nothing extraordinary has taken place since yesterday when I mailed a letter to Aziz. More time in the grove that's coming back to life, more butterflies collected, more photographs developed.

A strange and exciting foul smell wafts into my bedroom, a seductive blend of dead flowers and mildew. I jump out of bed and run out into the foyer.

The smell is stronger. My heart palpitates. Perspiration coats my upper lip. I dash into the kitchen, snatch a pair of shears, wet a dishcloth, and press it against my nose to keep the sultry vapors at bay. But, my olfactory cells having been seduced, I toss the towel aside.

The Amorphophallus must have come into bloom.

Plants and animals that share the same space with me react to changes in my life. The rhinoceros iguana of Haiti died because it couldn't bear the air of duplicity between Aziz and me. Sensing the depth of our joy, the red-eyed Madagascar frog, purchased on our honeymoon, croaked merrily and incessantly each night as we prepared for bed. A black-necked, fangless cobra got in the habit of crawling out of its box, its clammy body giving off the odor of dank moss as it slipped into our bed, stretching and twisting to interrupt our lovemaking. A pair of quetzals shipped from Guatemala flourished in our garden, carved a nest in an ancient tree trunk, and took turns incubating. The day I discovered Aziz and Butterfly in bed, the birds took flight, abandoning their eggs to the elements.

And now, the Amorphophallus titanum, having sensed the depth of my despair that thrust me into the arms of a *mullah*, is offering me the gift of its bloom.

Perched on top of the atrium, my Owl of Reason welcomes me with a staccato of barks. I wave and nod and make kissing noises, then gesture and clap loudly, hoping she'll fly off to hunt, or simply leave and conceal herself in the monkey tree, anywhere else but here. I don't want her around while I conduct my experiment. But true to her stubborn character, she pins her gaze on me and begins to claw at the glass panels.

"Do what you want, boss," I say, turning away and entering the atrium.

I gasp at the sight I face.

The massive leaf that once tightly hugged the towering stem of the Amorphophallus has slackened its grip and unfurled to form a tiered skirt of violet ruffles that curls like a giant fluttering wing around a trumpet-like flower of vibrant shades of lilac, hyacinth, and lavender. The heart of the flower is comprised of thousands of small blooms of livid purple that pulsate and ripple to attract pollinators. They smell like aroused flesh and the breath of dreaming animals.

I pluck out a bloom, releasing a stronger stew of scents—rotting meat, crustacean, and water urchin.

Beyond the glass dome, my owl lets out a chorus of strange hoots. I nod my understanding, acknowledge that I, too, am surprised at the splendid transformation and at the power of these pungent smells.

The flower shudders in complaint as I yank out another tiny bloom—a livid, mature purple from the outer tier—hold it up, and study it closely. The bloom reveals a few of the distinguishing features of poisonous flowers. It is covered with fine hairs and purplish black spurs. The pod is filled with tiny seeds. The odor of bitter almond is an added confirmation of my initial inference. A joyous spasm tugs at my heart. I pretend I don't hear my owl's cries. I don't want her to behold my joy, don't want her to guess what's passing through my mind.

Poisons have a way of lurking in unexpected places.

Flowers of the belladonna and opium poppy are both beautiful and lethal, yet have healing powers if ingested in small amounts. The foul-smelling ragworth is a poisonous plant that hosts striped caterpillars, but also heals mouth ulcers and joint pain. A few drops of valerian are a stimulant and an aphrodisiac, but in large doses, cause madness and aversion to lovemaking. Ancient cultures believed that love-in-a-mist, a self-seeding plant, cured baldness if applied to the head, but would dry the brain if rubbed vigorously.

My hand is cold and slightly shaking. It is not too late to walk out and double-lock the door behind me. Never look back. But where will that leave me?

I cautiously lick the edge of the Amorphophallus bloom to try to gauge the required dosage to bring about a quick and, preferably, painful end. A sap, neither sweet nor bitter, but somewhat salty and with a tart hint of capers coats my tongue. Nothing that can't be masked with rose petals, some strong honey, and a pod of cardamom. I bite off a small piece, a preliminary experiment, certainly not enough to cause me substantial harm, hold it in my mouth until nothing remains but pulp, which I spit out.

With a flurry of fluttering, my owl enters the atrium, zooms past my shoulder, and swoops down to land on the lip of the Corpse Flower's giant pot. I scratch her under the wing, poke her underbelly, try to pry her powerful claws open and send her off, but to no avail. Her cutting stare continues to probe me, her low, insistent hoots echoing around the atrium.

"Shoo! I just tasted a tiny bit. What's the big fuss? Go! I've had enough of you for today. Come back tomorrow. All right, you stubborn bird, you win! Stay here if you want."

I leave the atrium and slam the door shut behind me.

chapter 23

I DRINK HALF A GLASS of milk to flush some of the Corpse Flower out of my system, in case it proves highly poisonous. It would be disappointing if the plant I love, pamper, and feed ends up being nothing but a useless ornament. A twist at the pit of my stomach makes me pay attention, a slight pinch of nausea, but nothing alarming. I sip from a bottle of mineral water and glance at the clock. I will take note of any change in my heartbeat, taste in my mouth, temperature of my skin, or size of my pupils. It is exciting, this experiment, using my body as a laboratory, my veins as testing tubes to calculate how long it will take for the poison to take effect, after which I shall calculate the needed dosage of powdered Amorphophallus to create a most potent, fast-acting brew.

It is not so difficult to find out how poisonous plants react in our body. That information is accessible in books. I looked it up first in the comprehensive library in my house and then in the Beverly Hills Library. But how does one measure the damage that loss inflicts on one's body? My blood was laced with poison the night before I left for America.

I made love to Aziz that night. Loved him with my entire body, my head bursting with wine and grief. On the hardwood floor, facing our king-size bed, he folded me in his arms and murmured in my ear in his honey voice that seeped into my gut and turned me into pulp.

—Let's try again, Soree. Let's try to make babies. I'll come to America. We'll visit another doctor. Medicine is in constant change. New cures come up. I want your child, Soree—

He held me, consoled me, wiped my violent tears away, tears formed by the words I kept inside.

—Don't lose hope, Soree—

I, who had managed to convince myself for twenty years that a third addition would only disrupt our tight union, that a child would rob me of the precious time I spent with Aziz, found myself outmaneuvered by Butterfly.

—Don't be sad, *Jounam*. Come closer—

Our gazes snagged, tangled, and knotted. My nipples hardened.

—Give me your tongue, *Jounam*—

His manipulative tongue searched for mine, entering my greedy mouth, drinking my saliva. His betrayal did not alter his taste. Neither did my awareness that even as our saliva mingled, it was she whom he desired.

He lifted me in his arms and carried me to our bed that had so recently held the two of them. Or was it the three of us? Did he carry me in his head that afternoon?

He cupped my breasts, teased my nipples, his hand igniting sweet currents in my poisonous veins.

His gaze slid down my body, his fingers tracing each vertebra, hesitating at the lower curve.

—On my life, *Jounam*, you've the sexiest back in Iran—

His resourceful touch and seductive lies continued to thaw me, even as my mind raged against my treacherous body. I cuddled his erection, wondered whether he was aroused by me or the promise of a future fuck with her, whether he would penetrate me or remain loyal to her, even on this my last night in Iran.

His breath like pepper, his touch urgent, he parted my legs and eased himself on me.

My uterus clamped into a tight fist. I locked my thighs. "I've my period."

—Since when do you care, *Jounam*?—

Since the day you fucked my friend, in my house, on our bed, in front of my photographs, I wanted to scream. "I've terrible cramps," I whispered.

He rolled to his side, lifted himself on his elbow, and ran his fingers through my hair.

—I can't bear seeing you in pain, Soree—

I tasted red wine and longing in his mouth, and betrayal and deception on his tongue. I turned away and molded my buttocks into the crook of his body.

We fitted like two halves of a jagged bowl.

❦ ❦ ❦

I force another gulp of water down my throat. Curse the loud clock with its lazy hands. Is it just five minutes since I left the atrium? I press my head to the lacquered box that holds Aziz's unopened letters. Oh! God! I am lonely in America. I want Aziz.

The latest letter on top of the pile feels heavier, gives off a cloying smell. I drop the unopened envelope back in the box. Bad omens better remain sealed. I stare at it, lift it again, and weigh it on my palm. The same address, the same handwriting, the same stamps, yet a different smell. She is back to wearing Chanel No. 5. Aziz was with her when he wrote this letter.

Two sheets tumble out of the envelope. One in Aziz's handwriting, one in Butterfly's. The nerve! The audacity! I should read Aziz's letter first; hear his guttural, love-soaked voice; wallow in his "I miss you" and "I want you" and "Come back soon"; drink in the nicotine and olive soap scent of his hands that knew how to press on a nerve, stroke the length of a vertebra, trace expectant lips, then dismiss and abandon with a single wave.

A Monarch flutters through the window and lands on Butterfly's letter. It is early spring and Monarchs drunk on sunshine have abandoned the eucalyptus grove to warm themselves in the garden. Their invasion has painted my world many shades of orange. They feed on leaves and petals, blooms and host plants; drink from mud puddles and wet gravel; suck leftover fluids from the carcasses of insects. But above all, they are locked in a frenzy of mating. I've observed them with interest, timed them, marveled at their vigor, these frail creatures. It is a sight to behold, their courtship, the males pursuing females in the air, the females flirting to no end, the successful males luring the females down to earth to lock them in their grip for as long as it takes to impregnate them.

With a whisk of my hand, I shoo away the Monarch.

I unfold Butterfly's letter and read it first.

She framed the dried butterfly I sent her and keeps it at her bedside. She wants to know if I caught the Peacock butterfly myself. How sweet of me to dry it especially for her. She wants to know when my assignment will end. She misses me. Thanks me for inviting her to visit America. Of course she will come. When would be a good time?

Never, my friend. Never.

I remove Aziz's letter from the box and unfold it. I should tuck the letter back in the envelope and drop it in the box with the others. I should go out into the garden and visit with my owl. I should not allow Aziz to influence me. Not today that my blood is beginning to simmer with poison, yet I'm riveted to his confident handwriting, the places where the tip of his fountain pen ripped the paper. I shut my eyes to hold and hug the image of his hand inscribing the bold letters. What message do they contain?

My lovely Soree Jounam,

Come home! I'm lonely, the house empty, and Tehran dead without you. Why are you so seldom at home? Who's this Mansour who makes excuses for you? Since when has your work become so important that you would stay away on our twentieth anniversary? I'm jealous, Jounam. I need my woman.

You better call or I swear on my mother's soul, I'll come to fetch you myself.

I gave that frightful, dried butterfly to your friend. I don't understand why in the world you'd mail a dead insect to anyone, unless you're up to one of your Soraya tricks. Anyway, she asked me to mail her letter with mine.

I wipe beads of sweat off my forehead. I am exhausted and queasy, and my throat is dry. I force some more mineral water down my throat. Fifteen minutes since I tasted the Corpse Flower. I feel the onset of nausea and churning cramps in my stomach, but I am lucid. Able to concentrate on the progression of symptoms I am experiencing.

I count my pulse. A doctor is not necessary. Given time and lots of liquids, the body will purge itself of small amounts of toxins.

I compute—an exact mathematical equation—how fast I'm losing strength. How often I visit the bathroom. Dry mouth, nausea, exhaustion, dilated pupils. Symptoms set in after fourteen minutes. How long will it take for the poison to taint my blood? I am on the brink of a momentous discovery.

Will determine the required dosage to cause—*Oh!* Excruciating pain in my lower abdomen! A door slams. Footsteps in the attic. An army of discordant sounds drum in my head. Chimes reverberate somewhere. In my chest? The beat of "The Blue Danube." Lit candles stink stronger than Corpse Flowers.

Twenty-five minutes pass. They fucked to my waltz, to candles, and they—I am convulsing. Must call for help. The intercom. It's too far. The phone! Where is the phone? Where's Oni—Mansour? Crawl to the foyer. Cool marble. Ah! Cool. Breathe. Breathe. Don't faint. Delight. The Corpse Flower is fast. Lethal.

chapter 24

Blurry faces bend over me. My eyes can't focus on Oni, Mansour, the paramedics. My throat is locked up. I can hardly breathe. Why are they wasting time sticking me with wires? It's not my heart. I struggle to find my voice, form words, explain what happened.

"Don't fall asleep."

I yank the wire from under my left breast. Point to my mouth, to the atrium, to my stomach; struggle to cough out one word.

"Common procedure."

I don't have time for common procedures. I press my palm to my neck, inhale, and rasp out, "Poison."

They rush me into an ambulance, bound like a mummy, stuck with an IV. Sirens echo in my head. I can't lose consciousness. Help me, Aziz. Help! I conjure him up with the last vestiges of my slipping breath. His sleepy eyes, olive-soap scent, smoke-shattered voice, searching tongue…in her mouth.

Click.

Someone presses the oxygen mask to my nose.

Mansour's face is pale with fear.

I will not die. Not yet.

Senseless questions are thrown at me in the emergency room. What do they want? I am a foreigner without credit card or medical insurance. Without an identity. I possess an international driver's license and a new checkbook in my purse back home. Check number 28. My signature at the bottom of one check can purchase a wing of this hospital. But I have no credit history. They are having discussions among themselves as if I'm already dead. I've managed to escape my husband, but not my stupidity, the clamor in my head, or the laws and regulations of this strange country. I am a rich immigrant who will die in a UCLA emergency cubicle.

"Bank America." The words scratch my throat. I can pay cash. A piece of plastic card shouldn't be worth more!

"Your name?"

"Soraya."

"What day of the week is it?"

As hard as I try, I can't recall what day it is, yet I am able to summon the scent of candles and Butterfly's perfume with all of its cloying nuances. I fight the wedding band on my left finger. Twelve one-carat marquis *bleu-blanc* diamonds set in platinum. Mansour comes forward and gently removes the ring. I point to Mamabozorg's amber chain around my neck. He places the ring and necklace in the nurse's hands. Thirty-five exquisite amber beads, kernels of precious memories. A token of a once mighty Shah. And the nurse hands them back to Mansour as if they are plastic beads.

"Stay with us!"

"Don't sleep!"

"Maintain respiration and blood circulation…!"

"Exposure? Through the veins? Lungs?"

"Did you ingest something?"

They rinse my face with a cold liquid. I am shaken into semi-consciousness. Trembling. Sweating. Excited.

"Concentrate. It's important! What did you eat today?"

Today! What is today? I didn't eat anything. I try to think in the ensuing silence, to concentrate, stop myself from drifting away. Remember the name of the plant.

"Some kind of food?"

I nod. My eyelids are heavy.

"Gastric lavage!" someone shouts.

"Induce vomiting!"

"Twenty milligrams syrup of ipecac!"

I rest against pillows and sip cranberry juice, a cleanser. The nurse croons in a sweet, tiny voice, as if she's talking to a child. Her cherubic red curls surround plump, flushed cheeks and a heart-shaped mouth enhanced with lip liner. A single flap of fabric separates me from the chaos in the hallway and a patient in the next cubicle who asks for painkillers. A nurse reminds him that he has already been admitted, inebriated, three times this week and that she will not administer any more narcotics.

"I'm in pain, bitch!" he shouts.

I would have liked some narcotics myself to kill the dissonant waltz in my head, a cacophony of trumpets and rumbling drums that commands me to return to the flower before it dies. Find a way to preserve the potency of its poison until I lure her to America.

"I'm ready to go home," I tell the nurse.

She pats my hair into place. "No, sweetie, not yet. Drink another sip. You can't be discharged until a doctor sees you."

"But I'm fine. Stronger than ever," I lie.

"We'll let the doctor decide that," she replies.

My heart makes a double flip and refuses to settle. My liver or kidneys must have been affected. I ask the nurse what the problem is, but she tells me the doctor will answer all my questions soon. Soon seems an eternity in a foreign country, in an emergency cubicle, with a body that brims with poisons that no gastric lavage will manage to cleanse.

The doctor is far too young and too handsome to be allowed to examine female patients. Good-looking men should be banned from medical schools. They traumatize us. Suddenly, my hair feels oily, my legs too exposed, and I smell medicinal and bitter.

He appears no older than thirty, at least five years younger than me, but he addresses me as if he were my Baba. Does every patient regress to childhood here?

"Are you up for a few questions, Soraya?"

I am not. But I nod agreeably.

"Can you tell me what you ate?"

"I was gardening and a flower fell in my glass of water. I didn't think much of it first. Left it there. But then removed it and took a few sips."

"Could you tell what kind of flower?"

"Not really, but I know plants and this one looked harmless."

"How are things at home, Soraya? Are you under pressure? Any thought of…suicide?"

"Suicide! I am in love, doctor. Desperate to go back home to my husband. Why would I want to kill myself?"

"Yes, of course. Well, whatever you ingested was super toxic. Your condition deteriorated fast. We were very concerned."

I touch the bluish bruise on my forearm, noticing it for the first time. "You drew blood?"

"To identify the toxin." He rests his hand on mine.

"And?" I ask.

"Considering the circumstances, it's strange that we didn't find traces of poison in your blood."

"None?"

"None! Whatever caused the symptoms was excreted quite rapidly from your system." He pats my icy hand. "You were lucky. A few more sips of that water and you'd have gone into shock."

"Shock? Is that dangerous, doctor?"

"Yes, Soraya, very. It could lead to death."

I shudder at the thought, not so much of death, but at the thought of leaving my work unfinished.

The doctor gazes down at me. "Soraya, sometimes when the

body is under stress, one's immune system becomes weak and everything affects it faster. I will dismiss you on condition that you promise to rest."

I nod. A reassuring smile. I promise. Pull myself up and sit at the edge of the bed and wait for a spell of vertigo to subside.

chapter 25

A PROFOUND SILENCE HOVERS OVER my home, and the sky is darker than steel. This beast called smog, which, I'm told, is a combination of smoke and fog, chokes the hills, devastates the trees, and depresses the horizon.

I miss Tehran's sky, the imprint of a pale moon on the canvas of dawn. I miss the chilled juice we sucked out of a hole in a pomegranate during early morning hikes, the ritual of star watching at the base of the Alborz Mountains in the evenings.

—Make a wish, *Jounam*, and the stars will obey—

I've lost the ability to make wishes, but not the longing to hear Aziz murmur in my ear.

—I want to melt into you, *Jounam*, lick sea salt off your skin—

Mansour brakes to a stop at the gate and turns back to face me. He gestures toward the house at the end of the driveway. "I have to warn you, *Khanom*. There's a smell in the house. Oni washed and scrubbed all day. I even called a cleaning crew, but the *booyeh moteafen* stink is still strong."

"Thank you, Mansour. Any mail from Iran?"

"Yes, *Khanom*, I put it on your desk."

"Please drop me off at the door, and tell Oni to take the rest of the day off."

Mansour gives his forehead a hard slap. "Please, *Khanom*, you are still weak. You need to rest. Your life was about to slip away in the emergency room, God forbid, may my tongue be silenced. You'll need Oni to take care of you."

"I am fine, Mansour. Take the day off, too. Please drop me at the door."

I need to take a shower, wash off the smells of hospital, sweat, vomit, and the constant waltz that tumbles in my head like Iranian chickpeas in an American blender.

A slap of dank air assaults me when I enter the house, walk straight into the library, and lock the door behind me. I sort through catalogs, magazines, newspapers, and endless bills on my writing desk until I find the expected letter.

Butterfly's pinched handwriting strikes me with a painful rush of memories. Clutching my belly, I double over and shove my head into the wastepaper basket to vomit the bland hospital breakfast I forced down this morning. Vomiting is nature's warning, Mamabozorg believed, a sign that we've gorged on non-kosher food. I put my head on the desk and wait for my guts to settle before I return to the letter.

Butterfly is so very grateful, so very excited, hardly able to contain her joy at the prospect of seeing me. She accepts my invitation, of course, with great pleasure. She will arrive in a week.

I crumple the letter into a ball and shove it in my pocket.

Is there enough time to prepare for her? A plan is shaping. The guest bedroom has to be properly decorated, the children's quarters, too, for maximum impact.

I step out of the library and walk into the foyer. The odor of rotting flesh and vegetation slaps me in the face. I run ahead, afraid the Corpse Flower might have withered and been rendered useless in my absence. Rush straight to the veranda that leads to the courtyard and come to a halt at the top of the stairs.

I gasp at the sight below. The Corpse Flower's fecund smell has injected renewed life into every root, branch, and flower. Leaves are deeper green, flowers more vibrant, kaleidoscopes of butterflies basking all around.

I descend the stairs and tiptoe catlike into the atrium.

The Amorphophallus titanum has acquired an added magnificence as if, in my absence, it has been haunted by sorcerers and painters.

The flower is voluptuous, the stem proudly erect, the odor of bitter almonds gripping. But not for long. The flower, I understand, will hardly last more than forty-eight hours after blooming. Then, it will wither and fall limp, its active properties rendered useless.

Enough time has been wasted.

Returning to the library, I search the rows of encyclopedias for information. Poisons. Toxic plants. Conserving poisons for medicinal purpose. Distilling essence. Condensing sap. Bind the essential quality of the toxin in a few drops of alcohol and bottle. No. None of these will do.

My interest is piqued by a few legible, embossed letters on the spine of a tattered, leather-bound book. *A Book For Private Considerate…Reading…*Medical…Derangement…Herbal. I leaf through the table of contents: The Baseness of Medicinal Adulteration. Impure Vaccination. Consumption. Common Sense Herbal Remedies. Science of Poisons, Venoms, and Toxins: Autumn Crocus, Bleeding Heart, Angel's Trumpet, Monkshood, Castor Oil Plant, Delphinium, Giant Arum…

I can hardly contain my excitement. Giant arum is another name for the Corpse Flower. And right here, in Chapter XXI, are instructions for drying toxic plants for medicinal purposes. Dried herbs and plants have a longer shelf life, I know, and for my purpose this is of utmost importance.

> Dry flower on grates placed in a warm, shady area. Grind dried petals in a clean mortar. Store in sealed jars. Steep a teaspoon of dehydrated petals in slow-boiling water when needed. A thin layer of oil, distillate of the toxin, will float

on top. Use a half teaspoon to alleviate chronic dysentery, ailments of the gut, abnormal heart palpitation, and internal bleeding. Fatal in large doses.

Gardening shears in hand, I return to the atrium, walk back and forth and around to gauge which part of the Amorphophallus to behead so as to cause the least damage. If severed from the base, I muse, the heart might suffer and that will certainly cause the plant to wither and die. Then again, the plant's heart must be the reservoir in which most of its precious poison resides.

I unlock the shears with a metallic screech.

A flock of ravens darkens the sky outside. A rat scurries away. A squirrel scampers up the climbing jasmine. My owl's talons click on the glass dome overhead.

I keep my eyes down to avoid her yellow stare.

Khodaya! I hear Mamabozorg in the deepest chambers of my heart: What in God's name are you doing, Soraya?

I glare up at her and shout in a clear, loud voice that carries itself beyond the atrium. "I'm following your advice, Mamabozorg. Don't tell me you forgot! I'm not resting on my haunches while my life bleeds away. I'm taking control of my life. Isn't this what you wanted me to do? Now, shoo! Off you go. Let me be."

The owl flaps its speckled wings and rises to slowly circle the dome, so close its underbelly bumps with heavy thuds against one, then another pane, and for a second I'm afraid the glass will break. Finding me seemingly indifferent, she swoops down and settles on the door handle outside. I count the pecking sounds on the door, as if decoding Morse code that might explain her assessment of the situation or the level of her disapproval.

With a low, guttural bark of disgust, she finally takes flight, cutting through the fiery canvas of the sky, where the sun is still high among the colorless clouds. A flash of lightning breaks across the sky and the clouds shimmer unnaturally. There is a clap of thunder, but no rain. There is a disturbance out there.

I lower my head in the plant's presence and beg for forgiveness, pray with every remaining gram of compassion left in me for the Amorphophallus to survive the violation I am about to inflict.

Hands trembling, I summon the necessary strength and courage to amputate what took years of care to grow to this stage. I am not completely present because I cannot tell whether my eyes are shut or open when I embark upon the process of maiming the plant. I am not certain whether it will require one, two, or numerous attempts. I am aware of a *harjomarj* mayhem, but not certain if it occurs in my head or in the atrium. And then, I hear it with painful clarity. The drawn-out, mournful exhalation of the Corpse Flower. And I know that my job is done.

chapter 26

THE LAST SIX DAYS have been a whirlwind of action. The designer, Mansour, and Oni have carried out my orders to ready the house, the courtyard, and the gardens for Butterfly's arrival tomorrow.

Amorphophallus blooms are spread out on a wooden grate in the April shade. Every half hour, I stir the buds to dry them evenly. In the interim, I visit the courtyard to check on the plant, hum to it, and fertilize it, hoping it will forgive me and come back to life. I feed my owl extra helpings of juicy meat. Spray the flowers. Water the trees. Bribe the elements, I suppose, to continue to honor their regular rhythm.

Dew-laced spider webs sparkle like filigreed shawls among the coreopsis and purple cornflowers. Breezes carry the perfume of Autumn Joy and Ever Gold in the courtyard. The front garden is an aromatic tapestry of lively colors. The northern wall has vanished under climbing jasmines. Branches of the weeping willows graze the earth in supplication. And the recently arrived Monarchs are a different breed. They are thriving in the grove and seem immune to the rise and fall of temperatures, as well as plagues and all types of diseases.

I stir the blooms with a spatula, test some for consistency, and finding them dry, pour them into a mortar and begin pounding.

Images take shape, solidify, and become sharper with every sigh and rustle of the dried foliage under the weight of the pestle.

I refused to replace our bed for all twenty years of my marriage because I believed it served me well. Yet there they were, moaning and writhing on my black satin sheets, surrounded by walls crowded with my photographs, a collage of my life with Aziz among our exotic animals—in bed with the black-necked cobra stretched between us. Aziz wearing a tuxedo while feeding the rhinoceros iguana of Haiti. My face a portrait of laughter as the red-eyed Madagascar frog peeks out of my cleavage. And opposite our bed, a close-up of our lips, my most cherished photograph.

—Keep your eyes open and give me your tongue, *Jounam*—

The crescendo of the waltz might soften one day, the stench of lit candles diminish, perhaps. But never will I cease to taste Aziz's tongue in Butterfly's mouth.

I pour the fine-powdered Amorphophallus, what amounts to one cup of distillate, into the airtight jar.

❧ ❧ ❧

The black stretch limousine Mansour rented for the occasion heads down Veteran Avenue toward the airport. On my right, framed by clipped, geometrically precise blocks of grass, tombstones line a graveyard. Does it matter to the dead where they are buried? Do they care about the change of seasons? Mind that the grass never rests here?

I tap on the glass partition that separates Mansour and me and ask whether the cemetery is strictly for Americans.

"It's for war veterans, *Khanom*."

"Do Iranians have separate cemeteries in Los Angeles?"

"I don't believe so, *Khanom*. I know of two Jewish cemeteries."

"How long till the airport?"

"About thirty-five or forty-five minutes, *Khanom*, depending on traffic."

Once again the partition clicks shut, and Mansour and I become strangers in a country we don't understand but have, for our own different reasons, chosen as our refuge.

The limousine slides to the curb at the airport, and Mansour jumps out to open the door. I raise one high-heel-clad foot, then the other, and am grateful for the unyielding concrete underfoot because my knees are trembling, and I feel hollow inside my skin as if my bones and muscles have turned liquid.

I avoid the walking belt and take weak steps toward the designated gate. A sour-faced woman behind the desk assures me that Flight 34 is on time from New York, where Butterfly changed planes from Paris. I settle down, remove my compact from my purse, and study my face in the mirror. My makeup is in place, the dark circles under my eyes covered by concealer. Blush camouflages my pallor. My lipstick is bleeding, and for some reason, that adds to all the *harjomarj*. Small flames singe my throat, in search of a pocket of air, a breath of oxygen, the smallest whiff of fuel to explode into full-fledged rage. I pull out a handkerchief from my purse and tidy my lipstick, the cherry tint harsh against my pale complexion, as is the sharp glint of iron in my eyes.

—*Jounam*, you're up to something. The devil is in your eyes again—

I am, Aziz, I certainly am.

I pace back and forth, sit for a few minutes, and then situate myself a calculated distance from the gate, where I can easily observe Butterfly's entrance. My bladder is about to burst, but I stay put for fear of missing her uncensored expression that might reveal minute details of her past hours, most recent sexual encounter with my husband, in my bedroom, on my bed, to the waltz of the Blue Danube, to the twisting shadows of scented candles, in front of my most cherished photographs that witnessed our kisses, Aziz and mine. Until Butterfly.

Who stands at the entrance of Gate 18.

My dear, pretty butterfly, with the life span of a moth, carries herself with unprecedented pride and confidence bordering on conceit.

An orange kerchief with black polka dots falls loosely over her hair, and for an instant she is a Monarch butterfly with not four, but many protruding eyes.

"May the Evil Eye keep its distance," I murmur under my breath, covering my mouth and pretending to spit off the looming evil.

A long-sleeved, caramel-colored coat skims Butterfly's thin ankles. Her *chador* is tossed over her shoulders like a cape. She is not wearing her *chador* the conventional way Iranian women do—to conceal her sexuality and render herself chaste and asexual—but as an accessory to heighten his erotic pleasure, the pleasure of slowly peeling one layer after another to reveal the woman underneath. Her face, although masterfully painted, appears free of makeup, and her silhouette, despite being concealed under her coat, is a fluid motion of solicitation.

"Soraya!" she cries out, drawing her *chador* snug about her, and running toward me, her high heels sending her crashing into my wide-open arms.

I break her fall. Squeeze her to my breasts. "My friend! I missed you." And to my surprise, I have. I miss our closeness, our exchange of secrets, our past innocence, shared tears for unrequited loves, and the gossip-laced laughter of women with nothing to hide.

Butterfly holds me at arm's length. "Let me see you, Soraya. You look wonderful. America's been good to you."

Liar, I think, as she hugs me and kisses my neck, which she can hardly reach without my bending. Frail Butterfly in Soraya's embrace. Who is the elephant, who the mosquito buzzing in the poor elephant's ear?

I press her harder against me, inhale past the smell of her scarf and *chador* to reach other aromas trapped in her hair, analyze her top and base notes with their layered nuances that trace back to her most recent hours. Her heartbeat echoes in my chest, steady and strong and oblivious. Nestled in her hair is the scent of Aziz's olive soap and tobacco. So fresh, his sperm must be swimming in her.

My throat tightens to stop the rising bile even as my arms lock around her shoulders, squeezing her in a tight grip to conceal my face from her view. My gaze travels above and beyond her head, past the benches, the information desk, and a flight attendant rushing past another forming line of passengers.

Aziz stands at the gate.

He has come to fetch me.

Thank God I trimmed my hair, painted my toes, and wore my sheer paisley dress. Thank God I'm wearing the high-heeled sandals he likes. He walks toward me with calm, measured steps. His overpowering presence obliterates the surrounding mayhem, blots out everything but his delicious appearance and the outline of his strong mouth that parts with pleasure at the sight of me. He has lost weight. His cheekbones are more pronounced, his features more chiseled. A patina of sadness renders him even more desirable.

His loose tie is slightly askew. After a day of traveling, his white shirt remains spotless and his approaching scent tempting. The hairs on his chest show through his unbuttoned shirt. I glimpse a few gray strands that were not there before. A stir of contradictory emotions! Rage. Sadness. Delight.

He opens his arms. Our tongues greet. "My Soree. *Jounam*, my life."

My uterus contracts. Warm blood trickles down my thigh. No! My menstrual cycle is not due for another week.

A sweeping tide washes over me, and I yield to a vortex of blessed darkness.

chapter 27

I AM LYING ON THE sofa in my library, my head in Aziz's lap, his hand in my hair. I feel weak and hardly able to speak, the trip from the airport back home a flurry of hazy recollections. My giddy heart and confused brain fight one another.

What am I to do now? What am I to do with the album of my collection of men on the table in the drawing room and with the butterflies in the cabinet? What am I to do with the china cups and the jar of Amorphophallus tea locked behind glass cabinets in the kitchen? I had prepared for Butterfly's arrival, had an explanation for the album and my new photographic style. But Aziz is here now. And everything feels off balance and in desperate need of readjusting.

He helps me rise from his lap. I twirl my wedding bands to stop myself from falling into his arms, hanging around his neck, and pounding my fists against his chest. I want to trace the outline of his lips that seem drawn by chocolate, stroke his lashes, seize his nicotine-stained fingers, and bury my face in his scent of smoke and olive soap.

I want to take him by the hand and lead him out, splash his face with cold water, help him freshen up and change into comfortable clothing, because I can't bear to witness the fatigue shadowing his lovely eyes. Instead, I sit on the couch in my library with all the books and the grandfather clock that chimes "The Blue Danube" and gaze at him like a stunned *ashegh* lover. "Where is Butterfly?"

"I don't know," he replies absentmindedly. "I got you a gift for our anniversary." He unfurls a silver ribbon from around a box and tears off the gray wrapping, revealing a case with an embossed emblem of the House of Buccellati.

A pearl pin in the shape of a phoenix lounges on a bed of satin. A precious jewel I admired years ago, when Gianmaria Buccellati invited us to a private tour of his atelier, recounting how he first visualized a pearl as the body of a phoenix, its feathers yellow, orange, and green diamonds.

I own golden pearls from Burma, black and green pearls from Tahiti, white South Sea pearls from Australia, and bracelets made of the rarest of conch pearl. But this extraordinary piece of jewelry is more precious than anything I've ever owned.

Aziz fastens the phoenix brooch to my sweater. His touch is soft, and his tender smile transforms him into the innocent husband I once knew. "Our first anniversary away from each other. Let's make sure it doesn't happen again."

A hundred and thirty-six carats of the most rare and magnificent gems in the world are attached to my sweater, and I only have eyes for him.

"Come, *Jounam*, come tell me why you didn't answer my phone calls." He utters this without a trace of accusation.

"Of course, I called, Aziz. I called many times. But sometimes it's difficult to get through."

"Yes, the authorities are increasingly censoring calls. Especially from America." He shifts slightly away, scrutinizing me with his sharp gaze. "You lost weight, you know. Interesting, how missing our love affects us in strange ways."

My husband's words and their subtle nuances roll under my tongue. I can't tell whether he is joking or serious, whether he is referring to my love for him or his for Butterfly.

I put my head on his shoulder, stroke the phoenix like a nice, grateful wife. Why such an expensive gift? To stir the ashes of our love? To solder the irreparable shreds of what was? *Baksheesh*, I suppose, absolution money. I want to plant a hundred kisses on his treacherous eyes, then yank them out of their sockets and hand them back to him in his Buccellati gift box.

"My Soree, *Jounam*, call me selfish if you want, but it was lovely of you to faint in my arms. See why you need me? To catch you."

He touches my lips with the tip of two fingers, and I want to stroke the fingers that are embers thawing the chill in my bones. Instead, I reach out for the bell and summon Oni.

Tray in hand, she slithers into the library, soft-footed and apologetic. Her suspicious, tight-lidded eyes observe our houseguest, an unprecedented event. She bows twice to Aziz before putting the silver tray with gold-rimmed porcelain cups and a bowl of sugar cubes on the table, next to a vase of English lavender buds that resemble violet bumblebees. Their scent is supposed to mask bad odors and repel insects, but Butterfly steps into the library, her *chador* wrapped around her as if to conceal her shame in its folds.

"I love your place, Soraya. Did *you* name it Paradise of Butterflies?"

"Yes, it had a different name."

Butterfly's face lights with gratitude. "Thank you, my friend."

"No, no need to thank me. It's the least I could do for you."

Oni holds out a box of assorted tea bags for Butterfly to choose from.

"How negligent of me!" she exclaims as she flops down on the sofa. "I should've brought tea leaves. You must miss Persian tea."

I miss more than Persian tea. I miss Mamabozorg's guidance that was full of compassion and wisdom. I miss Madar's devotion that I once considered stifling, but that was displayed in the most affectionate ways. I miss my garden with the resplendent family of quetzals, the Mandarin duck, and my psychedelic, proud-necked iguanas. I even miss the absurd television shows that conceal faces of male singers behind painted flowers in fear of arousing women.

And I never thought that one day I'd miss the *pasdaran* Morality

Police, who could be bribed now with a few *toumans* and subtle flirtation to disregard a touch of lipstick and a dash of mascara. I miss Baba who loved, hardened, and protected me the best way he knew. And I miss Parvaneh, my former friend and confidant, the woman who mirrored my triumphs and faults.

But above all, I miss my husband, Aziz. Deeply miss what she stole from me. "Yes, Parvaneh, I miss Persian tea. What would you like? Orange spice tea? Mint? Apple cinnamon? Try champagne rose, my favorite."

"Morning Thunder, please."

An expression of subdued amusement dances in Aziz's eyes. "Morning Thunder? I'll have that, too. Will keep me wide awake and at my wife's service!"

Did I hear Butterfly stifle a sigh?

Aziz turns to her and cocks an eyebrow in the seemingly discreet language of traitors.

Oni tiptoes on her slippers. She glances at me with exaggerated wrinkling of her eyes as if to warn me of impending doom.

"Thank you, Oni. Prepare supper for our guests."

She bends her knees and lowers her head, her leather soles swish-swishing out the door and across the corridor to the asylum of the kitchen.

The moment Oni is out of earshot, Butterfly asks, "*Laleh*? Is she mute?"

"No," I reply. "The shock of her husband's infidelity, *zabanash ra dozdideh* stole her tongue and made her speechless."

Butterfly casts her eyes down. "Poor woman. But how do you know? Does she sometimes talk?"

"No, but she has that pinched, betrayed look."

Aziz begins to say something and then changes his mind.

An awkward moment of silence lingers, until I come to my senses and stifle the urge to speed the process of shaming and hurting. Patience, Soraya, do not deviate from your plan! "Come, let me give you a tour of the house." I want them to see where

I live, what my life has come to. I want Aziz to see what I have become in his absence. Want him to acknowledge our loss.

The chandelier in the drawing room splashes everything with lethargic hues—the gray walls, pale-colored settee, angular armchairs, and hard, cold granite table. This morning's airport chill is giving way to a warm evening, and through the French windows, a heavy fog is descending upon the gardens. The bong of the grandfather clock gives me a jolt.

"Not your taste," Aziz says. "This house. The décor, the furniture. Everything."

"It's expected, isn't it," I reply with a smile, not certain whether he is being judgmental or surprised.

"Expected?"

"For my taste to change when I am out of your sight."

"Perhaps, *Jounam*. But it won't happen again! I won't let you out of my sight again."

Every muscle strains to keep the smile on my face.

Cup of hot tea in hand, Butterfly settles down in one of the black, wooden chairs around the table.

My red album, 1999 stamped in gold on its spine, lies on the table like a bloody centerpiece.

She sips tea, slides the album toward her, and lifts the cover.

I approach from behind and slap the album shut. This is not for her. This special gift, the men enshrined between the covers of my album, is for my husband.

I cross the hall and walk straight to my studio. Place the album on the counter with my photographic paraphernalia, close the door behind me, and drop the key in my pocket.

Butterfly stares at me with surprise. "What do you have in that album, Soraya? Since when do you keep secrets from me?"

"No secret. Just a special surprise."

"For me?"

"And Aziz. Be patient, darling, it's worth it. Come, I want to show you my beautiful butterflies."

"These butterflies on the walls," Aziz exclaims, with a sweeping gesture of two hands that encompass the entire room. "It's so morbid."

I take him by the hand and lead him to the display cabinet. The glare from the chandelier makes it hard to see inside. He cups his hands around his eyes to take a better look through the glass panel.

"Aren't they beautiful, Aziz?"

His voice is low in my ear. "Ugly, *Jounam*, and useless."

"Don't say that!" I hiss back. "My best friend's name is Butterfly."

He throws his arms up. "So don't stick pins in them."

"I didn't. Told you the owner of the house is a lepidopterist."

"Yes, you certainly did." Then without warning, he plants a kiss on the back of my hand. Like old times when we couldn't keep our lips from touching. But the words he murmurs into my cold palm send a shiver across my spine. "You have changed, Soraya. And I don't like it one bit."

I want to say that I don't like what happened to us, either, to my husband, to our lives. Instead, slyness creeps into me, the desire to know more, know every sickening detail, so I ask, "How have I changed, Aziz? Tell me."

"Look around you, *Jounam*. This isn't you. And why in the world do you need such a large house in the first place? Why aren't you at the Peninsula? Something's up with you."

Butterfly buzzes behind us like an annoying mosquito. "What are you two whispering about?"

"Telling my Soree she's full of surprises." Aziz circles my waist and draws me closer to his lingering scent that never fails to rattle and unmoor me.

"She certainly is," Butterfly says, "*Yadeteh*, remember, when you dyed your hair red because a stupid professor said redheaded Jews are descendants of King Solomon and lack a common-sense gene?"

I burst out laughing at the memory. "I can't even remember the fool's name. Remember when Baba threatened Aunt Tala?"

"*Khodaya*! How can I forget? She fed me so well after that. I became plumper than a lame goose."

"The things we did. I can't believe I pulled down your bathing suit in…"

Butterfly gestures with a finger to her lips. "Not in front of Aziz."

"Come on, Parvaneh, tell. Was it in the *hamam*? No, no, in our pool on our twelfth birthday." I pinch her playfully. "You were as flat as a skillet."

Oni steps in and gestures that supper is ready, leading us into the dining room. I move the food around on my plate—baby spinach and heart of palm salad, roasted chicken and steamed broccoli—and nibble on a piece of lettuce, pretending to eat. I will never know if Butterfly will pile Aziz's plate with the juiciest piece of chicken, spoon out tender heart of palm, and grind a pinch of pepper on top, because Oni, with great pride, has taken it upon herself to serve us.

The curtains quiver in the warm breeze that makes its way in from the courtyard, transporting the odors of the Corpse Flower, wet and cloying as a traitor's slap.

Butterfly's nostrils flare. "Strange smell!"

"Yes. Stink of goldfish. I bought them for the New Year. They didn't last more than a week. All fifteen died. Tossed them in the garbage disposal." I don't say that on the first night of Noruz, instead of following custom and having goldfish swim in a bowl of clear water for good luck, instead of partaking of the delicacies Mansour had set on the table, food that started with the letter S for happiness, prosperity, and long life, I had gone out hunting for a *mullah*.

Aziz folds the napkin on the table and plants a kiss behind my ear. "Show me the bedroom, *Jounam*."

The dreaded moment is here at last, and I am not prepared. Aziz wants me all to himself. I hold his face in both my hands and look straight into his fickle eyes. "Make yourself comfortable, my love. I'll be back after I show Parvaneh to her room."

chapter 28

I GUIDE BUTTERFLY INTO THE foyer of bedroom suites, every detail of which I personally oversaw. We step into a pink-colored fairyland, antique crib and changing table, miniature dining- and living-room sets. An electrical train snakes its way from one room to another. Battery-operated dogs and cats tumble and roll, bark and meow. China dolls dressed in lace and velvet gowns sit, stand, or recline on shelves. Open closet doors reveal tiny patent shoes with bows, small straw hats with satin ribbons, girly beaded purses with rhinestone clasps, and taffeta evening dresses for babies.

"*Khodaya*! My God!" Butterfly screams, jumping around, hugging me, and planting a kiss on my arm. "You're pregnant! Success at last. So happy for you. *Mobarakeh*, congratulations!"

At the sight of her genuine joy and excitement, a heavy weight settles in the pit of my stomach. One by one, I lock the closets as if to deadbolt my cruelty in there. Pick up the battery-operated toys and turn them off. The racket of electrical train, barking dogs, and nursery rhymes dies down. "I'm not pregnant. Oni must have done it. She likes to wind up the mechanical toys. I don't know why."

Tears flash in Butterfly's eyes. I wipe a tear off the tip of her lashes. She sobs, falling into my arms, her body shaking with the force of her grief. "Sometimes I think I should leave Hamid and marry someone who can have children."

I murmur how sorry I am for her, how deeply I feel her longing. And I do. I run a hand over her stomach and feel the muscles tighten under my touch. We exchange glances the way we did not long ago, when we shared silent secrets.

I yank the blanket off the crib and toss it over the row of dolls on the shelves. "If it didn't belong to the owner of the house," I lie, "I'd give them all away. Come, let's get out of here!"

"I want to be like you, Soraya. Accept my fate and move on."

Chera delam misouzeh? Why the burning in my heart for her? Why do I pity her, when she has no compassion for me?

She wraps her arm around my waist and wipes my cheeks with the gossamer *harir* fabric of her *chador*, which has turned dark with my tears. "Don't worry, Soraya. I've learned to cope. I'm fine most of the time."

"Of course you are, my friend. Come. Let me show you your room."

Butterfly observes the black sheets on the bed in the guest suite, purchased for her arrival, the scented candles flickering on the bedside tables, the bottle of Chanel perfume on the dresser. She cocks her head and listens to "The Blue Danube" playing on the CD player. A slight twitch at the corner of her mouth betrays her feelings; an attempt to scratch her thigh transforms into a fist she conceals behind her back.

"It's lovely here, Soraya. Thanks. Feels like home. Where did you find the sheets? They remind me of Tehran."

Of course, they do, my friend. You had sex with my husband on similar sheets, wore the same perfume, lit the same candles, played the same music.

"Chanel! My favorite perfume." She raises the bottle from the dressing table, removes the stopper, and dabs perfume behind her ears.

I open the windows and draw in a few deep breaths, linger there, hoping and praying to hear my owl's voice of reason above the surrounding chaos. "I hope you are staying long, Parvaneh."

She flops on the bed, arms and legs splayed in a defenseless posture. "Ten days. Don't want to leave Hamid alone for more than that. It's the first time I won't be celebrating the Thirteenth with him."

From ancient Zoroastrian times to the present, it is customary for Iranians to gather outdoors on the thirteenth day of Farvardin, the end of the New Year celebrations, to honor nature and its rebirth. Blades of green sprouts that graced tables are tied, then cast into running water, a ritual intended to bring good luck in the coming year.

I attempt to riffle through her words to reveal their true meaning, but the overpowering scent of Chanel is confusing. My sense of smell numbed. I'm lost, blind, unable to identify the undercurrent of odors that would reveal her true emotions.

"Don't look so sad, Soraya. Ten days is a long time."

Yes, my friend, it is. You'll have a wonderful and exciting ten days. Like a "Butterfly Week," beautiful, but short-lived. Even the best of times must end.

A spark of an idea occurs to me. Why not take care of business tonight? Then there won't be any tomorrows for her to follow me and Aziz around and intrude on what must occur next. When she comes down with cramps, I'd tell Aziz that she must have had bad food on the plane, that another cup of tea would calm her stomach and that a doctor is unnecessary. And soon, after another cup of special tea, peace and harmony will be restored.

But, no, I am not ready to forego the pleasure of observing the two of them react to the prints in my studio and the swarms of Monarchs in the eucalyptus grove. Not ready to forego the pleasure of watching Aziz react to Butterfly's transformation in America as I tempt, even force, her to discard her *chador* and reveal the whore concealed underneath. My album of men is an altogether different matter. That must be presented to Aziz at the right time, once Butterfly is gone and he is at his most vulnerable.

We face the dressing table with its framed mirror and gaze

at each other, Butterfly and me, as if we are still teenagers and scrutinizing our budding breasts, forming curves, and new growth of pubic hair. We might as well be naked. We know each other too well, the two of us, not only every inch of our bodies, but our shared hopes and dreams and shattered illusions.

Butterfly's arched brows resemble a lark in flight, the peach fuzz on her upper lip that she bleaches with harsh chemicals glitters in the light above the mirror. The red beauty mark on top of her right eyebrow, which I found exotic once, looks like a drop of congealed blood. I cup her face between my hands and gaze at her brown, admiring eyes. Stroke the outline of her naked lips; press the plump center with one finger, forging a different kind of a bond. I draw her closer to me and press my mouth to the lips Aziz likes to kiss.

A moment of hesitation, a soft intake of her breath, before she steps away. Pats her lips with her *chador* and then manipulates it around her waist.

"Put the *chador* away, Parvaneh. You won't need it here."

"You sound upset, Soraya."

"Not at all. Just that it's considered backward to wear a *chador* here." I take the *chador*, spread it on the bed, and fold it carefully, slipping it in back of the closet and out of sight. "You won't need the *manteau* either."

"Until tomorrow?"

"We'll see how you feel about it tomorrow." I walk to the bed, lounge on the covers, and pull myself up to lean against the headboard. Aziz will have to wait while I slowly undress my friend to reveal the woman he finds more attractive than me, to study the intimate turns and grooves of the woman he caresses, licks, and whispers endearment to. Yes, he will have to wait while I reveal the hypocrisy of a woman who wraps herself like a mummy in public, yet has no qualms about transforming herself into a one-penny whore in his arms.

She removes her coat, exposing her ankles and wrists, the most tempting parts of a woman, according to the *mullahs*. Is Aziz drawn to her small wrists, the two delicate veins that run up her ankles, her narrow waist cinched with a silver chain-link? The hem of her blue dress flares out as she walks toward the closet to hang her coat. She unbuckles her belt and rolls it neatly on one of the shelves. She turns her back to me. Struggles to unzip her dress. The silk slides open to reveal the delicate bones of her shoulders, the black gossamer bra and matching lace panties that arouse my husband.

She unclasps her bra and steps out of her underwear for Aziz to crush her tiny breasts, lick her thighs, peel off her panties.

I ought to turn away. Spare myself. But I am hypnotized by the fragile chain of her vertebrae that leads down to the curve of her waist, mesmerized by her lifted arms and the manicured fingers that unclasp a horseshoe-shaped hairpin to loosen her braid, mesmerized by the suggestive shake of her head and the dark curtain of curls that tumble to the childlike buttocks Aziz cups in his hands.

She turns to face me. My fist springs up to my mouth to strangle the gasp in my throat. I struggle for a gulp of air. Plump breasts. Arrogant. Lustful. Breasts larger than mine! What dramatic event in her life could have caused this transformation? Why didn't I notice it the afternoon I caught them together? The body I had evoked in my husband's arms was that of a teenager—boyish breasts and girlish thighs and angular all over, the Butterfly I remember from years back. After all these years in my husband's care, she has bloomed into the maturity of a thirty-five-year-old woman, endowed with tempting curves, all softness and desire.

She sighs and shivers as she snuggles under the covers next to me.

I pass my hand over her damp forehead and hear myself asking if she sweats during lovemaking.

Her laughter is childlike, nervous perhaps, but when she answers I do not detect a trace of suspicion. "Of course I sweat. Like a dog! You know I like a good and dirty fuck."

“Yes. But something’s different. You’re more beautiful. More content. And your breasts! Implants?”

“Don’t be silly. I wouldn’t dare.” She weighs her breasts in her cupped hands. “They are bigger, aren’t they? Did I gain weight?”

“No. Just here.” Her breasts yield under my touch. Her nipples harden between my thumb and forefinger, goose bumps frame her areola. “It happens sometimes, you know. Breasts can become flush with love.” My husband. His love and passion. His betrayal.

“Mystery solved, then!” she announces with a yawn. “Now I know why Hamid can’t keep his hands off my breasts. Aren’t you tired, Soraya? Go, before Aziz hates me for keeping you so late. It’s midnight. Go, darling!” She covers her eyes with one hand and her lips move in a silent prayer.

What else is left for her to ask of God?

chapter 29

Aziz murmurs that my bedroom, with its small bed and cold colors, is too dreary for words. Enough to render impotent the most virile of men.

I glance at his bulging crotch that is immune to this frigid environment and declare that I am so miserable without him that I neither notice or care about my surroundings. He stops in front of the dressing table. "A broken mirror? Very strange, Soraya. Not like you!"

I shrug my shoulders and tell him that I simply didn't bother to order a new one. I do not tell him that the mirror was left intact to stoke my rage, to hone and polish my memories into crystalline slivers. I do not tell him that every morning after I wake up, and every evening before I go to bed, I study my cracked reflection in the mirror as I lose weight and my eyes acquire the hard glint of a predator.

Our split image in the mirror, mine and Aziz's, is a collage of broken bits and slivers. If only normalcy could be restored by shifting and setting the shards of glass differently on the mercury backing.

"Talk to me, Soraya, now that we're alone. Tell me what is happening." His stare dissects my image in the mirror, lingers here and there, before transforming into an expression of puzzled concern as if his wife removed her mask, and he has just become aware she is a stranger.

"Talk about what, Aziz? Decorating? I didn't want to waste time and money on decorating a temporary house."

"Look at this! You brought it with you?" He holds up the embalmed iguana and checks the chipped leg. He pulls a tiny shard of glass from the back, then another two. He puts the pieces on the dressing table. "Soraya, who broke the mirror with your iguana?"

"I did. I was alone. It was late. I wanted you. There was the iguana reminding me of my birthday when you told me these animals don't fuck if they're not in love. And I'm in love and wanting to fuck, with you on the other end of the world. So, I felt like breaking something."

"I'm here now." He draws me to him. A chilly breeze flaps the curtains, and I tremble. He strokes me with two hands as if to put me back together, as if to repair the insult he caused. His tightening arms are not gentle, but possessive and deliberate. He lifts me, weightless as air, I think, because it doesn't feel as if I am the one he is carrying to the faraway bed.

—Keep your eyes open, *Jounam*—

And I keep my eyes wide open to probe the depths of his betrayal, brush my nose against his neck, where the curve meets his shoulder, and the dimple of his arm where perspiration tends to pool, and he smells of desire and his tongue tastes sweet.

And he, who has become a master performer, cuddles my breasts in his hands and whispers: "I want you, Soree, *Jounam*, my life."

And I, who have never, ever desired another man, melt into his warmth, into the longing in his mouth, the sweet bitterness on his tongue.

That's why despite the threat in his touch, despite Butterfly asleep in another room, despite all the dead butterflies in the cabinet and the live Monarchs in the eucalyptus grove, despite the

Corpse Flower in the atrium and the black and blue vein in the crook of my arm, despite the warning barks of the owl all night, I open my thighs wide and invite him in.

chapter 30

THIS MORNING, AZIZ IN deep sleep, I prepare myself for the day, toning down my image to allow Butterfly to stand out and shine. It is a permissive society, America; it has a way of breeding temptation. And Butterfly is ripe prey. It will not take long, perhaps no longer than a day, before I succeed in exposing the real woman concealed behind the façade of modesty Aziz drools over.

A cup of steaming tea in hand, I tiptoe into Butterfly's room. The half domes of her breasts swell under the silk-stitched edging of the sheets, and her hair spreads on the pillows. Her eyes flutter open. She yawns and curls like a snake on warm sand.

I put the cup of tea on the side table. Arrange and fluff up her pillows against the headboard.

She pulls herself up with a contented sigh and snuggles back against the pillows.

I hand her the steaming cup, and she selects a sugar cube from among the three on a corner of the saucer, drops it in her mouth, and sips chamomile tea laced with cardamom and orange peel. We are back in Iran, in her kitchen, two close friends sharing intimate details of our lives over cups of aromatic tea, until her words shatter my memories.

"I didn't sleep very well."

Saliva pools under my tongue. Of course, she couldn't sleep. She couldn't bear Aziz spending the night with me. "That's what you get for drinking Morning Thunder! I'll brew you a special tea tonight. You'll sleep like an angel." I hand her a pigeon-blood-colored robe of mine and ask her to toss it over her nightgown because I've something interesting to show her.

She follows me out of the bedroom into the hall that leads to the drawing room, my satin gown trailing her like tempting plumage. We must be a sight, Butterfly and I, she clad in screaming red—barefoot and all flushed with curiosity and excitement—and me all in black—high-heeled and silk-clad and cracked beyond repair.

We step onto the balcony that wraps around the open-air courtyard in the center of the house. My friend's eyes widen with wonder at the sunken panorama below. The marble daises displaying Greek goddesses, Grecian columns supporting granite benches, the majestic monkey tree on the far right. And the atrium in the center, home to my Corpse Plant.

Butterfly descends the steps, her gown sliding behind like an invitation. She strolls about, enjoying this warm spring dawn, so different from the blazing summers and snowy winters back home. Humming under her breath, my friend, the seductress, glittering and colorful and ruthless like butterflies that land on flowers, tease and cuddle each receptive petal, then suckle it dry, strokes leaves and petals of snapdragons, bleeding hearts, and yellow honeysuckle, wide open in anticipation of impregnation.

She dips a finger in a glass feeder, brimming with sugar water to entice butterflies, and sucks her finger, then raises her bare arms overhead and shuts her eyes. I avert my gaze from her groomed, hairless armpits, from her neckline that outlines her plump cleavage.

"It's liberating, Soraya, isn't it? Not to worry about showing some skin. But I feel guilty too, as if I'm doing something wrong. I wonder why!"

"Because the *mullahs* have brainwashed us to feel like prostitutes if we don't cover ourselves."

"Exactly! Have you heard about the Spider Murders?"

"No, tell me."

She shakes her hair, already more uninhibited and at ease than last night. Is this not what I've been striving for? Then why am I bothered?

The tiny, bleached hairs on her arms stand up on end. "It's scary, Soraya. All women talk about these days are the twelve prostitutes strangled in the streets of Mashhad. A headscarf knotted twice to the right side of their neck. Called Spider Murders because of the way the bodies are draped in *chadors* before being dumped into streets and canals."

"What's the significance of the knots?" I ask.

"Who knows!"

"The answer might be found in the *Koran*. The right is farther from the heart, for example, but closer to some part of the brain that controls our reasoning. Not sure…or it could be an act of revenge…"

"The authorities say it might be the work of religious vigilantes. It's terrible. Families of the victims are embarrassed to come forward and claim the bodies."

For the second time this morning, I am about to get sick. Women who support their families the only way they can are denied a simple burial, yet the adulteress, Butterfly, is free to roam at will and create further havoc. I pluck a black leaf, dappled with dew, and press it to my flushed cheeks.

She bends to observe a Stalachtis phaedusa suspended upside down on a bleeding heart.

"It's harmless but can change color to resemble toxic butterflies to deter predators. Smart, isn't it? Like us. We camouflage ourselves, too."

"But we must," she replies in her innocent tone. "We're women! How else can we survive?"

I study a male Anteros kupris that maintains territory in the canopy of magnolia leaves, intent on trapping yet another mate. Interesting, how this species managed to find its way here from the Ecuador lowland forests. No hurdles are insurmountable, I suppose, when one is hunting for sex.

"Soraya, since when did you become so infatuated with butterflies?"

"Interested, not infatuated. Homage to you, my friend."

"You're full of it!" She grins, pulling a lock of my hair. "What's with the butterflies? The truth!"

"It was all here and it reminded me of you," I lie. "When the owner wouldn't rent the house if her butterflies weren't taken care of, I promised to take care of them. And you know what? I've been seduced. Come, see why. This one is a male Oleria quadrata. Belongs to the Clearwing family. It feeds on aster and then passes its alkaloids to females during mating, after which the female tastes bitter to other males. And that's it! Kaput! No more sex for them. Fascinating, isn't it!"

"Are you serious? *Khodaya*! You are serious. I love the idea." She approaches to take a closer look at the butterfly.

"If I had alkaloids," I say, "I'd inject Aziz with a healthy dose. And voila! I'll never worry about him wandering off."

Her face drains of color; an unguarded second of hesitation passes before she comes up with a reply. "Not a good idea. Then he'll taste bitter to you, too. Think before you start doling out your precious alkaloids."

I inhale her smells of orris and ylang-ylang, stir them in my nostrils, churn them in the pit of my stomach. She smells rotten and beyond repair.

My Owl of Reason swoops down with a startling bark and settles on my right shoulder.

Butterfly jumps back and cries out in fright.

Despite her weight and powerful grip, my owl has learned to land with graceful agility on my lap, arm, or shoulder without hurting me in the least. I like the sturdy grip of her claws, the comforting weight of her underbelly that helps me maintain a semblance of equilibrium.

"Soraya," Butterfly whispers, "Is that Mamabozorg's owl?"

"Don't be silly! We're miles and miles away. How could it be the same owl?"

"*Vayii*! I don't know what I'm saying. But it looks exactly like Mamabozorg's owl."

"Yes, it does. Pet her. She's friendly."

Butterfly recoils with a low gasp. "I'm scared."

"Scared? Of what?"

"I don't know. The eyes, I think. They're so large and yellow. They're frightening."

Butterfly is right. Sunlight has turned my owl's eyes into glaring, yellow orbs, bright and fierce and judgmental.

I run my thumb down the parting in the center of the bird's chest, the plumage smooth and oily on the surface, yet unyielding at the roots, stroke the plush down on her head, and a low hoot of pleasure emanates from her. "See, she's harmless. Come closer. Yes, try not to startle her."

Butterfly reaches out a trembling hand, then changes her mind and gently combs her fingers through my hair, down the long blond strands, so different from her dark curls.

I wrap my arm around my friend, all fluff and beauty, rays waltzing on the tendrils escaping her curls, this other sunlit Butterfly I knew as an innocent child, vulnerable girl, rebellious teenager, and now the close friend I have lost.

She tucks her arm in mine and, once again, as in the past, I feel a strong urge to protect her as we walk toward the atrium that seems to be on fire from the rising sun, reflecting on every glass panel. I open the door and stand aside for her to enter.

"*Khodaya*, help me!" she cries. "Get it out!"

A hummingbird is entangled in her hair. She jumps around, struggling to free it, her nervous cries ringing about the courtyard.

I thrust one hand into her curls.

"Careful, Soraya, you're hurting me."

"Stand still. Don't move. I almost got it!"

I take my time to free the hummingbird, trapped in Butterfly's net. There is a certain pleasure in tugging, plucking, and untangling, a certain melody to the drone of the alarmed bird vibrating in its net. Male and territorial, it pecks frantically at my fingers as if to drive away rivals from its breeding ground. This one requires careful handling. Like a packet of dynamite.

Freed, the disoriented hummingbird, dazzling green and fine as gossamer, lingers above Butterfly's head to recover its equilibrium, before buzzing away in anger.

From inside the house, the low voice of Mansour, the opening of a door. Aziz calling my name. The sun is higher in the sky and the atrium a fiery globe of glass.

Butterfly surprises me again by murmuring that it is high time I leave this madhouse and return home, and then she ambles into the atrium as if entering the familiar safety of her own home. A strong smell of carrion hits us like a punch. The tragic reality of where our fate has led us strikes me with renewed grief. I want to warn her that this is not home. Far from it. This is a shrine to her enemy.

My owl, too, hoots and barks and flaps in protest. She has never liked the atrium, but I want her close by now. I tempt her with handfuls of seasoned meat, juice-soaked nuts, and dried fruit from bowls Mansour replenishes daily and leaves all around, his way of bribing the owl to keep her evil eye at bay. I murmur in my most soothing voice, tickle the damp feathers under her wing, hold her gently down on my shoulder so she won't escape.

She resumes a ferocious fight to free herself, letting out a strange, piercing bark of pain. I loosen my grip and she takes off with agile speed, loops around my head once, flies around the atrium, then swoops down with great precision to land on Butterfly's shoulder.

"*Vayii*! *Khodaya*!" Butterfly cries out to God. "Soraya! It's hurting me! Send it away!"

I grab the bird with two hands and hold her dense, sinewy body tight. She wiggles free and flies out of the atrium like a feathered arrow.

Butterfly's face has turned the color of stale turmeric, her words tumble over each other. "I'm scared, Soraya. Keep your owl away from me. Please! I've never liked owls. Not even Mamabozorg's."

She turns her attention to the Corpse Flower, her hand shielding her mouth and nose against the smell of rotting flesh. "What a strange plant. *Bougand mideh* it stinks."

I point to the heart of the flower from where, just a few days ago, I had plucked most of the petals. I explain that when, if ever, the plant blooms, its seductive smell attracts pollinating bugs that congregate in its core. I explain that the plant has devised ingenious ways to tempt all kinds of innocent creatures to approach it and perform what amounts to sexual acts. "It sure knows how to trap to satisfy its sexual appetite."

Butterfly's body shakes with laughter. "God, Soraya, you're something else. I love your imagination."

Yes, she does. In that she resembles Aziz. And for that reason, they are the only two I feel comfortable sharing my dreams, fantasies, and photographs with. To the world, my photographs are the creations of a weird mind. To Butterfly, they are the product of genius, talent she supposes she lost at birth because she entered the world bent over and nearly strangled by the umbilical cord. To this day, she believes that those crucial moments of struggling for breath stumped her creativity.

She strolls around to check the Amorphophallus from all angles, a plant that resembles her in so many ways—her man-eating smell, voracious desire for what is not hers, her colorful, yet poisonous appearance. "Piff! It stinks in here, Soraya." She grabs my hand and drags me out of the atrium. "Can't bear the smell. Don't come here too often. It can't be good for you."

"As far as I'm concerned, out there is more dangerous than in here."

She releases my hand and aims a questioning stare at me. "Why is the world suddenly so dangerous? You're acting strange, Soraya! It's America, being alone, I don't know. Forget about the project and come back home. It isn't as if you need the money. Tell the magazine you've changed your mind. Say something, anything, lie if you have to."

"You want me to come back home?"

"Of course I do. Life is too short, Soraya. Let's wear it out together!"

I hold her at arm's length, observing her with genuine surprise. "Really! Since when?"

She lets out a mirthless laugh that belies her pontification. "Since forever, Soraya! Since I lost my parents and was stuck with Aunt Tala. Why are you surprised? You are the one who encouraged me to live life to its fullest, rather than shrivel up and become a wrinkled spinster. So, there! You are to blame."

"All right! I'm responsible. So, let's get out of here and do something fun and crazy. Let's start with shopping for clothes we can't wear back home."

I murmur promises of a thrilling day. A day immersed in a culture fraught with possibilities of freedom to spread your wings, my friend, to take off, soar, and live the day to its fullest. You are my guest, after all, and good manners and decorum require that even poisons be served sugarcoated and with great pomp and ceremony.

chapter 31

FRESHLY SHAVED AND WITH wet hair combed back, Aziz ambles into the drawing room. He winks conspiratorially, raises my chin, and plants a kiss on the tip of my nose. "Slept well?"

"Better than in a long time."

"And you, Butterfly?" he asks. "Did you sleep?"

"Not really," she replies shamelessly.

"Jet lag," he murmurs, turning away to observe my crocodile high-heeled shoes that add extra centimeters to my height, my silk skirt and sleeveless blouse that make me look even slimmer than I am. He runs his palm down my bare arm. "My sexy wife."

"Doesn't she look beautiful?" Butterfly interjects. "I love what you're wearing, Soraya."

"I'll help you dress like this."

"But I'm not you, Soraya. It won't look good on me."

"Don't be silly," I say, checking her chocolate brown, custom-made pantsuit, her braid tucked into her blouse. She left her *chador* behind, but further coaxing is required for her to discard her *manteau* and headscarf. "Take your kerchief off. It's ugly and it's hot. You don't need the *manteau* either."

She quickly discards her kerchief and coat, happy to be rid of the unnecessary confinements the authorities force upon her back home.

"You have beautiful arms, Butterfly. Show them off. Leave your jacket behind, too."

"But it's sleeveless. I can't remember the last time I walked out like this in public."

"You're not in Iran," I remind her.

"But I am going back," she protests as I unbutton her jacket and peel it off her back. A sly expression slithers across her face, and I know that it will not require a great deal of convincing to strip off the rest of her façade and expose the temptress underneath.

Aziz throws his hands up. "Parvaneh is right, Soraya. Don't forget you're going back to Iran, so don't get too used to these freedoms. Anyway, ladies, what are you two up to?"

"Going shopping," I reply. "Care to join us?"

"Not really."

"Please come," I say. "It'll be fun. We'll go to Rodeo Drive."

"Fun, it won't be, *Jounam*, but go enjoy yourselves. I'll meet you later for a drink."

I reach out and press one finger to his lips. "Stay close, Aziz. You promised to catch me if I faint again." I study his expression, his silent indifference and boredom, and wonder if he will walk away and abandon us to our wiles. And then, I nearly slap myself awake. Of course, he will stay near. He will do this for her. I rest a hand on his shoulder because a storm of raging emotions—anger, indignation, disgust, but most of all anticipation—has rendered me speechless and faint.

He takes my hand and presses his lips on the back and then, with a grand flourish of his arm, he bows low from the waist. "If you insist, Madame."

Butterfly is fascinated by the impeccable landscaping in Beverly Hills, the elegant architecture, and the extravagant women, tanned legs, exposed breasts, leopard-print and leather miniskirts, tattoos.

White orchids, mink bedspreads, and gold-handled guns are

displayed in the Aria Boutique window. Photographs of the designer, his ex-model ex-wife, and his present-model girlfriend look down on us from among the meticulously displayed shoes, negligees, clothing, and giant perfume bottles. Aria's yellow Mercedes, parked in its usual spot on the street in front of the store, is reflected like a luxurious mirage in the window. Our reflections, too—mine, Butterfly's, and Aziz's—flicker and quiver in the window, connecting and disconnecting illusions.

"I'm thinking of Aria's Yellow Orchid Boutique," Butterfly says.

The Yellow Orchid in Tehran was where the two of us spent hours selecting the approaching season's wardrobe. Then, the revolution happened and Aria was forced to abandon his boutique.

"Aria's story is unbelievable," she says. "A dream comes true."

"That's America! You can realize your dream, too."

"Me?" she asks, attempting to arrange her face into a detached expression. "I don't have any! Mine all came true."

Aziz squeezes my arm, slightly too hard. "This isn't for me, *Jounam*. Take your time. Meet me at the Beverly Wilshire bar when you're done." And, to my surprise, he turns on his heel and walks away.

"Is he upset?" Butterfly asks.

"Bored," I reply, certain that it must not be easy for him to witness his wife and mistress exchanging memories.

A stiff-necked doorman ushers us into the plush opulence of Aria's boutique, with its winding double stairs, glittering chandelier, and crystal perfume bottles.

A tall, lanky salesman, clad in a navy striped suit, discreetly follows us. He dabs at his upturned nose with a large, checkered handkerchief.

Aria studies us from the landing at the top of the stairs, dressed in a single-breasted, cream-colored suit with a yellow dress handkerchief in his breast pocket. He approaches the banister, rests two hands on it, and offers us his famous smile.

"Will he remember us?" Butterfly whispers.

Before I have time to wonder, Aria is descending the steps and walking toward us, his capped teeth flashing under the light of the chandelier.

The salesman discards his haughty attitude and stuffs his handkerchief in his pocket as Aria directs him toward a cane-brandishing middle-aged man decked out in cowboy boots, sequined vest, and heavy gold chains.

"Soraya! Parvaneh!" Aria exclaims in his heavy English accent. "My good friends! Welcome, welcome. How are you? How is the family? How long have you been here? Come, come, let me give you the VIP grand tour."

We exchange pleasantries, thank Aria and assure him that we will come back another time for the VIP tour, then solicit his help in updating Parvaneh's wardrobe. Designer shoes, perhaps, high-heeled sandals, something she won't find back home.

"I am your man," Aria exclaims, turning on his heel and returning with a tower of shoe boxes. He kneels down and hugs Butterfly's foot in his lap as if it belongs to his beautiful mistress herself. One after the other, he removes sandals from boxes and holds each pair up for us to assess. I shake my head in disapproval again and again, until Butterfly announces that she is in an adventurous mood and would like to try red shoes.

On one palm, Aria presents a pair of open-toed, sling-back, stiletto-heeled sandals with rhinestone-studded buckles.

Both of us nod our approval.

She struts around the store, waltzes from one mirror to another, pirouettes, glances down and behind, and then parades in front of me in the impossible-to-walk-in, attention-seeking sandals. Her lashes flutter in mock coquetry and her hips swing in rhythmic sensuality, giving life to her other shameless self. "Oh my, my! I really like America." She raises her foot for my benefit. "Tempting?"

"From all angles," I reply.

We laugh at a shared memory. Her belief that it is essential for whatever we wear to tempt from every observed angle.

Our differences, Butterfly's and mine, brought us closer with the passing years and with each experience, especially when it was an important endeavor such as purchasing a pair of shoes. She was practical, refusing to waste money on any article of clothing that could not be used as bait. She believed that since we were forced to cover ourselves from head to toe, surrendering the advantage of manipulation with the lure of flesh, what we chose to wear had to call attention to our sexuality by creating an aura of mystery.

Today, we are of the same opinion. She likes the red sandals that represent her newfound freedom. And that serves me well.

"I know the perfect dress to go with your special shoes," Aria exclaims, leading us to the back of the store.

He walks toward a rack of clothing and holds one up, a black evening dress with lace sleeves. I point to a transparent shell to replace Butterfly's long-sleeved blouse. He pulls out the spaghetti-strapped, low-cut shell and holds the see-through lace up to the light. "A museum piece, I assure you! Hand made in Italy. Especially for the House of Aria."

"You can't be serious!" Butterfly protests. "I refuse to wear this flimsy thing in public."

"But it is all the rage this season, this color and style," Aria coaxes. "A special order for Princess Caroline of Monaco, but I'd rather see it on your beautiful figure. Do try it, my dear. I'll bet on my beardless face that you'll fall in love with it."

Butterfly giggles. "That's what I'm afraid of."

I offer Aria a grateful smile as he leads us to the dressing room, where I peel Butterfly's blouse off, facilitating her transformation. Then I roll the delicate fabric of the shell down over her head and slanted shoulders, smoothing it around her breasts. I feel her warmth, the tender flesh Aziz caresses, where the material clings like second skin, her lace bra peeping out from around the swell of her breast, the dark nipples and the slant of the humid armpits he licks.

Wiping off her morning lipstick, I am all love and encouragement, taking my time to apply a coat of Coco Red lipstick, emphasize her mouth with dark lip liner, powder her cheeks with Violent Blush, and thicken her lashes with two coats of mascara. As I remove the elastic hair band, it breaks with a painful ping against my fingers, which get to work with added fury to undo her braid and fluff her curls about her shoulders.

She steps out of the dressing room to assess herself in a different mirror, pouts her lips at her image, adjusts her breasts in her bra. She likes her transformation.

She gestures toward the salesman, who is on his knees, in the process of hemming the cane-flourishing customer's trousers. "Remember when Aziz kissed your feet on your wedding? He is so special."

"Do you love him?"

She gulps in a large dose of air and begins to cough. Could one choke on one's secrets? Mamabozorg believed that lies lodge in the throat, turning into *badeh yoman*, a coil of black wind that swells up until it eventually suffocates.

I pat Butterfly on the back to dislodge the longing in her throat.

"Love?" she manages to spit out, at last. "Who?"

The tips of my fingers are thermometers at the small of her back, five sensitive lie detectors recording her emotions. "Aziz. I asked if you love him."

"Of course, I love him. Like my own brother." She rummages around in her purse, searching for something, a weak ploy to hide her true emotions. She finds a tissue and wipes her mascara-smudged eyes.

I wrap my arm around her shoulder, the fragile birdlike bones and naked skin. "You look beautiful, my friend. Let's go face America!"

She squints against the harsh sunlight outside. "Are you sure Aziz won't mind the way I'm dressed? I don't know, Soraya. This is a mistake. You go. Have a good time. Mansour will drive me home."

"Why should Aziz mind, Parvaneh?"

"I don't know. He's Iranian, after all."

"Suppose he does. Do you care?"

One artificial dry laugh breaks out of my poor friend. "Why does it feel as if I'm being questioned on Soraya's witness stand?"

"Don't be silly. Come! I'm not going without you. What happened to the adventurous you? You're here, you know, away from home and can have any man you want."

"I love Hamid. I don't want anyone else."

"Liar." I smile and tug at one of her curls. "What about your lover? You want him, don't you?"

"My lover? Oh, him! *Tamam shod*. He's over! Done! Finished. That's that, and I don't want to talk about it anymore."

"Not even to me?"

"No, Soraya, not even to you. I can't even think of that time without burning with shame. Do you understand?"

I want to cry out that I *do* understand, understand better than she could imagine. Instead, I attempt to push away the image of her with bits of my flesh between her teeth, snap my purse open, fish out my handkerchief, and sneeze my rage into its lace folds.

"Are you okay, Soraya?"

"I'm allergic to something around me."

"Want to go back inside?"

"It won't make a difference." No, it won't. I am allergic to her sharp teeth and to her lies and to the boutique we just left and to this ostentatious street and this suffocating smog. I don't want to be here. What I want is to be back home, serving tea the way a good hostess must, scalding hot and steeped with aromatic petals. Yet, I've been taught that nothing worthwhile will come to fruition without the patience of Job and the diligence of Rostam.

I've been taught that justice is hard to come by, but if and once it comes, it is as sweet and tender as love itself. The echo of Baba's stern voice rings in my head: Don't forget yourself, Soraya. Remember that even the harshest of sentences must be handed out with a respectful bow and velvet-gloved hands.

So, once again, I slip into the role of the wiser friend who initiated Butterfly into adolescence, into womanhood, and now coaxes her into the throbbing, smoke-filled Beverly Wilshire bar. The tinkle of glasses punctuates the surrounding chatter. The inviting gurgle of wine, champagne flowing into crystal flutes. The humid scent of aroused bodies, expensive perfumes, apple and cinnamon and passion. The notes of a piano can be heard from somewhere close by.

Aziz observes the two of us as we approach his table. Soraya, tall, lean-figured, and blond; Butterfly, petite and dark-haired—a diverse feast indeed.

Butterfly settles in the chair on Aziz's right. He studies her through narrowed eyes: the deep color of her mouth, the pink cheeks, the provocative attire. He directs a look at me. Is it questioning or reprimanding? "A stiff drink is in order," he announces. "What about you, Parvaneh?"

"A glass of wine, please," she replies.

"But you *must* have something stronger." Sarcasm drips like stale honey from his voice. "Two shots of vodka, perhaps, to complete your get-up."

"You don't approve," she asks, a new defiance in her dark eyes.

"It doesn't matter," I snap, regretting my lack of diplomacy and control. The elastic band of my luck is stretched to the limit. Another tug and it will snap. This is the worst time to raise suspicions, now that in the last forty-eight hours, I've successfully navigated my way through the explosive shores of our tangled relationship.

I pucker my lips and send an apologetic air kiss toward Butterfly. "Wine it is, then, for you. A martini, straight up, for me."

Butterfly runs her fingers through her hair, arranges one leg alongside the other, and adjusts a bra strap that slips down her shoulder, appearing to enjoy the luxury of who she has become in this country. She raises her wineglass and clicks it against mine. A shared smile passes between the two of us, before her wandering eyes, those globes of adoration, flicker away to rest on Aziz in an instant of unintended recklessness that she quickly harnesses. She redirects her gaze around the room, resting here and there and nowhere in particular.

The temperature in the room is rising, a certain heat caused by the promise of what the night might bring—forbidden passions, excitement, and endless expectations.

She turns to me and mouths "handsome," arching an eyebrow and gesturing toward the entrance to the bar.

The clink of goblets and flutes and the notes of the piano cease. A muted commotion somewhere behind. A chill creeps into the room. The throbbing of my heart beneath the thin fabric of my blouse.

Mullah Mirharouni stands at the threshold.

He has abandoned his religious robe and turban. He wears a dark suit and white shirt left open at the collar. His face shows signs of a newly grown beard. In preparation for his return home, perhaps. His gaze swivels around the room. A glint of recognition flashes across his lizard eyes, followed by a cunning smile he quickly stifles.

A *sheitoun* devil takes sudden hold of me, and as if I am alone and the *mullah* a welcome and expected guest, as if nothing out of the ordinary had transpired a few days ago between the two of us upstairs in this very hotel, and as if I had not changed my mind at the last minute and left him high and dry in the throes of sexual arousal, I rise from my chair and wave, inviting him to join me.

A moment of hesitation. He buttons his jacket.

Warning bolts flash in my thrashing heart. This will not end well, not at all. But it is too late.

With quick, confident strides he is crossing the room toward us.

"Who the hell is he?" Aziz hisses under his breath.

"*Salam, azizam* my dear," the *mullah* greets in Farsi with a voice as slippery as an eel.

I settle back into the comfort of my chair. "*Mullah* Mirharouni. Aziz, my husband. And this is Parvaneh, my good friend who I talked about. I met *Mullah* Mirharouni on the plane."

Aziz narrows his eyes at me. "Already Westoxified?" he grunts under his breath.

Butterfly tries unsuccessfully to gather her curls and twist them in back, hug her bare arms, and conceal them under the table all at once. She sinks deeper into her seat. A *mullah* in a bar in America is not what she had signed up for.

Mullah Mirharouni occupies the chair next to her. He extends his hand, but the traumatized Butterfly, having so recently shed her defenses, her many layers of camouflage, keeps her clasped hands under the table.

His outstretched hand, left unshaken, lingers for an instant in midair before Aziz grabs it. "So you met my wife on the plane, *Mullah* Mirharouni!"

"I had the supreme honor, *agha*."

"Enjoyed her company?"

My cheeks scalding embers, I brace myself, torn between hoping for a truth that will hurt deeply, yet terrified of the irreparable damage.

The *mullah* tugs at one sleeve, then another, as if trying to pull the answer out. "Allah be great, *agha*. A servant of God is not worthy of such company."

I hold my breath. The ritual of Iranian double-layered *taarof* and sitting on ceremony sounds sincere on the surface but conceals a truth none of us will like. I wait with morbid curiosity to hear what type of company I happen to be that the *mullah* considers himself unworthy of—a Jew, an infidel, a woman, or simply a tease?

"Such company?" Aziz taunts. "Enlighten me please."

"I congratulate you, *agha*. Your devoted wife hardly looked up from her book. That she remembers my name is a mystery."

Aziz drinks half his glass. He knows his wife better than to believe this.

Having delivered his lies, the *mullah* turns away from me, shifts his chair closer to Butterfly, snaps two fingers, and orders a double shot of vodka straight up. The clamor in my head prevents me from hearing what he is telling her. Color mottles her cheeks and rises all the way to her hairline. Please God, flirt, be yourself, Butterfly. Reveal your true colors.

The *mullah* tosses his head back and gulps down his vodka with the ease of someone who has spent a great deal of time in bars. Tiny beads of moisture appear on the bridge of his nose. He aims his glance at Butterfly's hands under the table. "*Rahat bashid.*" He encourages her to be comfortable.

Aziz shifts in his seat, muscles tense against the insult, a lion bracing for the kill.

Butterfly casts her gaze down. She tweaks and smooths a crease at the edge of the tablecloth. Her hands creep up and rest in her lap.

The room is foul with roiling emotions.

Aziz's voice is loud and harsh. "My dear *agha*, please correct me if I'm wrong, but doesn't the Koran forbid alcoholic drinks?"

"Ah! Yes, of course," the *mullah* replies. "You are absolutely right. Alcohol is forbidden, especially to a man of God. But we are all human and in need of diversion now and then." He aims a conspiratorial wink at Aziz. "I'm sure you understand."

"No!" Aziz replies. "I don't."

"Perhaps you do not want to," the *mullah* retorts. "That, too, is a human trait."

But I do understand. So does Aziz, I'm certain, even if he pretends otherwise, unaware that the *mullah* knows about his affair with Butterfly. Sweat trickles down my armpits at the kindled memories of having shared such intimacies with a stranger on the plane on my way to America.

Did the confession afford me some level of catharsis? Did it help me unburden? I'm not certain. What I know is that the *mullah*'s calm reaction that day, which I recollect with chilling vividness, and his matter-of-fact pronouncement—"It happens more often than you think, sister"—was an explosive fuse that sent me hurtling deeper down the path I am on.

The *mullah* raises Butterfly's glass and hands it to her. She touches her lips to the rim of the glass and puckers her face. I observe her closely, the slight lift of one eyebrow, the subtle flare of her nostrils reacting to the smell of alcohol, the hesitant grip of her fingers as she raises the glass and takes a dainty sip. She puts the glass back on the table. She seems fascinated by a man of God who, in the span of fifteen minutes, has shattered every image she has had of *mullahs*. Never before has she found herself in such close proximity to a *mullah*, let alone in a bar, and with one who drinks the forbidden alcohol as if it were rosewater sherbet.

I latch my gaze on her, willing her to redirect her attention toward me. And she does. The two of us are masters in the art of silent communication. I wink, smile, nod my encouragement, raise my glass to her health and to what the night might have in store. I shut my eyes, throw my head back, and sip my drink, hot and burning like an insult. I am here, my friend, behind you all the way. Don't you worry your pretty little head. Expose your hidden self, the woman who puts the red-district whores to shame.

She raises her glass, dips a finger in the wine and licks it, takes a sip, then another and another.

The *mullah* hands his credit card to the waiter and orders another round of drinks for the table.

Aziz calls the waiter back and, without uttering a word, takes the *mullah*'s credit card and hands the waiter his own. He plants the credit card in front of him. "I'll take care of my own."

This drink Butterfly accepts with less resistance. A smile of adulation brightens her eyes as she exchanges pleasantries with the *mullah*. They laugh. Such effortless laughter, so full of shared understanding and tinted with wine and vodka and anticipation. Please God, let them walk out together. Right now. Right here. Right in front of Aziz.

And soon enough, as if Aziz and I are part of the furniture, the *mullah*'s forefinger taps the back of Butterfly's hand, a playful, flirtatious gesture. I send her another encouraging wink and a discreet lift of my glass. She seeks his gaze with the intimacy of potential lovers, and, yes, she will rise on her drunken feet and leave with him. She certainly will. I breathe again, a breath so deep and fresh and full of hope that I can't remember the last time I enjoyed one.

Aziz throws his napkin on the table and abruptly rises to his feet. He growls under his breath that he has had enough of this charade between a Jewish woman and a Muslim stranger.

I smell his base note of jealousy in its raw and primitive state, devastating and explosive, smell Butterfly's top notes, black honey and brown sugar, sweet and cloying and more than a touch dirty, as she follows us out of the bar.

chapter 32

I FLIP THE ELECTRICAL SWITCH on, and a harsh light saturates my studio and glares off the row of photographs suspended from a wire. My throat tightens at the sight of my forgotten album, abandoned like a bloody stain on the counter. The thought occurs to me to step back out and shut the door behind me, tell Aziz and Butterfly that this is not the right time. Then when *is* the right time, if not now, I wonder, opening the door wide and inviting them in.

I reach out for the album and hand it to Aziz. "I couldn't wait to show you my photographs. Result of my hard work here. Hope you like it as much as I do."

Butterfly approaches the opposite counter. She steps back with a start. I hear the sudden intake of her breath at the display of Aziz's ravaged photographs spread on the counter. Her face turns the shade of bleached bone as she grips the edge of the table to steady herself. Last night's encounter with *Mullah* Mirharouni has left its mark, and she is back to understated makeup—a touch of blush and mascara—a long-sleeved pantsuit, and a foulard tied around her neck. Perhaps my plan backfired and she has raised her guard even higher.

Aziz has opened my album and, oblivious to his surroundings, is turning the pages, absorbed in the collections of my photographs, studying the image of every handsome man, American and

Iranian, in one or another suggestive pose, every lusting gaze fixed on the photographer. Will he understand how the act of hunting, collecting, and trapping men in snapshots—bullets aimed at his heart, which might have become immune to such threats—has kept me sane?

I watch him run the pads of two fingers around the edges of a photograph and pray that if the Lord exists somewhere up there or down here, He will have the photos serve their purpose. Don't let it be too late, Lord. Don't let me lose my husband to the curse of indifference.

Aziz's lips acquire the pinched look I know well, and for an instant I am so delighted he still cares that I am about to hug and assure him that although he can't have Butterfly, I am here to stay.

And then he slaps the album shut and pushes it away. "Rubbish! You are a better photographer than this, Soraya."

Never has he uttered my name as if it's an annoying insect he can't wait to flick away. I don't like it. I expected jealousy and devastation, not such indifference, accompanied by a gesture of his hand that dismisses and erases me all at once. I struggle to keep my emotions from playing on my face. I don't want him to see my enormous disappointment at this final discovery. Here I am, after endlessly casting my net here and there, yet now that the butterfly is at last caught, it's not the one I expected.

I stroke his cheek with the tip of one finger. "You are angry, Aziz. Why?"

"Not at all, *Jounam*. I just don't understand why you'd waste your time on these silly photographs."

A flood of answers renders me momentarily speechless. I can tell him the truth, of course, tell him that I am doing this because I want to hurt him, ruin his heart and face, and make him weak and undesirable. But he is neither of these now. On the contrary. He is more desirable in the way he seems to distance himself from me as he turns away to study the enlarged photograph of himself. He scrutinizes it with a furrowed brow and a frosty gaze.

He shoves aside print tongs and dishes on the counter. With one fast motion, he unsnaps the print from the film clip and drops it face up on the counter. He bends to examine his massacred image—the acidic eyes, turmeric complexion, inflated lips, and dagger-hair painted with coloring brush. He traces the image of one of his ears, outlined with black, wide-tipped marker. I have often imagined the joy of watching the expressions of pain and anger duel on his face, the dredged-up cesspool of emotions. But that is not what I see. Plastered on his face is nothing but a look of disappointment.

"Do you like it?" I ask him.

He tosses the photograph away like a worthless piece of trash and stares at me as though I've gone mad like the Majnoun lover of Persian fairy tales.

"It's an experiment," I feel the need to explain. "An exaggeration to make a point."

The corners of his lips crinkle in a bitter smile. "Really? And what point is that, if I may ask?"

"To show what happens when you don't censor yourself. You create art that solicits all type of reactions. But judging from yours, I've failed."

"I'm not sure how to react anymore. Your art. This place. Last night. I didn't believe that slimy *mullah* for a second, Soraya. I know you better than this. You'd never sit in a plane for twelve hours without striking up a conversation with someone next to you."

"Please, please," Butterfly implores. "Don't fight over last night or a stupid *mullah*. It's all my fault. I shouldn't drink so much when alcohol affects me like that. Can we just stop this and get out of here?"

"We are not fighting," I silence her. "This is between me and my husband."

Regressing to her childhood habit, Butterfly cups her left breast in her hand, weighing a guilt-heavy heart.

In the artificial light of the studio, Aziz's pupils have widened and darkened like a cunning animal, this man who knew me well once but does not know what to make of the woman he created. I want him to be afraid for us, afraid for all the years cloaked in secrecy, for the stink of deception that tons of attar can't wash off. In the menacing silence, I count three drips from the faucet. The house creaks and moans, attempting to settle around us.

Aziz sits on the stool by the sink, crosses his arms in front of his chest, and glares at the photograph.

Wanted alive and competent to stand trial.

"Well, *Jounam*, here I am! Alive and competent to stand trial. What am I on trial for?"

Sour odors saturate the studio. Mine, Butterfly's, and Aziz's, whose eyes have turned darker and harder than onyx. He slaps the print facedown on the counter. "Well, it doesn't seem like you're prepared for trial, Soraya, so pack your bags. I'm taking you home. No! No more excuses! I'm sick of them."

Butterfly grabs the print and waves it in the air like a shameful banner. "Burn it, Soraya! Burn it now!"

"Take your hands off my picture!" I pounce toward her and seize her by the shoulders, shaking her like a lifeless rag doll.

Aziz jumps up from the stool. "Enough! What's gotten into you, Soraya? Leave her alone."

Something stirs in my guts. Fear? No! I don't often experience fear. But I recognize a nagging sense that Aziz is tugging at the remaining threads that hold the torn pieces of our relationship together and is slowly and persistently unraveling the entire fabric.

Suddenly I feel like a dumb *ahmagh* clueless donkey. My husband is deeply in love. But not with me. He is in love with *her*. He did not make this trip, all the way to America, to take me back home. He is here because he can't bear being away from *her*, not even for the ten days she came to America.

No, I will not come undone and disappear. I might have lost my aura of mystery to you, but I've held on to the power of my secrets. I have a surprise for you, Aziz. None of us are going back home. I will cause you grief. Deep, devastating grief. Once Butterfly is gone, with no trace of foul play in the autopsy, I will not abandon you, Aziz, but be here to nurse you back to health as a good wife must. Watch over you while you suffer, damaged by shame and remorse and loss with no one to turn to but your faithful wife.

I hold my breath in until I can't bear the pressure in my lungs, exhale slowly and deliberately before facing the two of them, already huddled at the threshold, ready to flee, ready to leave me behind in my studio with nothing but my memories sealed in films and locked in black plastic cylinders lined up on the top shelf, abandon me to the stench of processing solutions, developing chemicals, stop bath, and failure.

I summon my sweetest voice and say, "I'm really sorry, Aziz. I shouldn't have done that to your lovely face. You, too, Parvaneh. Forgive me, will you? Let me make it up to you both. Go freshen up. I'll serve you delicious tea in my garden."

chapter 33

THE SIGHT OF MY garden seems to disgust Aziz. He murmurs that he has never seen such *harjomarj* mish-mash of plants and flowers thrust together.

"But it's adorable." Butterfly's eyes sweep the landscape in wonder. "All the different flowers and butterflies living in harmony."

I smile agreeably because I don't want to admit to the sleepless dawns, the long hours of work, the love and hatred I've raked, planted, and watered into this foreign soil. Don't want to admit that I like what my garden has evolved into, the lewd excess of raging colors, overpowering scents, and dizzying array of butterflies reminiscent of a whore's den. A violent kaleidoscope of climbing jasmine overwhelms the gazebo. Rodents nestle in dense bushes, water lilies in ponds, mites in blossoms, and grasshoppers on the birds of paradise.

And at the farthest end of the grounds, I like the lush eucalyptus grove that, despite being struck by a second plague—this one at midnight like a guilty thief, the drone of invading wings startling me awake and sending me to the grove with Mansour before the pests had a chance to inflict much damage—continues to be a haven for devious Monarchs.

Yes, I like the thorny patches and tangled branches, like the climbing philodendron, the floating nightshade in the fountain, and the entire family of screaming flowers that reflect the shape I'm assuming.

But above all, I like the grave that occupies its own lonely space in unassuming grandeur at the end of the eucalyptus grove, unaware that a companion is on the way.

What I don't like is the strange silence of my Bird of Reason. She has abandoned her throne on the monkey tree in the courtyard and flown into the garden to perch on top of the entrance to the gazebo, regal, silent, and still, as if cast out of some type of mottled alloy. I whistle three times to announce my presence. But instead of evoking the usual flurry of acknowledging flaps before she comes to land on my arm or shoulder, she remains motionless. Dignified. Grand. Disapproving.

Aziz and Butterfly take the path to the eucalyptus grove, and I enter the gazebo to prepare tea. From my vantage, between the branches, I watch them stroll among the trees. Monarchs flutter above them like sunny halos, as if to bless their union. But no rabbi, priest, monk, or ayatollah would officiate such a wedding.

They must be exchanging impatient love-complaints, their first chance to sneak away alone. He, lying that he did not and does not want to make love to me, begging her to be patient. She, reassuring him that I suspect nothing, whispering under her breath that she will die if she doesn't have him to herself.

Bowls of fruit, dates, rock sugar, and pistachio are set on the wrought-iron table. A silver samovar gurgles on a side table. A jar full of Amorphophallus tea stands next to a box of Darjeeling tea bags. Three cups are carefully arranged on a tray with arabesque carvings. Two gold teaspoons lie at an angle on two saucers, one for me and one for Aziz. A silver one in Butterfly's saucer.

Mamabozorg reminds me that no matter where I am in the world, I shouldn't forget that I am Iranian and that it is important to steep and serve tea properly.

"In my many years of experience," Mamabozorg says, "I've never been involved in a business, the signing of an agreement, the promise of marriage, or made a vow, affirmed a friendship, or shared a secret without holding a cup of tea in my hand. For us, Soraya, a cup of tea is like a trusted friend between two hands. Use it to advantage, sip or stir slowly when you need time to think, add sugar when the news is not good, click the cup on its saucer when the need arises to startle."

My friend ambles among the Monarchs, seeming childlike and pure, yet rich with mystery and deceit. She has experienced her own form of metamorphosis, managed to survive the rigors of the last two nights and days, cast off her skin, and evolved into a seductive butterfly.

But I am not deceived. I recognize Butterfly for what she is: a poisonous caterpillar that has invaded my habitat.

I pry the jar of Amorphophallus tea open. A loud hiss and, with it, the masking aroma of rose petals. Do toxins expand when left unattended?

Fine tea, Mamabozorg believes, is like premium wine. The color and bouquet are important. When held up to the light, tea must not be too weak so that light passes through without exposing the character, nor too dark to conceal the cognac gleam of its heart.

Aromatic leaves of the highest quality are selected, preferably from the mountainous regions of Ceylon or Darjeeling where the plants grow slowly, allowing time for the complex flavors to develop. A multitude of herbs and spices—cardamom, ginger, black currant, mint, jasmine, or rose petals add a pleasing aroma.

The process of brewing is a delicate art of precision and control that requires the proper accoutrements. Water in a silver samovar must reach a boiling point before being poured over tea leaves in a china pot. Once the leaves are submerged in hot water, the teapot is filled to three-fourths and placed on the neck of the samovar to brew for no less than twenty minutes and no more than half an hour. Otherwise, the color will turn muddy and a thin layer of foam will appear on top that would render the entire mixture worthless.

Narrow-waisted glasses with filigreed holders are preferable, and handles are essential to avoid burning the fingers. The glasses are set on small saucers with miniature spoons placed on the right of the glass. Glasses must be arranged in perfect order on a tray, the handles facing guests, the tray held low and at a comfortable serving level.

"Always serve tea in transparent glasses, Soraya, always. Tea that reveals its shade and character speaks of an open-hearted hostess. Those china cups with tiny rose designs on them are good for the British, who have a lot to hide. Never, ever serve lukewarm or cold tea. You want the warm liquid to soothe your guest's throat and stomach as it's sipped through a sugar cube. And never refuse a cup of tea. It's rude, unless, of course, it's offered to you by your enemy."

Butterfly's laughter, loud and carefree and shameless, reaches me all the way from the eucalyptus grove.

It was over mint tea years before that Butterfly disclosed her affair to me.

Later, I went through a list of possible candidates in my mind, single or divorced, friend and family, but failed to come up with the right fit. I wondered why she would keep her lover's identity a secret from me, wondered how any man could have so swiftly and completely infatuated her. I pressed her to tell me. She would not. Years passed. In time, whoever he was in my mind transformed into a mythological being, a romantic hero larger than the Romeos and Majnoons of classical literature.

Then, I found him with his eyes closed shut and his mouth glued to hers, on my sheets, surrounded by my photographs, my bedroom pulsing with notes of "The Blue Danube." They didn't notice me. Of course, they didn't. The Devil himself might have carried them off to the bowels of hell, and they wouldn't have broken their tight hold.

So began the deadly struggle to reconcile the ideal lover I had seared in my imagination with the traitor in my bed, who came inside me the very next day after I discovered his betrayal.

I take my sweet time to separate and remove the dried rose

petals from the Amorphophallus leaves, a last-minute decision to render the tea more potent, then fill the teapot with hot water from the samovar and add fresh tea leaves. A drop of the dark liquid spills on the tabletop and I blot it with my forefinger.

I summon my steadiest voice and call out, "Tea is almost ready!"

Their approach transports the menthol scent of eucalyptus leaves. Despite their attempt to readjust their expressions, their hooded eyes reveal more than they can imagine. Yellow powder from the wings of Monarchs has settled on Butterfly's cheeks. Aziz dusts the powder off with his handkerchief.

Such a simple act. Such an intimate act.

Let him stroke her one last time, if he must. In the end, he belongs to me. I am the one he will need once the tears, the remorse, and the appeals for forgiveness spill out.

We occupy the chairs around the table, drop napkins on our lap as refined guests must do. Aziz takes my hands and, finding them cold, blows on them. His expressive face is sad under the shadow of afternoon stubble, his lower lip is curled like a question mark. I raise his palm and study his heart line, the straight and curved grooves that speak of deceit and betrayal, a heart line that ends below the index finger, reflecting a nature easily shaped by others, easily hurt by others. Poor Aziz. Hard times are in store for you, but I'll be there to love, nurture, and console you.

"Look, Aziz, this line stretches uninterrupted. You'll live a long life. I wonder if other lines might predict the quality of our lives. Are we going to be happy? Content? Or sad and miserable?"

"I don't believe in this nonsense, *Jounam*. If the old you comes back, my life will be just fine."

"Old me!" I grin, making light of his comments. "What's wrong with me now?"

A hesitant moment passes. A bee buzzes its way in and lands on Butterfly's shoulder. I flick it off. The samovar lets out a series of burps. I check my watch as if nature is holding her breath and there's a deadline for what is about to occur.

"Read mine," Butterfly interrupts, reaching out an open palm that smells humid and demanding like the water hyacinth. The day Mamabozorg warned me about the "green plague," the beautiful, but voracious water hyacinth that strangles every growth in its path, she must have known that the green menace would follow her beloved granddaughter all the way to the edge of the world. Shape your own fate, she advised. God holds back His blessings from those who allow their lives to go to waste.

I run my thumb the length of Butterfly's lifeline. She is not wearing her wedding band. Whereas I continue to sport my two wedding bands that were meant to strengthen my love bond, now a constant reminder of my failure. I stroke the grooves of Butterfly's crooked palm. Not a straight line to her name. "I can't find your lifeline."

She snatches her hand away, spits to her right and left, and murmurs incantations under her breath. "Bite your tongue back, Soraya. Don't invite bad luck."

I glance up through the jasmine branches to find my Bird of Reason perched on top of the gazebo outside. I clap twice. Whistle a Persian tune. I want her to come inside. I want her to keep me company.

"Have you seen her owl?" Butterfly asks Aziz. "It looks exactly like Mamabozorg's owl."

"That owl?" Aziz nods and gestures up as if to say that he has seen the bird somewhere out there. "It's not as handsome as Mamabozorg's owl."

"Time for tea," I announce.

"Can you buy Persian tea in America?" Butterfly asks.

"Everything can be bought here, from *shireh morgh* to *janeh adamizad*—chicken milk to human life."

Butterfly claps happily. "It's almost like home."

Her kitchen in Iran, on Africa Avenue, was our living room, dining room, and therapy office all in one. This was where we gossiped and cried and laughed and sipped tea. I can still conjure up the taste of her elaborate recipes, even to a sprinkling of cinnamon on top of her rice custard *shirberenj* and a pinch of saffron in her *halva*, to the taste of her chickpea cookies with slivers of pistachio, and grape leaves stuffed with nuts and dates. I can still hear her say, "A man's desire begins in his stomach." I did not agree with her then. Yet, she proved the clever one, after all. Did she seduce my husband with her cooking, too?

I lift the teapot from the neck of the samovar, tilt it high above the cup, and observe the liquid, deep amber and laced with potential, pour from the spout and form a rich puddle in the cup. "Dark tea for you, Butterfly."

I drop English Darjeeling tea bags in cups for Aziz and myself. She knows that Aziz and I are not tea drinkers in the traditional sense and that we prefer light tea prepared with tea bags. I place Aziz's cup on the table in front of him.

A blade of sunshine makes its way through the branches and glints on the samovar. A lizard falls off the overhead branches and lands at my feet. I give the animal a gentle shove with my shoe.

Butterfly reaches out for the sugar bowl, drops two sugar cubes in her tea, and stirs absentmindedly.

With a great swoosh of spread wings, my owl glides through the branched archway and into the gazebo, raising a faint scent of wet feathers. Silently, gracefully, she settles on the table next to the grumbling samovar. She shifts from one leg to another, puffs up her chest, her bespectacled eyes boring into me.

The phoenix brooch on my collar feels heavy, weighted down by much more than precious stones and metals, the smooth pearl in the center, the cold diamonds on the wings, one hundred and thirty six carats of brilliance. A token of his regret? A gift to assuage his own guilt? No! *Baksheesh* money to shut me up. But it is time to speak, to suffer together as we hear accounts of years of betrayal. Once intimate details are voiced, digested, and absorbed, we will all be irreparably damaged together.

I disengage the pin from my sweater and attach it to Butterfly's jacket. Her breath smells of the odorous, buttery substance civet cats secrete when in danger.

"Soraya!" Aziz growls. "What are you doing with my gift?"

Butterfly unfastens the brooch from her coat and drops it on the table as if it's burning her hand.

"I saw the two of you together in my bed," I whisper.

"Saw who?" Aziz demands.

"Saw you, Aziz, with this whore, copulating in my bed."

He lifts his hand and bangs it on the wrought-iron table, rattling the china cups. "What the hell are you talking about? You've gone mad, Soraya!"

"*You* are the crazy one!" I cry out, jumping to my feet and holding onto the table, afraid the teacups will break and render everything useless. "I saw everything, Aziz. The candles. The wine. Heard the music."

Butterfly's eyes dart around to seek a safer place. Her trembling legs take small backward steps, but there's nowhere to flee.

I grab her hand. Force her back into her chair.

Aziz pulls a crumpled packet of cigarettes out of his coat pocket—Oshnoo, strong and filterless. It is his first cigarette since his arrival ninety-six hours, two-thousand eight-hundred and eighty minutes ago. He draws deeply, letting out a spiral of smoke behind which his narrowed eyes and pinched mouth obtain a haunted expression.

A white halo frames Butterfly's pale mouth, cleansed of the last trace of lipstick. She slides the cup toward her, but unable to summon the strength to lift, pushes it away, too close to the edge of the table.

I slide it back to safety.

My heart settles. My hands no longer tremble. My voice is calm now that we have arrived here at last, hurtling toward some uncertain but inevitable closure. "I want to know everything, Aziz."

His once grand body succumbs to the seat cushions. "Why, Soraya? Why destroy the rest of what we have left together?"

"Not destroy, Aziz. Salvage."

He wipes sweat off his face. "I came home early that day. I can't tell you how often I wished you'd been there instead of:..."

"This, this...Parvaneh?"

"Yes."

"What time of day was it?"

"What difference does it make now?"

"The exact time."

"Early evening like now. We had lost power in the office. You were working."

"What did you do first?"

"I changed, like always. Poured a glass of wine. Turned on the music. Read the papers."

In the gathering dusk, in my garden, I listen with morbid interest, my rage mounting at his remembrance of every minute detail. When in love, the body secretes pheromones that sharpen the senses, alert the mind, and hone our sense of smell. When in hate, we suffer the same changes. I, too, will forever live with the memory etched in the crevices of my wounded heart, "The Blue Danube," the stench of candles, their hungering mouths.

His cigarette burns his fingers. He tosses the butt underfoot and grinds it with his heel. His gaze seeks Butterfly, who is shrinking in her skin. Her eyes have lost their shine; her teeth have disappeared behind her tight-lipped expression. Aziz's furious fingers fish another cigarette out of the pack and drum it on the tabletop. "The doorbell rang and I thought you'd forgotten the key to the house. She was sobbing at the door. Problem with Hamid she wanted to discuss with you."

I see Butterfly, timid and slightly sheepish, appear at the door and fall into my husband's arms as if he was the only safe haven remaining to her, the god who will wave a benevolent arm and wipe out all her troubles. I have known her far too long not to have witnessed the seductive, almost erotic moments of her vulnerability. Aziz is not to blame. Had she not trapped me into friendship in the same smooth, slick manner?

Aziz lights another cigarette with a flick of his lighter. "One moment we were sitting there discussing Hamid, the next…" He drops the lighter on the table. "Believe me, Soree. It had nothing to do with love."

I fight with all of my might to maintain the fading remnants of my trust. I want so much to believe him, even though he is lying with a face wiped clean like a just-painted wall. "What then? What was it?" I ask the question, but pray that he'll have the dignity and wisdom not to answer.

He shuts his red-rimmed, dry eyes and rests his elbows on his knees, cradling his head between his hands. I want to reach out and stroke his hair that tumbles over his face, touch his eyes, this man whose pain and grief is tucked away so far and deep that he has forgotten how to cry. I wish you were man enough to cry, Aziz. If not now, then when? When is a good time to shed tears for our senseless loss?

He raises his head, and his stare slashes through me like a shock of ice water. "You really want the truth, Soraya?" He leans forward to make his point. "If you have to know, Parvaneh needed me that night, and it felt good, really good, because you never do."

"And why is this bad?"

"A man," he replies with a bitter smile, "wants his wife to need him. Your independence, Soraya, make me feel unnecessary sometimes."

And instead of telling him how wrong he is and how very deeply I need him, even now that he has betrayed me, I lash out, swearing that I refuse to become my mother, who can only see herself in her husband's reflection. My mother, who can only exist under my father's overreaching shadow. "No, Aziz, I won't become a martyr and resort to deception. Become someone I am not." I say this with defiance but little conviction because I *have* become my mother, after all.

Butterfly sobs in her cupped palms. The stench of civet grows stronger. She pulls the saucer with the cup of tea toward her. A stream of the caramel-colored liquid spills from the porcelain lip, trickles down the side of the cup, and pools in the saucer. She sets the cup back down again.

I push it further away from her, not wanting her to drink her tea before I am done with her, wanting nothing to break our fall until we land with a loud thud, sullied, bruised, and forever lost. "Don't try to fool me, Aziz. It wasn't that one night. You fucked her and kissed her and loved her for years and years. Parvaneh told me herself."

"Please, Soraya," she begs. "Don't."

"What the hell are you talking about?" Aziz's voice is almost lost beneath a series of intrusive barks from my owl.

"That Noruz night when Parvaneh ran into the streets. You remember, of course. She pretended to take a bottle of Valium and we rushed her to the hospital."

"Soraya! Stop it! Not in front of Aziz," she pleads.

"Why not, my friend? He is your lover, after all. The man you were ready to commit suicide for! Yes, Aziz, she told me she'd lost 'her man,' her exact words that night. She said she hoped 'her man' would pity her and resume the relationship once he found out she attempted suicide. But how would he find out, I asked, since only Hamid, you, Aziz, and I were there that night. Here's what she said: 'He will find out. Trust me, he will.' And you did, Aziz. Of course you did. You were there."

A roar, like the howl of an animal, reverberates in the garden. The cry of my husband's anger. And on his face an expression of utter shock and disbelief. "What in the world are you talking about?"

"*You* tell *me*!" I scream back.

The metal legs of his chair grate underfoot as he pushes away from the table. He looms over Butterfly, his anger more menacing than any curse. "What did you tell Soraya?"

Her face speckled with tears and mascara, she recoils from the furious flare of his eyes. Her hand crawls toward the teacup. I snatch it away from her and put it back on the table. Not now. Not now that Aziz and I are momentarily united, the sheer force of our rage about to annihilate her.

She jumps out of her chair and runs out of the gazebo, fleeing into the fecund canopy of eucalyptus.

The hiss of her fighting lungs, crackle of breaking branches, and snap of leaves under her steps alert us to her flight ahead as we follow her into the tangle of trees. Then silence. Such profound silence that Aziz and I stop and glance at one another. For a sweet instant I allow myself to believe that despite Butterfly, despite the lies, mine and his, he still belongs to me.

The sound of retching sends an orange cloud of quivering butterflies off the surrounding leaves.

Aziz's features harden again, dark and indifferent and remote.

I thrust the boughs aside, damp earth giving way under my shoes as I advance deeper into the creeping vegetation, the invasion of moss and fungi, the clamor of insects and flurry of Monarchs. Sunlight filters through the caving canopy of branches overhead, the low-limbed trees and dense tangle I break into.

Butterfly is doubled over with the effort to empty her stomach of an indigestible mountain of deception. Bile splashes against the slab of pink marble of the grave at the end of the grove and, like brown quicksilver, clings to the engraved gold letters—*Beloved Friend and Husband, Your Memory Forever Lives.* She steps back, alarmed, trying to escape the grave, but heaves and coughs anew and retches on the block of marble until nothing is left but foam.

We wait, Aziz and I, observing Butterfly clutch her belly. She was not prepared for this. She thought she was going to get a holiday in Los Angeles. She thought there was nothing to do here except lounge about, gossip, and recharge herself for him.

She breaks eucalyptus leaves off a nearby branch and wipes her mouth.

I am struck by a fresh wave of grief. I step closer and lean over her. "Parvaneh?" The smell of mud, vomit, and deceit is nauseating.

Her face is streaked by splintered shadows of branches and strands of hair loosened from her braid. Her neck is mottled red.

"How often did you fuck my husband? Weeks? Years? Every single day?"

"Tell Soraya the truth!" Aziz booms.

Butterfly rises and leans against me, resting her head on my shoulder as if it is old times and we are in the hospital after her stomach has been pumped of nothing.

Mosquitoes buzz around my ears. I slap one dead against my cheek. I want Aziz to wipe off the bloody mark, a small affectionate gesture. But embroiled in his own theatricals, he continues to feign ignorance and demand the truth from her.

She lets out a great sigh. Falls lifeless on the scattered leaves underfoot.

"No!" I scream, shaking her. "Breathe, Parvaneh, breathe." I want her conscious and accountable. I want to watch her squirm and writhe and suffer. I want to serve her a nice, large glass of Amorphophallus tea.

I wipe her face clean with the palm of one hand. She will recover, this catlike woman with more than nine lives.

I struggle with her weight as we walk out of the claustrophobic grasp of trees and the grave that moans and sighs behind our retreating steps.

Aziz grunts and I am not sure whether he is concerned for his lover or doesn't understand why I am helping her. I am certain he wouldn't want me to leave her among the eucalyptus, lifeless and soiled in mud and vomit. He refuses to lend me a hand as, with great difficulty, I maneuver her limp body into a chair in the gazebo. I adjust her collar, push her wet hair off her face, and stop myself from offering to apply lipstick on her pale mouth to honor a semblance of decorum. I fill a teacup with water from the fountain and rinse her face, pat her dry with my sleeve.

She is not allowed oblivion. Not yet. Not in this world.

chapter 34

"How long have you been fucking my husband, Parvaneh?"

I sit here in the gazebo, wedged between Butterfly and Aziz, demanding an answer from my stone-faced friend.

Frogs croak and crickets scurry among the carpet of flowers. Minutes or hours pass—time has lost its meaning—as I reflect upon our losses, Aziz's, Butterfly's, and mine. I am torn between wanting to wrap a consoling arm around my friend's narrow shoulders or else stabbing her blind with sharp fingernails. I long to offer Aziz a glass of rosewater sherbet, long to bring a spark of life back to his eyes, even as I want to prolong this painful wait that is stickier than *gaz* nougat.

Outside, unexpected winds swallow the breeze, and beyond the hills, the sky is heavy with convoluted clouds. Night is falling. A chill in the air. Tea is brewing in the teapot. When all is told, we will have the rest of our messy lives to resettle at our homes, search for a sanctuary in foreign lands, or ask for absolution in other worlds.

I steal a glance at my owl, begging for her approval. She has not moved from her post by the steaming samovar. She continues to gauge me with huge eyes, the fiery shade of hammered gold, seething with wrath and wisdom. I want her to flutter and bark and groan, fly away if she has nothing better to offer than this incriminating silence.

Butterfly and Aziz's bodies are turned away from each other like rattlesnakes coiled into themselves. When secrets are exposed, lovers become enemies, unable to face one another. Aziz's once inebriated eyes are sober, his once plump mouth is a threat. A cigarette is idle between his fingers.

I want to stroke his pale face, the dark shadow under his chin, bring drunkenness back to his beautiful eyes. I want to touch my lips to the artery at the side of his neck that pumps nervous blood and tell him that I need him more than he will ever understand. I move my chair closer to Butterfly and study her for a long time. She knows I want the truth, knows that I have it in me to wait forever if necessary, that I will not release her until I hear every painful detail of how she robbed me of everything I hold dear.

She tugs at the collar of her blouse as if it's suffocating her. "No, Soraya! I won't say another word. You can't make me."

Aziz's voice startles us all. "Talk, woman! You are killing Soraya!"

Butterfly stares at the strands of hairs she pulled from her head. "*Khodaya*! God! It's bad. You don't understand."

I believe her. I certainly do. It will be bad, this spilling out of secrets. Once she uncorks herself, she will not hold back the most painful details until nothing is left but the remnants of our ruined lives.

My owl's head rotates a full circle. Its weary eyes reflect disgust as they come to rest on Butterfly as if to say: here we go, at last.

Butterfly's breath permeates the gazebo with the biting odor of civet. Her low voice silences the clamor in the garden. "Aziz told you the truth. That evening…in your house…it never happened again. It was a terrible mistake."

They all say that, don't they? The cheaters with their roaming eyes. Thieves with filching hands. All of them, with their wandering hearts, they all say it was a terrible mistake and expect a forgiving kiss on their erogenous spot in the center of their foolish little heads.

"You have to believe me, Soraya!" She pants as if she has been running for hours to reach this place. "This…this…our…Aziz and me. It only happened once."

"You lie," I cry out. "I don't believe you!"

"It's the truth, Soraya. It's no excuse, I know. Even that I'll regret until I die."

I shut her down with a piercing glare and a gesture of my raised hand. "What about the Noruz you pretended to take sleeping pills to scare Aziz? Do you think I forgot that?"

"*Khodaya*! God! It's not what you think, Soraya."

"Really! Then why wouldn't you tell me his name? Tell me who he is?"

In the twilight, her face is the hue of the jasmine creepers that claw their way up and around the gazebo like thieves in the night. She clutches the Buccellati brooch forgotten on the table, nicks the tip of her finger on the wing of the phoenix, and lets out a small cry. A drop of blood sprouts on her finger. She licks it with the tip of her tongue.

I grab her face between my hands and hiss right into her lying eyes, "Tell the truth! Or I'll strangle you in front of your lover."

"Back off, Soraya!" Aziz roars. "Let the woman speak!"

My owl hops to the edge of the table and cocks her head. Her round-eyed stare sweeps the length of our bodies. She tosses her head this way and that, and then, to the accompaniment of a low rumble emanating from deep inside, rotates her neck one full circle, the back of her head dismissing us.

"I want to die," Butterfly groans. "I caused you such pain, Soraya…and now…Oh! God! Are you sure? Just tell me to shut up! It's better than the truth."

The winds howl in my ears. A chill pierces my bones and settles in my marrow. Perhaps I should not solicit added grief, should not replace suspicion with certainty that will lead to more pain. Yet I open my mouth like a dumb marionette and say: "I want to know everything, Parvaneh. Everything!"

"It was another man, Soraya."

"I don't believe you. If it was, why would you keep him a secret from me?"

"Because I can't tell you."

"Of course you won't tell me you are fucking my husband!"

Aziz curls his hands into fists and I think he might strike her. "You are a cruel woman, Parvaneh! Cruel and shameless. Tell the truth. Now! Or I'll kick you back to where you came from!"

"All right! If you want to know I'll tell you." Disjointed words seep through her lips. "The other man, Soraya…the other man…" She stares directly at me, as frightened as I've ever seen her. "The other man was your Baba."

I jump up. My chair topples behind me with a dull clang. "Baba? Baba! *My* father?"

Aziz towers over Butterfly and shouts, "You *doroughgou* liar! How dare you!"

"I don't believe you either," I scream. "You evil woman. My Baba would never have an affair with someone his daughter's age. Why, Parvaneh? Why are you lying like this?"

Her fingernails draw bloody threads along her cheeks. "I wish it was a lie, Soraya. Remember when Baba became interested in your flowers? When he asked for the copper planter you bought in Paris, the one engraved with the dragon and bamboo shoots?"

Of course, I remember. Every one of my plants and their containers are etched in the archives of my memory. But how could Butterfly, who'd never stepped into my greenhouse, know the flowerpot I had purchased from Marché aux Puces?

"You planted Silver Beads in it, didn't you? The plant has silvery leaves and black stems."

"Daddy Long Legs!" Aziz murmurs, exchanging a glance with me. But this time we don't laugh at our secret joke. The tangled stems that looked like our chief rabbi's signature don't strike us as funny anymore. I lavished such care on this plant that Aziz threatened to "dismember his rival."

Aziz draws from his cigarette. Smoke drifts out of his mouth and spirals in front of his face. The spark of shared understanding is extinguished.

"Baba wanted the plant for me," Butterfly says, "as well as the other ones you gave him. Go back and trace the dates he asked you for a plant or some type of flower. The dates fall on my birthday."

Her words settle in my bones like toxic mercury. Fragments click and connect like synapses, every incident, every detail becoming transparent with fresh meaning. Long-ago events should have alerted me. I should have suspected that day when Baba began driving Butterfly home from high school. When he, who never meddled in other people's lives, went on a crusade to punish Aunt Tala. When he started to visit my greenhouse and show interest in my plants. And I should have suspected something when Baba changed his will in favor of Butterfly.

Yes, I ought to have suspected that Butterfly, too, in her own timid way, was on a journey to shape herself into the woman Baba admired, meek and dependent and clinging to his every word.

But above all, I should have known that when Madar, in silence and without explanation, moved out of Baba's bed, a momentous event had forced her to acknowledge defeat at last, transform herself into a martyr, and bury her pain under a carapace of silence. We each react differently to betrayal.

Butterfly's voice comes from somewhere far away, a calm tone that comes with the knowledge that there's nothing left to hide. "Soraya, it was all my fault. Baba was like my father and mother in one. The family I never had. I was lonely. He helped me become a woman. No! Please, wait. Not only in that way."

My shoulders ache under the weight of the arm Aziz wraps around me. My eyes burn; my lips are chapped. I raise one hand and command Butterfly to stop. "I would have recognized my plants in your house. I never saw any."

"He gave me a spare key to his secret apartment. I kept the plants there."

"Baba has a secret apartment?" I say this once. Then again. And once again. Snap! The last frayed remnants of my denial break.

A mascara-tainted tear rolls down the corner of Butterfly's eye.

We share another moment, Aziz and I. No need for words. The dining-room set with high-backed chairs, the china plates and teacups with the design of tiny irises, the queen-size bed with the carved walnut headboard, these were not to help Baba furnish his partner's bachelor pad. They were for his secret apartment.

"Don't blame Baba. Please, don't." Butterfly repeats it a few times, and I don't know if she's trying to convince me or herself. "I became so clingy. Refused to let go. I wanted something of what you had. He was horrified when Madar became suspicious. He stopped seeing me after that. I reacted like a spoiled child who had lost another father. So, I pretended to kill myself. Oh, Soraya, what did I do? I betrayed everyone I love! *Elahi bemiram*, I want to die."

Winds make their way into the gazebo, seep through my forming cracks, and whistle in my guts, dashing through my veins and swelling everything out of shape. Nothing looks the same. My garden that once throbbed with life is curdled with regrets now. Their world gutted, the butterflies have lost their luster and droop listless on dull fauna and flora.

A subtle shadow flutters at my peripheral vision, and my *Morgheh Hagh* comes to life like a forgotten wish. She levitates above our table, and I wonder if she is flapping her wings in a silent farewell. I don't blame her. Why would she remain behind to witness this unfolding insanity? For once, Mamabozorg was wrong. This Owl of Reason did not settle in my garden to bring good luck.

She whooshes past me, soars over and above Aziz, grazes Butterfly's hair, then sails ahead to hover in place at the threshold of the gazebo. Behind, the remnant of a bloody sunset stains the horizon.

I ignore my owl, draw a deep breath, and summon the strength to lift Butterfly's cup. It is lukewarm, useless, and undrinkable. I empty the tea underfoot and, for an instant, expect the poisonous brew to bore a hole into the earth.

"Sit, Soraya!" Aziz says. "No one wants tea."

I turn my back to him, lift the teapot, and pour my friend a cup of fresh tea, strong and dark and lethal. This she deserves and more, I argue with myself. She deserves this for what she did to us—me, Aziz, Baba, and my Madar who suffered in silence all these years. But what about Baba? What about the wiser, more experienced accomplice? Does he deserve to die, too?

I tell myself I'm here now, on the other side of the world, and don't care if I'll ever see him again. But I do. I care very much. I tell myself to forget this selfish man who betrayed Madar and, in the process, tainted my relationship with her. Forget this man who did not even have the decency to keep his slimy hands off a clingy, immature girl. But even as I say this, I know that I will never forget my Baba.

Butterfly holds the cup of hot tea between her hands. She stares into the dark liquid as if baffled by my inexplicable gesture of hospitality. Her lips touch the rim of the cup.

A hard fist forms in my stomach.

My owl zooms past me and with brutal force lands on Butterfly's forearm.

She screams as hot tea spills over her breasts and splashes on her thighs. She collapses on spattered tea, her face squashed against broken shards of china on the tabletop. When she raises her face, it is a network of fine, bloody cuts. "I'm to blame, Soraya. Baba didn't want to…well, it doesn't really matter now."

In that she is right. Nothing matters now. The cup is shattered. Tea spilled. The stink of burnt Amorphophallus leaves scream from the teapot that sizzles and spits dry on the neck of the samovar. They can all explode into a consuming fire, for all I care—the teapot and the samovar, as well as this gazebo.

chapter 35

We exchange silent glances, Aziz and I, in our first private moments together after Butterfly has fled our company in the gazebo to pack for their early-morning flight.

It is quiet around us as if the turmoil of the last hours evaporated when Butterfly left us. The sun has set. The shards of china on the table are gray in the dusk. I raise the phoenix and attach it to my blouse. I like this moment, alone with my husband.

Aziz rests his hand on my arm, his touch fierce and unrelenting. "I can't make sense of you, Soraya. Was I blind? Are you the same woman I married?"

I remain silent because I am not the same woman, of course. How could I be when so much has happened?

A breeze makes its way into the gazebo and tosses his hair onto his forehead. A series of emotions chase each other across his face. "Tell me, Soraya. Did you never love me?"

An angry sob escapes from my throat. I attempt to gulp a breath of damp air, double over with dry coughs. Never, ever did I expect Aziz to question my love for him. Never, ever did I expect this intolerable injustice. "I will tell you what real love is, Aziz. Prove how much I love you." My throat feels raw and I think I might lose my voice. "My pills, Aziz, my pills."

He comes closer. "What pills, Soraya?"

"My pills."

"Pills?" A flash of concern in his eyes. "Are you sick?"

"My birth control pills."

"Your birth control pills?"

"Yes. I did it for you, for us. This is how deeply I love you."

"What the hell are you talking about?"

"About the birth control pills I've been taking. You know why? Because I can't bear to share you, Aziz. Not even with our own child."

"What are you saying, Soraya?"

"We breathe together. We cry and laugh and think together. A third addition would damage us. Shatter what we have. We are one, Aziz."

An imperceptible change takes over, a hardening of his mouth, a darkening of his shuttering eyes. "How long has this been going on, Soraya? How long?"

"Ever since we married."

"All these years, you could have had my child?" An artery jumps at the side of his neck that is mottled with anger.

"I don't need children, Aziz. You're all I need."

He picks up the bowl of sugar and hurls it onto the tabletop.

Shards of glass rain down. One last piece of china clings to the iron rim of the table, then falls silently. Sugar cubes and bowls of dates and pistachio and rock sugar scatter underfoot.

"Baba's betrayal pales compared to what you've done to me, Soraya!"

I turn toward him like a furious god, my hand darting out to press on his mouth, my voice harsh, cracking. "Don't you ever compare me to Baba!"

"I fear for you, Soraya. You're not well. You need help. I'm taking you home."

My husband is right. Not that I need his help, but that I am not well, broken beyond repair and harder to put together than the shattered pieces of glass and china underfoot. Still, it feels good to see Aziz step in and offer to protect me.

My gaze seeks my owl, but finding no solace, I say: "I'm not going back, Aziz. There's no home to go back to."

"Destroy what's left. Go ahead." His face muscles tighten as if stitched too tight. His raises his hands to buffer me from what is to come. "I am filing for divorce."

"Because of Parvaneh?"

His voice is hardly audible above the din behind my eardrums. "No, Soraya, this is not about her. She holds no power over *us*. It's about the pills. It's about you deceiving me for all our married life—and you don't even get it, do you? That's it! I am done. I'll mail you the divorce documents."

My owl lets out a short, deep bark, spreads her wings, and flies straight toward the jasmine creepers. Her dappled wings get entangled in the branches, flapping violently. I can't tell whether she is in pain or simply disgusted. I rush to her aid. Struggle to free her with numb fingers that refuse to cooperate. I rub my hands together, blow on them, and manage, at last, to break the confining branches.

Freed like an arrow, my owl glides overhead and then, with unprecedented care and finesse, lands on my shoulder. Her sharp claws close into a tight grip. My blouse rips with a hiss. She puffs her chest and her every mottled feather stands on end. She lets out a piercing, apocalyptic bark as if to end this night that is longer and darker than the biblical Night of Noi.

Aziz leaps out of his chair. His left hand comes down in an iron grip over the bird's head to keep it from inflicting further damage. His right hand is as gentle as ever. One by one, he pries her talons open and dislodges them from my flesh.

My owl nuzzles the top of her head against my right cheek, a soft, fleeting gesture, an apology perhaps. Our eyes meet. An instant of shared understanding: it is time to part ways, Mamabozorg. All has been done, all said. She spreads her wings and whirls twice above my head, then flies out of the gazebo and straight into the bruised horizon.

Four pool-drops of blood bubble up on my shoulder.

"What have I done to you, *Jounam*," Aziz murmurs.

chapter 36

A WET SMELL OF WASHED carpets and cheap aerosol lingers inside the rented black stretch limousine that glides down the silent Bel Air streets. It is a pearl-gray dawn and dew clings to the car windows. A breeze from the ocean ruffles the feathers of a crow that lands in front of the car. Mansour pounds his foot on the brakes and the car swerves. Butterfly's arms spring to the dashboard for support. She has had the good sense to banish herself to the passenger seat in front.

We sit in silence, all four of us—Mansour, Butterfly, Aziz, and myself. Nothing left to say. Friendships are broken. Promises shattered. Love soiled.

Aziz is leaving me.

Free to pick up the rest of his life and do as he pleases. Abandoning me to gather my shattered self and do what I please with my haven of butterflies, collection of photographs, and cesspool of memories.

Mansour clicks the glass partition between the front and backseat shut. Perhaps he sensed my wish, a wife's last wish to have a private moment with her husband. I want Aziz to be mine on this last ride, this very last time I will see, smell, and hear him. His shallow breathing beats in my chest. In my heart. Not wise of me to inhabit his skin in such an intimate manner. But, this I did. Lost myself in him. Forgot my soul and identity.

I stroke the amber chain slung around my neck, the Star of David heavy on my black dress. Two amber beads screech between my restless fingers. Mamabozorg knew then that a tiny mosquito can kill an elephant, yet I did not heed her advice to be watchful of petty betrayals, my own included, until they became insurmountable *badbakhti* miseries. But even she, who was my Bird of Reason, ended by betraying me. Our wise matriarch should not have turned her back on us and gone into seclusion. We needed her.

We leave Sunset Boulevard behind and enter the 405 freeway. It is an ugly stretch of concrete and cement, this freeway that replaces the proud mountains and ancient plane trees of my previous home. The sky here is dulled and suffocating, pressing down like a blanket of ash. Somewhere beyond lurk emerald mountains and a turquoise ocean, but this is my reality now, a freeway flanked by depressing blocks of low, industrial buildings. In Tehran, the Shahyad Monument—memorial to the Shah—greets visitors with its pre-Islamic arches, ornate domes, and intricate arabesque designs. It once suggested a gateway to the future and a celebration of the past. Now, it is a symbol of the Shah's aborted grandeur. But to me, it remains a monument to the best years of my life. I am exchanging that for my haunted house with its battered butterflies, abandoned monkey tree, and lifeless Amorphophallus titanum.

Will Aziz plant a farewell kiss on my cheek or will he withhold even that last gesture of...what? Love? Kindness? Mercy?

—There's nothing a tongue-kiss won't solve, *Jounam*—

But what he says now is: "Will you ever come back, Soraya?"

"No, Aziz. Nothing left to come back to. I've lost everything. Baba, Madar, my country. And you."

He covers my hand with his large hand, then slides his wedding band off my thumb and rolls it down his own finger, taking back the last piece of his heart with him.

The limousine glides to the curb in the airport, and Mansour jumps out to open the door for Butterfly. She gathers her *chador* about her, making her way around the limousine and distancing herself from us with short, quick steps. Her hair is covered with the same orange polka-dotted kerchief she wore when she arrived here. Her *chador* floating behind her, she enters the terminal building. The *chador* gets trapped in the automatic sliding doors. She does not wait for the doors to open and release her *chador*, but abandons it to trampling footsteps as she continues on her way ahead and out of my life.

Aziz's hand is on the door handle. One last time, he turns his sleepy eyes my way with that expression that says—you're up to something, *Jounam*, the devil is in your eyes again—and for an instant I don't see anything but the delicious outline of his mouth because I think he might kiss me and our tongues might meet one last time.

Sounds tear out of him that I've never heard before. This man who does not know how to cry. His chest heaves and I think his heart is about to break. My right hand rests on his heart to catch the broken pieces. I don't look away because for the first time in our life together I see my husband crying.

Tears roll down his cheeks and wet his lower lip and stain his white shirt. I wipe tears off his mouth and suck my finger.

This is not the salty taste of guilt.

The car door is opening. He is stepping out; one decisive foot after the other takes him away from me. He does not look back. I notice an imperceptible wave of his lowered hand and a dismissive shake of his head. And just like that, Aziz is gone.

Unbidden tears and helpless wails pour out of me as if a fist shattered my chest open. I hold my head between my hands and cry out with all the force of my rage and remorse.

Mansour turns to offer me a bottle of water. A policeman tells him that he needs to move the vehicle. Mansour shoots him an angry look and gestures toward me as if to say we have an emergency on our hands. "She is not well, officer."

The policeman peers in through the window and then orders Mansour to move on.

"Shall we go, *Khanom*, or do you need more time?"

More time for what? I stifle my scream; I've run out of time. "Go, Mansour, go now!"

The limousine slowly pulls away from the curb.

My head is aching with a thousand images of my lost husband. Aziz is lurking in my greenhouse, snipping branches off Daddy Long Legs, arranging them in funny positions. We laugh. Now we swim in the Caspian Sea and it is a bright day and he fixes me forever in his gaze. Now his image is merging with mine on our wedding day on the dance floor and we are flushed with love.

Now, it is our last night together in my bed in America. We are curled away from each other, our backs touching lightly. The rhythm of his breathing tells me he is awake. Hours pass. It is midnight. The clock in the hallway plays "The Blue Danube." My mind roils with regret. Forgive me, I whisper. Forgive me. I want him to turn around and hold me close. But all he offers is his indifferent silence, until the sun rises and we have to face the day.

The limousine jerks to a halt.

The door opens and he slides inside like a shadow, swift and silent and with no explanation. He reaches for my hands and locks them between his; it feels like a warm cocoon.

"My Soree, *Jounam*, my life."

I slide close to him and nuzzle my cheek against his shoulder. His scent of tobacco and desire is devastating.

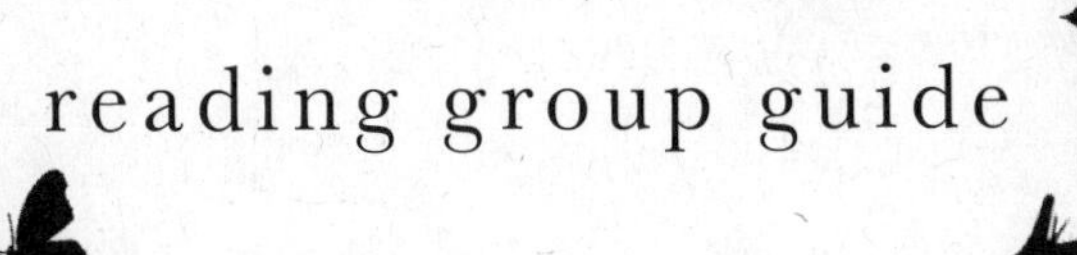

reading group guide

1. How does the protagonist's introduction set the tone for the novel? What do you think it means when Soraya's father says that the day she called herself an artist was the very same day she lost touch with the reality of their culture. Do you agree or disagree? Explain your opinion.

2. Soraya says of her difficulty letting go of clothing restrictions that "a habit of twenty years can be as stubborn as a handful of bloodthirsty leeches." What other habits does Soraya have trouble discarding? Do you have habits within your own life that would be extremely difficult to break?

3. While seated next to the *mullah* on the plane, Soraya feels that "the urge to take action is blinding." What kind of action is she considering? Why?

4. How did you feel when you learned that Soraya had been taking birth control pills even while enduring fertility treatments and tests? Did her reasons match your expectations? Why or why not?

5. Through her story, Soraya details how women have suffered oppression by men in Iran but also how oppressive love can be. Explore the ways in which oppression influences the characters in this novel. How much control do they each have over their situations? In what ways do they seek to exert that control?

6. Discuss how the politics of Iran's 1979 revolution and the fall of the Pahlavi dynasty influence the characters of the novel. What exactly does "Westoxication" mean in the context of this story? How did the term first strike you?

7. The relationship between Soraya and Parvaneh is a complicated tangle Soraya seeks to unravel during her time in California. She explains on the very first page of the novel that she's here in part because "I can't free myself from Parvaneh." Do you trust her interpretation more or less after discovering the truth at the end of the novel?

8. How does Soraya compare the life cycle of the butterfly to her friend's transformation over their years together? In what other ways does Soraya draw comparisons between the butterflies of her garden and Parvaneh?

9. Discuss the significance of names in this novel. Why do you think Soraya's father was against naming his daughter after a constellation? What other names have particular meaning? Why do you think the author chose these names?

10. Soraya's obsessions while in California revolve around butterflies, plants, and photography—a collection each time. What relation does each of these pastimes have to the other? How does Soraya use them as a means through which she struggles to deal with Aziz's and Parvaneh's betrayal?

11. Soraya is charmed and thrilled to discover a rare Corpse Plant in her new gardens. Discuss the irony of a plant by this name being the prize and jewel of the atrium and grounds. Compare and contrast her various descriptions of the Corpse Plant with Soraya herself.

12. Soraya describes her photo album on page 39 as a "testament to how I will trap men like moths in my net, suffocate them in jars, pin them in cigar boxes." Yet, despite her appreciation of

the "appetizing morsel" of a man she encounters in Franklin Canyon in chapter 6, she ultimately refuses his invitation and returns home with only photos. Why? What is she really after?

13. What is the "scent of butterflies"? How does Soraya describe it? What is the significance of this phrase as the novel's title?

14. Revenge is another prominent theme in this novel. Soraya explains of her plans, "Scores must be settled gradually and patiently. To savor the sweet nuances of dessert, it must be allowed to slowly melt on the tip of the tongue." How does Aziz's surprise visit upset this approach? Discuss how events might have unfolded differently if everything had gone according to Soraya's plan. In what other ways do the characters of this novel take revenge on one another?

15. Just when she's longing for home the most, Soraya discovers a Barking Owl, also called "the Screaming Woman," in her atrium. What is the significance of the owl as a symbol and for Soraya in particular? Discuss the differences between how Mansour and Soraya each view the bird.

16. What is it that bothers Soraya most about Aziz's betrayal with Parvaneh? Why does the sight of them kissing seem to hurt her more deeply than the fact that they are lovers, or even that they are in her and Aziz's bed?

17. When Parvaneh arrives in California, Soraya notices for the first time how her friend's breasts have swelled. How does she explain this to herself? How else do you think Soraya's tendency to see Parvaneh only as her childhood friend affects Soraya's ability to see the truth?

18. Soraya never wavers for a moment in her surety that Aziz has been unfaithful with Parvaneh for years. Were you as surprised as she to find out what had actually happened? Looking back, what clues did the author leave you?

19. Discuss the difference between Baba and Madar and between Aziz and Soraya. Are Baba's and Aziz's betrayals equal? Why or why not? Could you have forgiven either one of them if you were Soraya? How do you feel about Madar's and Soraya's betrayals of their husbands?

20. Soraya's dark plans include hurting and humiliating Aziz by sleeping with other men (or making him think that she had, in the case of the photo album) and then killing Parvaneh. Why do you think she was unable to fulfill the first part but went as far as serving Parvaneh the poisoned tea, which she continued to try serving her even after she discovered who Parvaneh was really in love with?

21. Mamabozorg is a character who has lived through two very different Irans. Identify the lessons she seeks to impart to Soraya and discuss their influence on the plot of the novel. Do you agree or disagree with her decision to isolate herself in her own home? Explain your opinion. What would you have done?

22. Superstition and religion influence the characters of this novel in many ways. Identify the role of each using examples from the novel to illustrate your points. For example, why do you think the author chose to make Soraya blond, tall, and so different from everyone around her? How does the author blend the cultural proclivities of the Jewish Iranian people with post-revolution Iranian Islam?

23. Why do you think the author chose this ending, even after Soraya discovers that her worst fear—that Aziz and Parvaneh are in love—is far from the truth?

24. As the story progresses, how do Soraya's gardening efforts reflect who she is and who she is becoming? Discuss the irony of Soraya's own transformation through her obsession with

Parvaneh's. Do you feel, as Aziz does, that Soraya has become a completely different person—or have her experiences simply brought out latent characteristics? In what ways is Soraya unable to change?

25. Why do you think Aziz acts the way he does at the very end? Where do you see their marriage going now that Soraya has decided never to return home?

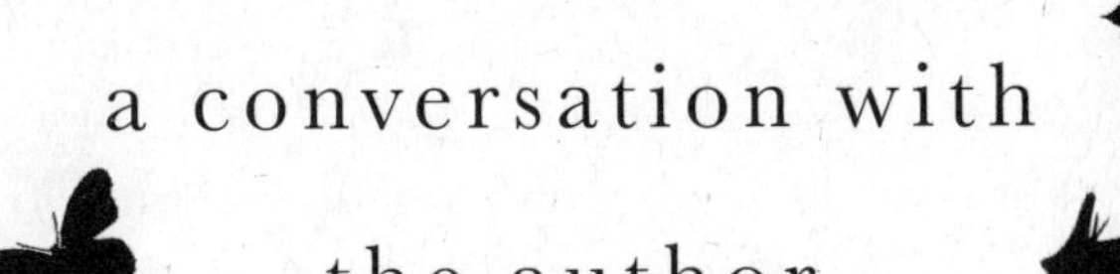

a conversation with the author

1. In the opening pages of *Scent of Butterflies*, Soraya recalls that her father once told her that deciding to call herself an artist marked the moment she "lost touch with the reality of our culture" (page 1). What is it about her artistry that disconnects her from her culture?

   Dora: It is unfortunate that in the Iranian community, being an artist—a photographer, painter, musician, singer, etc.—is considered a low-level profession and artists are rarely given the respect they deserve. This is especially true for women, whose rightful place is supposed to be at home, taking care of their husband and raising their children. But Soraya is different. She refuses to conform to the acceptable, albeit unfair, mores of her society. Consequently, her father believes that calling herself an artist is an indication of Soraya's disconnect with her culture.

2. There is much discussion in the novel about the restrictive rules and social mores regarding women's clothing. Would you speak to this issue as you feel it affects modern Iranian life?

   Dora: I've been repeatedly surprised by the disparate views Iranian women have about the *hijab*, or modest clothing. Some women see this forced veiling for what it is—repressive and a type of misogyny. Others have embraced the *hijab* as a way of declaring their individuality. After the 1979 Islamic

Revolution, Iranian women found themselves at the mercy of the Komiteh, or the Morality Police, a bunch of thugs with nothing better to do than harass women for refusing to adhere to the strict demands of the Islamic Regime's code of dressing. But history has proven that it is difficult to break the feisty will of an Iranian woman, and a good majority of women today, especially the younger generation, have no qualms about wearing makeup and using the long overcoat and head cover as an accessory, rather than a means of concealing themselves.

3. Through Soraya's eyes, we experience the underbelly to Iran's professed piety, represented by the *mullah* she meets on the plane and with whom she nearly has sex later. Do you feel this is a kind of corruption, as Soraya seems to, or is it merely a creative application of the law, as the *mullah* might have explained? How common is this practice of taking on "temporary wives?"

   Dora: It is important to remember that Soraya's point of view is tainted by the devastating betrayal she has experienced. As such, she has a tendency to paint most men in a negative light and the *mullah*, of course, is at the top of her list of corrupt men. Having said that, there's no doubt that the religious authorities, under the pretense of piety, continue to take all types of liberties that are nothing short of corruption, including the practice of taking temporary wives, or *sigheh*. This practice was considered backward and discouraged during the reign of the two Pahlavi Shahs, but after the 1979 Islamic revolution, temporary unions were not only endorsed by the mullahs, but also encouraged as sexual release. Many women, especially after the Iran Iraq War, were forced to seek temporary marriages for financial support. Today, a large percentage of progressive Iranian women shun the practice of *sigheh* as nothing more than prostitution or being forced to share their husband with another woman. And a number of young women, who are not allowed to travel or share a hotel room with a boyfriend, have become creative and solve the problem by engaging in a *sigheh* with their boyfriend, which legalizes their union in the eyes of the authorities and gives them freedom to date and be seen together in public.

4. Through her story, Soraya details how women have suffered oppression by men in Iran, but also how oppressive love can be. What about this theme of oppression interested you?

    Dora: It is remarkable how deeply I've been affected by my childhood experiences and my first impressions of Iran, a country so different from Israel, where I spent the first nine years of my life. The image of the first *chador*-clad woman I witnessed in the streets of Tehran will remain with me forever. To my child's eyes, that black-sheathed woman symbolized negativity, backwardness, and oppression. I also remember how unusual, and unacceptable, it was for my mother to get her driver's license at the time and how she was harassed in the streets of Tehran. That, too, seemed a form of cruel punishment. And among many other incidents that remain with me, I witnessed the heart-wrenching pain of a close relative who, unable to bear children, was forced to share her husband with a second wife. So the theme of oppression, the many shapes it can take, sometimes blatantly overt and often under the pretext of love or religion, is reflected in each of my books, especially *Scent of Butterflies*, where Soraya appears to free herself from the barriers of her culture but remains a prisoner to her own obsessive love.

5. Though this story is not ultimately a political one, the 1979 revolution and subsequent fall of the Mohammad Reza Shah's dynasty clearly influence the characters of the novel. Could you talk a bit about what "Westoxication" means to you and how you used this story to explore the concept?

    Dora: I started *Scent of Butterflies* after I finished my first novel, *Harem*, at a time when the tumultuous events of the 1979 Islamic Revolution that forced me and my family to leave Iran were painfully fresh. So it is inevitable that the pain and confusion I struggled with at the time would be reflected in my characters. I have a scene in my book where Baba attempts to explain the reasons for the revolution and the fall of Mohammad Reza Shah. One crucial reason for the downfall of the Pahlavi Dynasty was the speed with which the Shah wanted to secularize and westernize the Iranian culture. But Iran had a powerful contingency of religious fundamentalists that throughout history have fought the dangerous influence of the "Imperialistic West" that they consider toxic, hence "Westoxication." Even today, thirty-four years after the Islamic Revolution, the term "Westoxication" is used in a negative way to refer to an Iranian American woman who, in the eyes of the older generation, has become too outspoken and independent and as such has disconnected from her Iranian roots.

6. The complicated relationship between Soraya and Parvaneh lies at the heart of this novel, giving shape to our protagonist's relationships with the two primary male figures in her life—her father and her husband, Aziz. What did you draw on to lend realism to the women's history and friendship? Have you any friends remaining from your own childhood?

   Dora: I often think that I would have become a therapist if I would not have discovered my passion as a writer. I am deeply interested in the psychology of all types of relationships, ones I witness firsthand and others I read about. I love biographies because they shed light on the lives of fascinating characters. I draw from the news, books, movies, whispered gossip, and, of course, real-life events to portray my characters in the most realistic manner.

   Thanks to Facebook, a good number of my childhood friends have been able to get in touch with me, some who left years after the revolution and who continue to supply me with firsthand information about Iran after the Shah.

7. Soraya draws many comparisons between the butterflies of her garden and Parvaneh throughout the novel. What first inspired you to play with this metaphor, and how did you ultimately arrive at the novel's title, *Scent of Butterflies*?

   Dora: As the book evolved and I paid attention to the signals Soraya sent me, I discovered the reason I named her Parvaneh, which means Butterfly in Farsi. It was then that the theme of butterflies found its way into the story. In addition, as Soraya is struggling to make sense of her loss and unraveling in the process, a type of transference is taking place, and she begins to imagine the butterflies in her garden as having the same qualities as her friend, Parvaneh, who she begins to call "Butterfly." Sense of smell is important to Soraya, and she differentiates the characteristics of butterflies by their scents. Here is a short excerpt from the novel, which takes place after Soraya traps a butterfly in her net: "Scarcely dead and still supple to my touch, she begins to give off the smell of public baths, humid and cloying and a bit dirty. And now, just this instant, limp and rendered harmless, she emits the bland odor of stale flowers." Hence the title, *Scent of Butterflies.*

8. Soraya's obsessions while in California revolve around not only butterflies, but also photography and plants, particularly the Corpse Plant she discovers in her new California gardens. Do you share any of these hobbies with your protagonist? If not, what prompted the decision to incorporate them into her character?

   Dora: My hobbies, alas, are not as diverse as Soraya's. My obsessions, at any point and time, revolve around an era, person, plant, animal, artistic medium, or subject matter I find fascinating to use as fodder for my stories. Years ago, I was introduced to the Amorphophallus titanum in an article in the *Wall Street Journal*. I held on to the article, certain that the strange Corpse Flower would find its way into one of my novels. When the plant bloomed in the Huntington Gardens in 1999, it made international headlines. I had to see the magnificent Amorphophallus, which is native to the equatorial rainforests of Sumatra. I knew that the bloom was short-lived and lasts approximately twelve hours and that I had to get myself to the Huntington Gardens while it was still in bloom. I was among thousands of people who gathered around the Corpse Flower, witnessing the plant at the height of its fertility and emitting an odor that has been compared to many things, including rotting flesh. Right then and there, the Corpse Flower was assigned a major role in *Scent of Butterflies*.

I am not a photographer, but my sister, Laura Merage, is a well-known and accomplished one, and I've learned to appreciate photography through her special view, which Soraya has inherited.

9. Themes of death and decay appropriately underscore much of this sometimes dark story. Were these issues particularly on your mind while writing the novel, or would you say that in some sense, because they are part of nature, death and decay are always with us and thus always influencing the way we engage with the world?

Dora: The literature of death and decay has been around forever. We live with the reality of death, and as such, it inevitably creeps into our stories.

The reality of death was especially close while I was writing this book, a time when revolutionary courts, in order to purge Iran of political dissidents and members of the old regime, were, without the benefit of a fair trial, ordering hasty executions to eliminate the threat of a coup d'état.

For Soraya, who believes she is experiencing the death of

her love, this theme has an added significance, influencing the way she engages with her world.

10. Revenge is another prominent theme in this novel: Soraya finds great delight in plotting hers. Is there a little bit of vicarious thrill going on there, or is this perhaps something you share with your protagonist? At this stage in your writing career, how much of yourself still ends up as fodder for your characters?

    Dora: It is safe, and often fun, to join your characters on a fictional journey you would never dare embark on in real life. I confess there are times I wish I possessed Soraya's courage to extract revenge on certain individuals, better left unnamed. But I am not as brave as Soraya and perhaps more sensible sometimes. Who knows! What I do know is that for now, it is much safer to delegate to my characters certain thoughts and actions I'd never imagine undertaking.

    It is difficult for a writer to identify what percentage of herself is instilled in her protagonist. From one side, I am nothing close to any of my characters—Rebekah in *Harem*, who sells her body to support her daughter; Madame Gabrielle in *Courtesan*, who is, well, a courtesan; the clairvoyant Darya in *The Last Romanov*; and Parvaneh, or Butterfly, in *Scent of Butterflies*, whose obsessive love drives her to acts I would never imagine. Yet! How could some subconscious characteristics of a writer not end up in her characters?

11. The Barking Owl, also called "the Screaming Woman," has much significance as a symbol in the novel. What does the owl represent to you, and how did it find its way into this story?

    Dora: Years ago, while writing *Scent of Butterflies*, I visited a hotel in New Port. One afternoon, a falconer arrived with four birds of prey—an eagle, a hawk, a falcon, and an owl—for display in the hotel gardens. I was mesmerized by the owl, the way it completely rotated its head, but mostly by its piercing, yellow eyes that seemed to bore through me. I was writing the scene where Soraya comes to Los Angeles, leaving Mamabozorg, her grandmother, behind in Iran. Mamabozorg is a compelling character, and I didn't want for her to be absent from the page. In addition, Soraya is close to Mamabozorg and in dire need of her advice. The solution came to me in the form of the owl, who represents Soraya's grandmother.

12. What made California the perfect place for Soraya to retreat and set to weaving her web? Do the locations in the novel have a real-life meaning for you?

    Dora: This is my only novel in which the locations have a real-life meaning to me. I have lived in all these places. This being my most contemporary novel, it made sense to set my characters in Iran and Los Angeles.

13. Superstition and religion influence the characters of this novel in many ways. Did you do any research to add this element to the story? Did you draw from your own experiences to create any aspects of the superstition or religious beliefs and practices coloring the novel?

    Dora: The superstition and religious beliefs influencing my protagonists are inspired by the colorful characters of my extended family—grandmother, aunts, cousins—and by a culture rich in legend and superstition. My grandmother sometimes used blessings and curses comprised of a mixture of Hebrew, Farsi, and even French words that were completely incomprehensible to me as a child. As an example, she hated storms and cursed them as "*Tifouneh Noar.*" It took me years to realize that she combined the words *toufan*, storm in Farsi; the Biblical Noah; and *noir*, black in French, to come up with "Noah's black storm," to curse a detested deluge of rain.

14. A unique aspect of the religious interplay in this novel is that you focus on the lives of Jews living in Iran. Describe for us

what it was like working to tell a story through the lens of a Jewish Persian people living under the laws of post-revolution Iranian Islam.

Dora: Although I was lucky enough to get out of Iran in time, I have been closely following the plight of the few remaining Iranian Jews who were too old or poor to leave the country. It is unfortunate that during periods of political turmoil Jews become scapegoats, and the Islamic revolution was no exception. The remaining Jewish community, who had enjoyed a short period of relative reprieve during the reign of Mohammad Reza Shah, sensing the tide of change, realized that it was prudent to show their support to the incoming regime, no matter their personal sentiments.

I can't think of a better example to demonstrate this forced show of solidarity than referring to a photograph in *Esther's Children: A Portrait of Iranian Jews*, edited by Houman Sarshar. This is an important book I highly recommend. The caption below the photograph says: "Chief Rabbi Yedidia Shofet (far right) and his son Rab David Shofet (center) participating in the general demonstrations leading up to the Islamic Revolution in Iran. Tehran, 1979." From my vantage as an Iranian American Jew, enjoying the freedoms America has afforded me, the sad, somber, and I'm certain fearful expressions of the rabbi and his son in the photograph is both enraging and saddening.

15. The novel ends on a somewhat surprising note. What kind of endings are your favorite to write, and what led you to avoid a "neat" ending for this novel? Did you know early on in your writing process how the novel would end?

Dora: I never know the ending of my novels until I've gone through many drafts and have moved events and chapters around to fit the story. I've often come to the end, when I'd realize that the beginning of the novel is actually the ending.

It is also very common for me to go back after I believe I have the ending and cut the last chapter because I'd arrived at the ending earlier than I realized. I don't like "neat" endings because that robs the reader of the gift of imagination, where the reader is allowed to imagine how the lives of the characters will unfold after the last page, which to me is not the end, but another beginning.

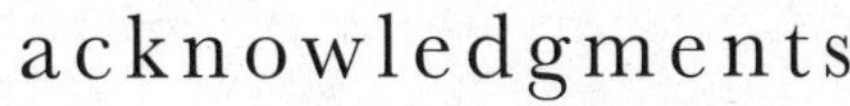

acknowledgments

My first thanks goes to my dear editor, Shana Drehs, who guided, advised, and inspired me with great wisdom and an astute sense of style.

Heather Hall, Elizabeth Pehlke, Angela Cardoz, Nicole Komasinski, Adrienne Krogh, Diane Dannenfeldt, and Sabrina Baskey-East, my conscientious team at Sourcebooks, continue to be a blessing. Your additions, subtractions, and suggestions have elevated this novel.

Many thanks, as always, to Dominique Raccah, the Grand Lady herself, who is always there to open doors and smooth the way.

Anna Ghosh, your patience and perseverance paid off. Thank you.

Thank you, Marcela Landres, for being such a steadfast and believing partner in the tumultuous journey this novel has endured.

My gratitude goes to Maureen Connell, Joan Goldsmith Gurfield, Leslie Monsour, Paula Shtrum, and Alexandra Kivowitz, my talented team of writer friends and supporters, whose invaluable comments and endless well of imagination have enriched this novel.

Every step of the way, from inception to publication—I've lost count of the years, fifteen or sixteen in all—I depended on the encouragement and support of my family, friends, and colleagues, who helped bring this most personal of all my novels to life.

A million thanks to my husband, Nader, who is always there to listen, calm, cheer on, and encourage, as well as lend his support in a million loving and much appreciated ways. Carolyn, Negin, David, Leila, Adam, Hannah, and Macabee, words cannot describe my love for you. You continue to provide me with a much-needed and appreciated sanctuary, a place to regain my spiritual and emotional balance when the need arises. Thank you.

My deep gratitude goes to my mother, Parvin, the unwavering matriarch of our clan, and to Ora, Nora, David, Solomon, and Laura, my biggest fans, who enrich every aspect of my life. My sister, Laura Merage, an incomparable artist in her own right, supplied me with invaluable details about the process of photography. Any errors that might have persisted, despite careful attention, are purely mine.

Jonathan Kirsch and Ann Kirsch, I am grateful for your wisdom, friendship, and guidance. John Schatzel, Lita Weissman, Aurick Canete, Jon Evans, Alison Reid, and Linda Friedman, thank you for caring in these times of change and for keeping our books alive on your shelves.

about the author

CHRISTINE MARIE PHOTOGRAPHY

Dora Levy Mossanen was born in Israel and moved to Iran when she was nine. At the onset of the Islamic revolution, she and her family were forced to leave Iran and settle in Los Angeles. She has a bachelor's degree in English Literature from the University of California–Los Angeles and a master's in professional writing from the University of Southern California.

Dora is the bestselling author of the widely acclaimed novels *Harem*, *Courtesan*, and *The Last Romanov*, translated into numerous languages. She is the recipient of the prestigious San Diego Editors' Choice Award and has been featured in various publications and media outlets, including *Sh'ma*, *Los Angeles Times*, KCRW, Radio Iran, Radio Russia, and numerous television programs. In 2010, Dora was accepted as contributor to the Bread Loaf Writers' Conference.

She blogs for the *Huffington Post* and reviews fiction for the *Jewish Journal*. She is working on *The Visionary*, her fifth novel.